# The Orpheus Trail

**MAUREEN DUFFY** is a notable contemporary British poet, playwright and novelist. To date she has published thirty works, including six volumes of poetry. Her *Collected Poems, 1949–84* appeared in 1985. Her work has often used Freudian ideas and Greek myth as a framework.

# The Orpheus Trail

## Maureen Duffy

ARCADIA BOOKS

Arcadia Books Ltd
15–16 Nassau Street
London W1W 7AB

www.arcadiabooks.co.uk

First published in the United Kingdom by Arcadia Books 2009
This B format edition 2010
Copyright © Maureen Duffy 2009

Maureen Duffy has asserted her moral right to be identified as the author of this work in accordance with the Copyright, Designs and Patents Act, 1988.

A catalogue record for this book is available from the British Library.

ISBN 978-1-906413-65-1

Typeset in Arno by MacGuru Ltd
Printed in Great Britain by CPI Cox & Wyman

Arcadia Books gratefully acknowledges the financial support of Arts Council England.

Arcadia Books supports English PEN, the fellowship of writers who work together to promote literature and its understanding. English PEN upholds writers' freedoms in Britain and around the world, challenging political and cultural limits on free expression. To find out more, visit www.englishpen.org or contact English PEN, 6-8 Amwell Street, London EC1R 1UQ

Arcadia Books distributors are as follows:

in the UK and elsewhere in Europe:
Turnaround Publishers Services
Unit 3, Olympia Trading Estate
Coburg Road
London N22 6TZ

in the US and Canada:
Dufour Editions
PO Box 7
Chester Springs
PA 19425

Arcadia Books is the *Sunday Times* Small Publisher of the Year 2002/03

*For Madge and Freddie*

It's evening, dusk already felting up the windows, before Harry realises his watch isn't on his wrist where it should be. He'd been out in the greenhouse watering the tomatoes, almost drugged by the heavy scent of the plants as he brushed against the leaves, until Jean called him in for tea. After their plates of ham and salad he'd gone out again to potter in his garden shed before settling down for the evening's telly.

'I seem to have lost my watch,' he says.

Jean looks up from the black handset with its rows of little buttons that should give access to unlimited choice but yield only disappointment as she searches for an old film, preferably black and white and prefaced by the swirling image of the Gainsborough Lady as she graciously inclines the feathered cartwheel of her picture hat.

'When did you have it last?'

'I remember looking at the time just before we came back and thinking that the evenings would soon be drawing in. I must have lost it on site.'

It was the end of the season. Soon they would all have to stop work so that the contractors could move in, cover over their summer's dig and begin to lay the new carriageway.

'Where are you going?'

'I thought I'd go back and see if I can find it.'

'You'll never spot it in this light.'

'I thought I'd take the metal detector.'

'Then I'm coming too. You're not going up there on your own. At least I can hold the torch.' Jean knows it's no good to argue.

They put on the boots they were wearing earlier, still clogged with Essex clay. Harry fetches the detector from the shed. Jean takes the big spotlight torch. They set off without speaking.

It's been a frustrating summer. After the first excitement of winning a reprieve of three months that allowed a local team to investigate the possible Saxon site where the graves of women had been found seventy years before, their combined efforts have turned up only a measly collection of pottery shards, a coin or two, a harness buckle, and part of a scabbard.

Harry leads the way, bending under the tapes marking out the site. Heavy rain had stopped work the day before and the earth is sticky, clinging to their boots as if wanting to drag them down. Already it's too dark to see. Harry switches on the detector, Jean the torch. They begin to go over the ground, Harry sweeping his probe from side to side, prospecting.

Something shines momentarily in the torch beam. 'What's that over there?' Jean says, trying to pick up the gleam again.

'I'm getting a definite signal.' Harry moves forward.

'I didn't think we were working this far over.'

'Keep the torch on it, Jeanie. It looks like we've found it.'

'Be careful. You'll slip!'

The detector is buzzing impatiently. Harry goes forward. 'It is my watch. I've got it.'

She sees him bend down stiffly, his hand outstretched. She hears a cry. Then she can't see him anymore.

Harry is falling. He leans heavily on the detector to steady himself as he bends to pick up his watch and suddenly its metal shaft sinks through the soft mud and goes on down, bringing Harry and the ground he's standing on with it. He remembers his old army training and bends his knees to break his fall. Then he lands soft and safe on crumbled dry soil.

He hears Jean calling him. Gulps and calls back: 'It's alright, darling. No bones broken.' Then chokes on a mouthful of dusty earth. Looking up he sees the light from the torch like a little moon.

'What happened? What shall I do?'

'See if you can find a ladder or something to get me out.'

'I'll go and get help.'

'No, don't do that. I'll feel such a fool.'

The little moon vanishes. Alone in the dark Harry puts out his hands, blindly feeling for a way out. He comes up against a hard surface. His foot strikes an object in the dust. He thinks he hears a metallic sound.

Light shines in the gap above his head. 'I've found a ladder.'

'Good girl. Can you lower it down?'

Jean puts down the torch and pokes the end of the ladder through the hole. It's almost too heavy for her but she holds on. She knows if she lets go and it falls on Harry it could injure if not kill him. She feels the weight suddenly taken from her.

'I've got it. Can you shine the torch down here? I want to see…'

'Come up before anything else falls on you.'

'I'm coming. Move the torch about a bit.'

In its light he can see he's in a large square hole, a little room. The floor is silted deep with the sandy dust that had broken his fall but he can see objects poking up through the thick layer. Cautiously he brushes away the sand from a small circle by his feet. For a moment in the torchlight there is the gleam of gold.

And that's how it all started with Harry Bates ringing me up at what felt like midnight, although the ten o'clock news was only just over, to tell me he thought he'd fallen into a chamber tomb. At first I wondered if it was some kind of joke. Then it crossed my mind that it was a ploy to keep the contractors at bay a little longer. But as he went on the details were too precise to be faked. How could Harry and Jean Bates have dug out a large pit overnight, and filled it with artefacts that would have to be convincing enough to be examined in the cold light of dawn? For that was what it was going to mean.

'I think you'd better meet us on site early before anyone else gets there. Then you can see for yourself.'

'Shouldn't you let Harris know?' Harris was the professional archaeologist sent down from London to oversee a team largely made up of local amateurs. There'd been some friction between them. Harris pulling rank and a little contemptuous of the local society's efforts. I'd gone along there as often as I could to try to keep the peace. He'd made it clear, as the only other pro, that he blamed them for the season's failure to turn up any significant finds. Not that he thought much of me either, as a mere keeper of the local museum, local government not national, with a small not very important collection to curate, apart from the old finds of three quarters of a century before, dug up carelessly by the first set of road builders. Harris felt he'd wasted a whole year, with nothing to show for it that would improve his chances on the career ladder attached to a well-funded university department with plenty of foreign sites.

And the way these things go he was probably right.

'I'd rather you saw it first,' Harry said.

These days you can't despise the amateurs or do without their extra man and woman power. After all what were the pioneers like Schliemann and Pitt-Rivers but wealthy amateurs in a way? There's the famous photograph of Frau Schliemann wearing the necklace her husband had dug up at Mycenae. No one would dare to do that now with a find of such age, fragility and importance.

So there we were next morning at six o'clock with only a few early cars going by on the bypass and the site still deserted.

'What were you doing up here so late?' I asked them.

'Harry lost his watch,' Jean said. 'And we came up to look for it.'

'In the dark?'

'I brought the metal detector and Jean had the big torch. It was just as I'd found my watch and was picking it up that the ground gave way.'

'He was lucky not to break his back or at least a leg.'

'There's a thick layer of dust down there that softened my fall. You'll see. We left the ladder there.'

'Right, here goes.' I began to lower myself down the rungs. As I reached the bottom I realised that the top of my head was only a few inches from that of the ladder but Harry was shorter than me, a little shrunk with age from the youthful height he must have had, and he hadn't had the benefit of a ladder when he fell.

I switched on my own torch to examine the pit.

Although it was daylight now only a faint gloom pervaded the tomb, as I saw it unmistakably was, as I shone the beam of my torch from one protruding object to another. The place was clearly stuffed with more grave goods than I'd ever seen all together, apart from in the British Museum. I saw exposed rims of what must be vessels of all shapes and sizes, and other pieces still in their coats of solid dust that seemed to call out to me to touch them, to open up their mystery and bring them into the light. Buried for over a thousand years with their owner, I felt they were asking to be looked at afresh. There were even objects hanging from the walls.

'Well?' The Bateses chorused together as I reached the top of the ladder and stepped down.

'It must be the best thing since Sutton Hoo,' I joked.

'You do think it's a buried chamber then?'

'No doubt about it.'

'And Saxon?'

'By its position along with the other material they found in the twenties, I think it must be. But we'll soon know. We have to call in Harris at once and apply for an extension. This'll upset the contractors.' I foresaw a struggle ahead to get them to suspend work for another, possibly unknown length of time while we carefully uncovered, documented and lifted everything we could. Already I was determined that what we found shouldn't just be lost in a national museum. Whoever it was who had been buried there, man or woman, might indeed still be there under the dust of the centuries. He or she belonged to us, was ours and should stay here, even if we had to build a special room to accommodate the finds.

'Okay,' I said, 'let's call and wake up Harris with the good news.'

'Isn't it a bit early?' Harry said looking at what must be the watch that had set it all off.

It was true. It was still only seven o'clock. Time had stood still, as it sometimes does when it isn't racing frenetically, according to some law of perceptual relativity.

'Harry and I usually have breakfast at a little place on the front,' Jean said. 'Why don't we go there and ring him at eight? If you'd like to come with us we can park on a yellow line until nine. I could do with a hot cup of tea. The mornings are getting so chilly now.'

So I climbed into their aging Vauxhall and we trundled sedately through the deserted town, not yet invaded by the traditional east London day-trippers down for the last taste of freedom and holiday sunshine. As I got out of the car I could just make out the flash of sunlight on waves at the distant horizon, beyond the wide stretch of ribbed sand, darkened by the receding tide, with here and there stripes of blackly gleaming weed, the rubbery swathes of bladder wrack. And

I thought that it was the same sea the tribes of Saxons, Angles and Jutes had come across to make landfall first in Kent and then on into our Kingdom of the East Saxons whose shore we were standing on. I imagined the boats coming in over the water with the sun glinting on the row of round shields hung over the sides, and grounding in the shallows, the men leaping over the sides with their swords drawn in their hands.

The Bateses belonged here. Theirs was an Old English name: the children of Bata. Not so mine. Kish, an incomer whose father had fled from Hungary after the first uprising though some of my colleagues thought me more English than the natives.

I could understand Harris's disappointment when I told him that what he had longed for all summer had happened without him.

'Are you sure?' he asked. 'They could be mistaken, over enthusiastic ...'

'Quite sure. I've been down there myself.' Another blow.

'I'll meet you there in half an hour.'

I don't know whether he decided then that if he hadn't had the gratification of discovery at least he would have that of final display.

'I'll have to get some extra people down from London. This is much too important to be left to well-meaning amateurs,' he said, ignoring Jean and Harry Bates, as soon as he came up from inspecting the tomb.

'I imagine we'll all have to chip in if it's to be done in time,' I said. 'Will you handle the council and the contractors or would you like me to?'

'I'll be much too busy rounding up a professional team at such short notice. You deal with the local bureaucracy. You're used to them.'

This was a great relief. I thought I could put a good case to my bosses for the tourist benefit to the town of such a find and they could take on the construction company.

Winter was only a few months away. We worked under arc lamps at night and a tent by day, to protect the site against the weather, as if we were researching the scene of a crime. No body was found. Only a little tooth enamel. But over a hundred objects were brought to light. I watched as they were packed up and carried away to be examined, cleaned and conserved by experts, who I found much more cooperative than Harris.

'I think we've got something to show you now,' the head of the conservation team said a few months later. 'Do come and have a look. I think you'll like what we've been able to do with your amazing haul.'

Hilary Caistor, chief conservationist, met me in the reception area of the London Museum's Archaeology Service. 'We've laid them out for you. Not everything of course. We've still got months of work but what's come up already is pretty fantastic.' Even then I wasn't prepared for what I saw.

Where there had been what looked to the inexpert eye lumps of Essex clay there were now recognisable objects: bowls and cups, blue glass jars, bits of gleaming gold in the shape of two tiny filigree crosses, a buckle, coins, a lidded flagon, even a couple of dice and a set of bone pieces for a game like draughts. 'We think we've got an iron folding stool and a sort of harp,' Hilary Caistor said as I studied the benches, crowded with pieces, in silence.

'It's not my specialist period. Can you tell me what you think it all means?'

'Well, it's obviously high status. I think it wouldn't be too far fetched to say probably royal. The stool is a giveaway, a first for an Anglo Saxon grave but known from princely graves on the continent and from representations of kings and emperors.'

'And the harp?'

'Oh, essential. Think of *Beowulf*, the feasting in the great hall of Hrothgar, or Caedmon having to leave when the harp was passed round because he couldn't sing.'

'I can see I'll have to brush up on all this stuff.'

'If I can help at all...'

Hilary Caistor wasn't conventionally beautiful, in fact she had more the look of a librarian, or primary school teacher after a long time at the chalk face: comforting, dependable.

'I'll take you up on that if I may. Now when can we have them back?'

'That's difficult.'

'I need to have something to show to the bosses.'

'Maybe we could arrange to let you have a sample collection for a while. There's insurance to sort out, and security of course. You see they're not just yours. You've unearthed a national treasure, I'm afraid.

But I'll see what I can do with the trustees, and the ministry. They've already been on the phone asking what it's all worth, as if anyone could say, especially at this stage.'

'Do we have any idea who it might have been?'

'It's definitely male. My money's on Saebert.'

'Saebert?'

'Prince or king of the East Saxons, under his overlord Ethelbert of Kent. He died in 616. It's all in Bede's *History of the English Church and People*, along with the story of Caedmon.' I nodded as if I knew. She went on: 'I had to look it all up too when I began to realise what we'd got. Bede says he was the first Christian king in Essex and that ties in with these.' She pointed to the two tiny filigree crosses. 'Maybe they were laid on his eyelids so he would be able to see his way into the kingdom of heaven guided by the cross. Bede also tells us that the great attraction of Christianity was its doctrine of life after death. He has a pagan Anglo Saxon priest say man's life under the old religion is like a bird flying out of the darkness, through the warmth and light of the great hall into the dark again.'

My head was beginning to reel. There was so much to take in. 'I think I'd better pick up a copy of Bede on the way home.'

'There's a translation in paperback. Bede of course wrote in Latin.'

'Not English?'

'No. He had to wait for King Alfred to come up with an English version.'

I picked up the book in my favourite high street shop that still sold real writing to a dwindling public. My own speciality had been the nineteenth century which fitted in well with charting the town's rise as a royal watering place when Queen Caroline started the fashion for sea bathing here, a craze taken over by east Londoners as the nearest bit of coast straight down the railway line. Now I had to venture on to something new.

Ever since I'd found myself at the bottom of Harry's ladder with the dust-shrouded funerary objects all around I'd felt a strange sensation as if I wasn't alone, as if I was being watched. I'm not a superstitious man as a rule but it was as though someone had come into my life. While I stood there, my eyes following the beam of my torch as it lit on one object after another, I felt an empathy with this vanished king or prince, as if some of his dust had entered my bloodstream, as if I'd breathed him in.

Since Lucy died I've lived alone, almost. We had a good but supportively unremarkable marriage for eight years with Lucy working at the central library, me at the museum, two decent local government salaries, security, and pensions on what seemed distant horizons. Then she found a lump and, after a rollercoaster two years of alternating hope and anguish, I was alone.

Or almost. We had no children and at first I thought I'd find a home for Caesar, the cat, and close the whole episode of a married life that had once fitted like a slipper. But instead I found myself looking for him after a day's work when I came home to an otherwise empty house, listening for the flip-flop of the cat door when he came in demanding food and attention while I worked at my desk in the evening or slumped in front of the television. I think he saved my reason and if sometimes I could laugh at myself, leading the life of an old maid with her cat, I had a job I loved and someone at least warm and breathing who cared whether I came home at night, if only to spoon out a tin of cat food.

Now I settled down with him stretched out in front of the fire and opened Bede's *History* at the index and looked up Saebert, hoping I'd remembered the name correctly. There he was on page 108. As I began to read I had that strange sensation again of not being alone or of being outside myself with someone else inside.

The story was fascinating enough. Ethelbert of Kent who'd been converted by Augustine and his monks, sent by Pope Gregory as missionaries to the still pagan Anglo Saxons in AD 597, had married a Christian princess. Saebert, his nephew, had been won over in his turn by Bishop Mellitus, charged by Augustine with taking on the East Saxons, but 'when he died his three sons who were still pagans,' Bede said, 'were quick to profess idolatry and encouraged their people to return to the old gods.' Mellitus was sent packing and it was another generation before Saebert's grandson was brought back to Christianity by St Cedd who founded monasteries at Tilbury and Bradwell-on-Sea. As I read, a whole world was opening up in my imagination, of petty kings and great halls where harpers sang stories of dead heroes, and firelight fell on gold, enamel and jewelled sword hilts or flashed from the blue glass jars whose use I couldn't even guess at unless it was for holy oils to anoint a dying king. Beside the king a queen might have sat, wearing the gold pendant with its star of red garnets from the 1920s Saxon dig that we kept in pride of place on display at the museum but that had never really moved me until now. I knew that I would look at it with newly opened eyes tomorrow.

Hilary Caistor had told me a story by Bede about a bird flying out of darkness through the hall into the dark again, and now I found that in the account of Ethelbert's own conversion. It was a powerful image of our brief lives but I thought too I could see another meaning, that people themselves were like birds flying into our lives bringing light and music, as the dove descends from heaven shedding sunbursts in the moment of creation, and then night closes in again, leaving only an empty darkened theatre.

Three months after my visit to the London Museum the story of our find was released to the press. Hilary warned me this was about to happen. I tipped off the local papers and made sure they covered the press conference. Then the phone began to ring. Members of the public wanted to know 'when the king was coming home'. I had to apologise to Jean and Harry Bates for not keeping them up to date on developments. 'Do you want me to tell people, the press for instance, how you two found the grave?' I asked Harry. 'It'll probably mean a lot of intrusion in your lives, reporters doorstepping you, that sort of thing.'

'We'll talk it over,' Harry said, 'and let you know.'

Then it was the chairman of the council's publicity and tourism committee wanting to know why we couldn't have 'our king' back.

'You'd need to make special, very secure arrangements. As it stands the museum couldn't cope. These objects would fetch a lot of money on the internet black market in antiquities.'

'Local people have a right to know what's been found under their feet.'

'I'll see what I can do and keep you informed,' I tried to soothe him.

'I hope you have the town's interest fully at heart, Mr Kish.' And the receiver was slammed down.

I rang Hilary Caistor. 'I've been looking into it,' she said, 'because we did discuss this before. How about a limited selection, including some of the more spectacular pieces of course, for a short period, say a month, while we study the long-term needs? Would that satisfy your people?'

'It would certainly help.' I hoped it might galvanise them into, at least, increasing my funding.

'Should I come down and look at your facilities?'

'Please do.' I smiled at the unintended innuendo, glad that we weren't using videophones.

Over lunch at the Pier Hotel we discussed the problems. It would mean clearing a room of its existing exhibits, tightening up security, getting in some extra staff who would have to be carefully vetted. I wondered aloud if the chairman would provide the funds. 'I'm grateful to you and the MOL,' I said. 'I'll let you know how I get on. I'll pop up and see you, if I may.'

The chairman would find the money. 'It's only right for the town.' I made it an excuse to see Hilary again; we were on first name terms now. I set about the arrangements 'to bring home our king' as the local press put it. It was to be a gala opening. I felt myself growing more excited each day at the thought of having those beautiful objects with their patina of a life lived, and a death, fourteen hundred years ago, still on them. At last the security van drew up in front of our building and the packing cases were carried inside. I left them as they were overnight. We would open them in the morning. I had the explanatory material, the postcards, booklets and leaflets all ready but I drew back from putting my hands on the things themselves. I needed a night's preparation as if for some religious ritual, a time of purification.

Caesar's presence, his demands for attention and food, helped to calm me down. After all they were only artefacts like those I handled all the time. There was nothing, apart from their intrinsic value, any different about them from my beloved royal dancing pumps with diamond buckles a queen had worn. And yet I felt there was.

In the morning I managed to control my excitement long enough to eat the proper breakfast Lucy had always insisted on. The presence of the team of two, responsible for our displays, ensured I appeared calm and in control. We unpacked the cases and gingerly lifted the exhibits into the light, arranging and rearranging them to show themselves at their best. In the small room we had been able to set aside for the exhibition the effect was almost overpowering, even to me who had seen them before.

'London's been very generous,' Lisa, the team manager said. 'Surely lots of people will want to see them.'

'Let's hope we can cope with the crowds,' I laughed. Already the school visits were booked. That evening there was to be a reception for the press and the friends of the museum, the chairman of course, even the mayor. 'I think that's all we can do for now.'

Locking the door behind us I suddenly had the feeling that there was somebody still in the room we had left, but, looking back through the glass door, I knew it was just an illusion brought on by the strange aura thrown off by the things themselves, and the simple beauty of the blue glass jars, the golden crosses, the gleaming buckle as bright as when it had been laid to rest belted to its owner's waist.

The reception had gone well. Everyone seemed suitably impressed. Jean and Harry Bates, who had decided to come out as the original discoverers, had been applauded and interviewed. I hoped they wouldn't regret it later. The last question had been answered, the last guest gone. 'I'll lock up and set the alarms,' I said to the receptionist.

'Goodnight, Mr Kish.'

'Goodnight, Phoebe. See you in the morning.'

Now I could have the exhibition to myself. I went back into the room and began a slow inspection of the glass cases. At the one containing the gold pieces I stopped. A trickle of dust had caught my eye. It seemed to be spilling out of the gold buckle. I got out the keys, unlocked the case and raised the lid. The deposit of fine silt was small but unmistakable. The buckle consisted of a long triangular case, a hasp with the metal tongue attached to it and the oblong rim for the belt to be threaded through. The ornate case had a back and front section held together with three decorated round rivet studs like gold buttons. Perhaps one or more of these had worked loose on the journey, letting the thin trickle of dust ooze out between the plates. With a shock I realised that this might be the king's own dust but I pushed the thought aside and went to get the gloves we always wear when handling objects.

Snapping them on I lifted out the buckle. I would need a brush to clear the trickle away before the public were allowed in. I held up the buckle between the fingers and thumb of my right hand. A little more dust spilled onto my glove. I turned the piece over. More dust fell as if from a broken egg timer, only this one had been marking the passing of centuries not minutes.

It seemed best to let as much of the brownish powder seep out as I could before putting the piece back in the display case. I picked up a leaflet and held it under the buckle until there was a little heap of the stuff and the flow stopped. I ventured a gentle shake. I didn't want to come in the morning and find more earth to be brushed away. As I did so I thought something moved inside. I shook it slightly again and this time there was a sound, hardly more than the broken filament of a light bulb makes when shaken but unmistakable. Something was entombed within the body of the buckle.

For a moment I stood there wondering what to do. Then I put it back on its display stand, blew away the dust and locked the case. My mind seemed to have taken on the sudden blankness of shock. Switching off the lights, I locked the door, set the security system and left the building, locking the door behind me; doing all the right things but on autopilot, in a kind of daze.

Caesar jumped down from his preferred chair when I opened the sitting-room door, and the touch of his warm body against my legs as he wound himself about me brought back some feeling of normality. I poured myself a whisky and dry ginger and sat down to think, letting my fingers scratch between his ears and under his chin as he liked best.

How should I handle this? Ask Hilary, came back the answer. Maybe she's come across something like this before. And when I got through to her in the morning that was her answer.

'I thought there was something more to that buckle. There was too much of it. After all you only need a tongue and an eye for fastening. Not that ornate body.'

'What would it be then?'

'Probably a reliquary of some sort, and hollow.'

'And inside?'

'Usually a bit of a saint's bone or hair.'

'Not hair. The noise was solid.'

'But I would have expected bone to have dissolved, given that we don't have any trace of a body.'

'Except the tooth enamel. Perhaps the buckle protected it, whatever it is.'

'But the dust got in.'

'Yes, the dust got in.'

'Should I come down and have a look?'

'Please, if you can spare the time.'

'For this, of course. It could be something really exciting, proving he was a Christian.'

'Then it would have to be Saebert. Bede is quite clear as you told me.'

'I'll come down this afternoon. Then we can have a look when the public have left. Don't let anyone else touch it.'

'It's safely locked away.'

There had been a steady stream of visitors all day, including two school parties. The exhibition didn't mean much to most of the children as far as I could see. Just a welcome break from the routine of school. But several of the adults, when I looked in from time to time, showed something of the suppressed excitement I had felt myself, even a little of the shock of last night.

Hilary arrived at four thirty and we went along to what we were calling 'The Royal Room'. The last visitors were drifting away. The museum closed at five and it was almost dark outside. 'You've laid it out very well,' she said.

'That's our Lisa. She's really much too good for us. I'm afraid we'll soon lose her. I've told the staff I'll lock up tonight; that we've got some work to do here. So we shouldn't be disturbed.'

'Good. Let's open the case.'

Once again I unlocked it. We both put on gloves. Hilary lifted out the buckle. She shook it gently against her ear. 'There is something in there. I heard a distinct knock.'

'Would it be sacrilege to try and open it?'

'It might be professional suicide.'

But I felt that whatever was in there wanted to be seen, let out, almost like the genie from the bottle.

'Aladdin's lamp,' I said.

'You mean try rubbing it. Who knows what we might find. A pity it wasn't opened during the cleaning process.'

As she spoke her gloved hand was stroking the buckle.

'Can you move the rim where the belt goes through?'

She pushed at it gently with her forefinger. 'I don't know if it's meant to move.'

Suddenly the hasp holding the tongue and rim in place slid backward. 'It's the weld,' Hilary said. 'It's come apart. I nearly dropped the whole thing.' The fore piece had fallen away, leaving the buckle in two parts with a long slit open between the riveted plates.

I took the hasped tongue and rim in my gloved hand. 'Whatever is in there must have been inserted before the other part was welded on.'

With a delicate thumb and forefinger she upended the rest of the buckle over her palm. There was a little flurry of dust. Then gravity did its usual trick and not one but two small objects, very small indeed, fell into her hand, one round, one square.

'I'll get a cleaning brush. Hang on.'

Carefully we worked at the surfaces of the two little enclosures.

'Perhaps the round one is a coin.' There had been coins among the finds from the grave, two gold tremisses of the Merovingian kingdom in France, dated to the early 600s.

'I don't think so,' Hilary said. 'Look, isn't it some sort of amulet? Surely that's the Chi-Rho in the middle. You know, the symbol of Christianity the Emperor Constantine saw in the sky before the battle he had to win on his way to Rome.'

'In this sign conquer.'

'That's it. But the words round the outside look like Greek to me and I don't know any, do you?'

'Not even a letter, apart from Pythagoras in maths, you know, $\Pi r^2$. Or was it that thing about the square on the hypotenuse? I always got them mixed up.'

Hilary turned the piece over and brushed at the other surface. A picture began to appear. There seemed to be some sort of musical instrument in the middle, like the harp we'd found in the dig but I couldn't make out the rest of the figures.

'What about the square thing?'

She brushed at it carefully. 'It's gold, very thin, a little folded sheet like a piece of paper and what looks to be more Greek letters. A prayer perhaps or charm. What do we do now?'

'We put the two pieces of buckle together as if they're still joined and lay them on the display stand. And we wrap the two inserts in cotton wool and lock them in the safe. Then we go and have a drink at the Pier while we decide what to do next.'

*

Circa 1300 BC
Hymn to the Lord of Lords, God of Gods Ahuramazda

*Tell me truly, O my Lord, this I ask:*
*Who was the creator, the First Father of the Divine?*
*Who laid down the pathway for the Sun and Moon?*
*Who causes the moon to wax and wane again?*
*How I long to know my Lord.*

*Tell me truly, O my Lord, this I ask:*
*Who established the earth firm below and kept the sky*
*From falling? Who made the trees and the streams?*
*Who yoked the swift winds and rushing clouds?*
*How I long to know my Lord.*

*Tell me truly, O my Lord, this I ask:*
*Who in His kindness made darkness and light?*
*Who in His goodness made sleep and waking?*
*Who ordered morning, noon and evening?*
*How I long to know my Lord.*

**The Avesta of Zoroaster**

*

'I think I should photograph our finds,' I said to Hilary when I rang her the next morning. 'Then we can get a preliminary reaction to what we've got before letting others loose on them.' I knew that the Museum of London would want to take them into custody and I wasn't prepared to give them up yet. I reasoned that, at the moment, they were alright where they were. Only the two of us knew of their existence, no one else had access to the safe without my permission and no one could remove anything without signing for it. 'I'll email them through to you today, but I'd rather you didn't let anyone know where they came from at this stage if you can.'

'I think I can manage that. I'll have to let someone see the pictures or they won't be able to help but I can probably keep the provenance quiet – though not for long.'

The safe was in the basement. I let it be known that I wanted to photograph the little gold crosses, removed one from the case and shut myself in with our digital camera. As a precaution I photographed the cross first. Then I took the two objects from the safe, set them up and shot as many close-ups of the surfaces as I could, sorry that I didn't dare open up the folded gold sheet to see if there was more writing on the inside.

Selecting the best images, I loaded them onto my personal laptop and sent them off. It was a risk that had to be taken. Ordinary post was too slow. But the longer it took to identify the texts the more I endangered both Hilary's job and my own. It was our duty to own up to the finds which were part of a discovery of national interest, although as grave goods, they couldn't be declared treasure trove. Indeed the question of ownership was technically rather complicated since they had been found on council land but the Bateses had been the discoverers. Jean and Harry had generously renounced any claim to the objects but would that stand up in court if they changed their minds?

I didn't really care about my career. I was sure I could always do something else but I was concerned for Hilary who was much higher up the scale in a job she obviously liked and that would be hard to replace.

'Could we meet?' she asked when she got back to me next day. 'There's someone I'd like you to talk to who can explain things better than I could. I realised when I saw the pictures that I had to let someone else in on it if we were to make any sense of what we've found. But he's tremendously reliable and rather tickled to be involved.'

Leaving work early I took the train to Liverpool Street and waited for her in the handsome new glass and chrome café above the station concourse.

'This is Professor Linden,' she said. 'We call on him when we've got a problem. He usually comes up with an answer.'

'You flatter me, Hilary,' he said extending a hand whose back was a delta of blue-corded veins. 'Call me Jack. It makes me feel not quite so ancient.'

'Alex Kish,' I said. His handshake was surprisingly firm. The voice, I thought, showed a faint trace of an American accent. 'The coffee's not too bad. Shall I get you some?'

I found them laughing together when I got back to the table with two frothing cups. The professor at once began to spoon milky foam into his mouth.

'Hilary's told me a bit about your find,' he said. He put down his spoon and took out an envelope with prints of my photos which he spread on the table. 'What do you want to know?'

'First, is it Greek, as we thought? Then what does it say?'

'It's Greek, alright. As to what it says, this one,' he tapped the picture of the round disc with its inscription. 'That in the middle as I think you already know is the Christian symbol of the Chi-Rho. The letters round the outside make up two words: Mithras and Ormuz.'

'Mithras I can do. The Roman god of soldiers, wasn't he? But the other… What was that again?'

'Ormuz. A later version of Ahura Mazda: the old Persian supreme god of Zoroastrianism, the equivalent of Jehovah or Zeus. Or just God.'

'And the other side?'

'That's very interesting and quite complex. In the middle is a lyre, as you've already identified I think. On either side are two dolphins and the figure lying across the top of the lyre is a sleeping hound.'

'Does it mean anything or is it just decorative?'

'They're all symbols of Orpheus. That's his lyre. The hound signifies his descent into the underworld; the dolphins his journey to the Blessed Isles.'

'So what does it add up to? Why are all these gods or heroes or whatever they are put together on this amulet, if that's what it is?'

'They are all expressions of a belief in resurrection. All of them, Christ, Orpheus and Mithras, return from the underworld, Hades, the bull's cave, and Mithras and Christ both promise an eternal life in heaven to their followers.'

'And Orpheus? Ormuz? How do they fit in?'

'Orpheus was thought of as a prophet, as poet and musician he explained the mysteries, the beliefs and the initiation rites of Dionysus, another resurrection god.'

'So he isn't a god himself?'

'No. He's just connected with Dionysus, aka Bacchus, his prophet if you like.'

'And the other? Orm… something?'

'Ormuz is supreme over Mithras, rather like the relationship of the first two persons of the Christian trinity, except that Mithras isn't an official son. Although Ormuz creates the cosmic egg and Mithras according to some versions is born from that.'

'And the gold leaf with its inscription?' Hilary asked.

'That's Greek. A few lines of poetry but I haven't had time to track them down.'

'From what you've said we're not looking at something Anglo Saxon or even very Christian.'

'I think, in fact I'm pretty sure, that these are things that were left behind when the Roman army pulled out. Or else they were gifts from somewhere.'

I thought of the coins from France, the flagon and bowl from Ethiopia found in the prince's grave.

'Trade? Presents,' Hilary said, 'or something found in a grave or ruined temple and used as a sort of good luck charm?'

'If Christianity didn't get the king into heaven maybe Mithras or Orpheus would.'

Professor Linden drained the last of his coffee, ran his spoon round the inside of his cup for its final coating of froth and stood up. 'I must go. Keep me in the picture and I'll let you know if I find out any more.'

His thin figure, like one of Lowry's stick men, vanished down the escalator. 'It's such a lot to take in,' I said. 'But it doesn't help with what we do now.'

'I'm afraid we have to own up to what we've found, with a few adjustments to our story. I imagine neither of us wants to be carpeted. I'll tell the Department. Who should you tell?'

'My chairman, I suppose. And he'll tell the local press. It'll be all over the media in no time.'

Then the Lord Cyrus, lord of lords, king of the Persians, Medes, and all Ionia after he had defeated Croesus, king of Lydia with all its wealth and splendour, determined to conquer Assyria. To this end he sent magi as his servants and the servants of Ahura Mazda, Lord of Lords, God of Gods, into the land to prepare the people, among whom were dwelling many enslaved by the Assyrians, such as the people of Jerusalem whom King Nebuchadnazzar brought into captivity. The Assyrian capital was then the great city of Babylon whose walls have a circuit of fifty-six miles with a hundred gates of bronze. In the middle of the city are the royal palace and the temple of Bel, the Babylonian Zeus, where there is a golden statue of the god, seated on a golden throne with a table of gold beside.

When the Lord Cyrus came to the city he diverted the river Euphrates into the lake which Queen Nicrotis had dug as part of the city's defences, and entered the city of Babylon along the riverbed as soon as the water was low enough. Then all the Babylonian empire as far as Egypt fell to the Persians and the captive peoples returned to their own lands.

'Thus says the Lord, your ransomer who fashioned you from birth: I am the Lord who made all things, by myself I stretched out the skies, alone I hammered out the floor of the earth. I say of Jerusalem, "She shall be inhabited once more," and of the cities of Judah, "they shall be rebuilt; and all their ruins I will restore." I say to Cyrus, "You shall be my shepherd to carry out all my purpose, so that Jerusalem may be rebuilt and the foundations of the temple may be laid." Thus says the Lord to Cyrus his anointed, Cyrus whom he has taken by the hand to subdue nations before him, I will go before you, I will break down gates of bronze, I will give you treasures from dark vaults, that you may know I am the Lord, Israel's God who calls you by name. For the sake of Jacob my servant and Israel my chosen I have called you by name, and given you your title, though you have not known me. I make the light, I create the darkness, author alike of prosperity and trouble. "I alone have roused this man in righteousness and I will smooth his path before him; he shall rebuild my city and let my exiles go free."'

The Unknown Isaiah

All hell broke loose as I'd feared. The chairman insisted on calling a press conference as soon as I told him what we'd found when, as I put it, we were making a routine inspection of the buckle to see why it was leaking dust, which was nearly the truth. Hilary phoned to say her boss had suggested calling in Professor Linden to help with identifying the objects and she had warned Linden to expect a summons.

'Tell me more about him. How does he come to be a specialist in this sort of thing?'

'Apparently he spent years in the field in the Middle East, before the Mullahs and Saddam, and the West's breakdown in relations with that part of the world. He was on joint digs with the people out there. Then things got so bad that all the projects were dropped and Western money, mainly American, was withdrawn. Of course he's horrified by what's happened to archaeology in Iraq. He blames America's thirst for oil and refuses to live in the USA any more.'

'Does he think the British are any better?'

'Not much. But just enough, which is handy for us.'

The press conference was a brilliant PR coup if that was what the town and the museum needed. Any mention of mysterious cults puts the headline writers into overdrive.

'Was the prince a pagan at heart?' was the mildest of them. The national press picked it up overnight and the next day the phone never stopped ringing. I did my best to answer unsensationally, knowing that anything I said would be souped up in the retelling. By the time we shut up shop I felt as if my brains had been picked over with a set of delicate scalpels and all my ideas and emotions lifted out, except for a dazed weariness that was almost catatonic.

Before locking up I went along to look at the exhibition. Now there was no need for secrecy, the two tiny objects, one round, one square, had been placed beside the buckle. Suddenly it struck me that they looked as if it had given birth to them, as if these were its offspring. I had felt myself being drawn down the corridor to the room by an invisible thread, and now again I had the same sensation as before of being watched, as if I wasn't alone. Quickly I switched off the light and left for the comfort of Caesar and a large whisky and dry ginger.

The chairman rang me in the morning. 'Have you seen the papers? They've really put us on the map.'

By lunchtime Phoebe was having to regulate the flow of visitors, all eager to see the latest finds. I hoped they wouldn't be too disappointed.

'Some of them were rather weird, Mr Kish,' she said later as she handed me the key to the king's exhibition room. 'New Agers I should think. Like those who turn up at Stonehenge on Midsummer's day.'

'With any luck it'll be a nine days' wonder,' I said, 'and then we can get back to our usual quiet life.'

'I wouldn't count on it. Goodnight, Mr Kish. See you in the morning.'

I'd hardly had the time all day to more than skim through the headlines so I took the papers home to read at leisure. Caesar didn't like me reading. He would jump up on the arm of my chair and dab at the pages of book or paper with a closed paw before trying to climb onto them so that I had to stop and give him my attention. This time however I pushed him off. Somehow one of the journalists had got hold of Linden. 'Specialist in Middle Eastern religions and mystery cults believes he has identified the writing on the folded golden sheet as lines from an Orphic poem. Orphism was a mystery religion popular in Roman Britain, and in competition with Christianity for dominance in the late Roman period. Orpheus was torn to pieces by the Bacchae for refusing to join in their dance in which they were also said to tear wild animals apart in their frenzy.'

No wonder the public had been queuing up to get in.

I telephoned Hilary. 'Have you seen the papers?'

'I have.'

'Did Linden tell you about this?'

'He rang me to apologise. He was just about to tell me he thought he had identified the text but the press got to him first. Of course he claims that wasn't what he said, and I do believe him.'

'So do I. But as a result we've had the weirdoes on the doorstep all day, clamouring to get in.'

A small queue had already formed when I got to the museum in the morning. I decided to use the back way into the building, only to be met by Lisa waiting outside my door.

'Could I have the key to the safe, Alex? I presume you thought the new finds would be more secure there overnight. Probably a good idea but we'll have to let the customers in on the dot. I imagine that's what they've come to see after yesterday's press so we'd better get them back in the case before we have a riot on our hands.'

'What do you mean, Lisa?' But already my heart was beginning to thud with my suspicions. 'I left them there in the case with the buckle last night. Then I locked up and went home. Are you saying they're not there now? Come on.'

I hurried along the corridor towards the king's room, Lisa almost running to keep up with me. The door was open. 'Who unlocked the door?'

'I did. I wanted to make sure we really had found the best layout for the exhibition.'

Even from the doorway I could see the buckle was now lying on its own. But I crossed the room and peered through the glass in the hope that the two small finds would miraculously reappear. Then I tried the lid of the case and found it was already unlocked.

'We'll have to call in the police. Can you put a notice on the glass saying the objects found in the buckle have been removed for further examination?' It went through my mind that I had been stupid to lift the lid, leaving my fingerprints on it and possibly obscuring others. But it had to be relocked in case anyone took a fancy to the buckle itself. The shock of finding the objects had really gone seemed to have stopped me thinking clearly. Now my brain began to re-engage.

'Cancel what I asked you to do just now,' I said to Lisa. 'I realise we'll have to close the whole room. The police may even want us to close the museum itself. Until we know put a notice on the door saying closed for relocation.'

'Someone will find out what's happened,' Lisa said. 'There's bound to be a leak.'

'I know but we'll keep it quiet as long as we can.'

Back in my own room I notified the police, then the chairman who seemed to take the disappearance as a personal disaster, and finally Hilary.

'I wonder what it means,' she said. 'I'll have to tell the department. I'm afraid they'll insist on everything coming back here for safety.'

I'd also been wondering what it all meant. Why those two miniature objects and not the gold buckle itself, of far more value just for the weight of the metal?

The rest of the day was spent being interviewed by the police and explaining to angry members of the public that the exhibition had closed early because of problems with the air conditioning, a fiction that couldn't be argued against.

The next morning a police expert on art and antiques theft turned up and shook his head. The chance of recovery was very remote. The objects had probably already been spirited abroad where there were collectors to pay a lot for anything with a whiff of mystery or cult attached to it. Then in the afternoon, as Hilary had predicted, London demanded the return of all the finds, and the chairman ordered an internal inquiry. My job was on the line.

I was suspended for three months pending the results of the enquiry into whether I was guilty of gross negligence. Fortunately the union found me a good lawyer who hoped to be able to convince any judge that I couldn't even have suspected, let alone known, that the new finds would be an immediate target. Meanwhile to pass the time I took myself to London with the idea of meeting Hilary for lunch but also to talk to Linden and to study some of the finds from other sites that might throw light on the two objects found in the buckle.

Linden and I had agreed to meet in the British Museum café, high up above the dome of what had once been the Round Reading Room where Marx and so many others had fed their imaginations. I had spent the morning peering into the glass cases that housed the Roman and Anglo-Saxon artefacts and marvelling again at the jewelled and gleaming Sutton Hoo Hoard, to which, the experts said, our own find came a close second. Our collection was now in the strongbox that is the Museum of London and we were unlikely ever to get it back.

'Tell me about the inscriptions.' I was watching slightly mesmerised as Linden went through his coffee ritual of capturing milky foam on his spoon.

'They're usually instructions to the dead on what to do when they get to the underworld to make sure they go to the Isles of the Blest rather than to Hades.'

'What sort of instructions?'

'Well, as usual the left is the sinister side so the soul is told to avoid the spring on that side and drink from the spring on the right. The soul has been purified in life by the right rituals and claims to be no longer mortal but a god.'

'So they were buried with the dead, these instructions?'

'Just like your finds. Come on. There's one here I can show you that you probably missed this morning.'

And I had. After a time of looking at small objects under glass, the eye and brain get weary and begin to miss even the very thing you're searching for. There it was now in front of my eyes when Linden had led me to the right room, and the right case in that room, or rather there they were: a slightly concertinaed thin gold plate with writing on it and the narrow pendant it had been folded up in.

'There are several of these from Southern Italy, mostly in the museum at Naples but just this one here. As far as I know none have ever been found in this country.'

'And now the only one that has is lost.'

'I've been keeping my eye on the internet sites but nothing has turned up yet. Usually there's a buzz when the traffickers get their hands on something interesting but nothing so far.'

'Why don't the police monitor this sort of thing?'

'Oh they do. But the thieves are very clever. They use codes and sites that change all the time. It's the modern version of the Willow-the-Wisp. As soon as you think you've caught it you find your hands are full of air or smoke. I've got something else to show you here. It's on loan from St Albans right now, which is lucky for us.'

Again he led me between the dizzying glass cases with their precious jewelled holdings like iridescent flies entombed in amber, until we reached a special exhibition of religious symbols lent by other museums around Britain. At once I saw the small round medallion, so similar to the one from the prince's grave, that had been in the buckle with the gold leaves. 'This one has the Egyptian sun god Ra in the middle instead of your Christian Chi-Rho,' Linden said, 'but the principle's the same. Hedging your bets that one of them will get you into the happy hunting grounds.'

A photograph showed the back of the amulet. 'That's different too,' I said.

'It's Mithras, not the same as your Orpheus, I agree, and instead of his usual birth from the cosmic egg he's coming out of the cave where he's just slain the bull or, as some authorities think, been born out of the primal rock instead of the egg.'

'This is fourth-century Roman.'

'So, I suspect, is yours. An earlier coin that's been reworked as a sort of lucky charm. The Christian symbol in the middle probably dates from later than the other motives.'

'If Saebert's sons were still pagan they might have wanted their dad to be sure of a happy afterlife. But wouldn't they have been the sort of pagans Bede describes, believing in life as just an interlude in the darkness?'

'As I said: no harm in hedging your bets with a good luck charm. Or maybe Saebert's own faith was a bit shaky still. The ancient world was prepared to see the numinous under all sorts of names and disguises. It's only the monotheisms, Christianity, Islam and their forerunner Judaism that said you had to restrict yourself to one story.'

'So what we've got is an Anglo-Saxon prince, an early Christian buried with a lot of symbols of foreign gods, Mithras, and the other one I can't pronounce...'

'Ormuz.'

'Ormuz and Orpheus, only he wasn't a god but some sort of pagan prophet. But what does it all mean?'

'Does it have to mean anything? Can't it just be a bit of fascinating Dark Age history?'

'It could have been,' I said, 'if the things hadn't been stolen. Somehow that makes it all different. Sometimes I feel as if a ghost walks over my grave.'

'I've felt that too, in old sites in Mesopotamia and Persia, as it used to be called, when we've suddenly come upon something that hasn't been seen for three thousand years or so, as if the people who were there are still keeping watch.'

'That's it. That's it exactly.'

'I think a lot of people have felt that sensation, that's why you get stories like the curse of Tutankhamen. Anyway I'll keep looking to see if anything turns up on the internet.'

Linden, I could see, wasn't going to tell me his precise sources and I could understand that. It gave him a stake in our discovery. I sensed he was lonely and that every new contact was important to him, even if he had to buy his way in with his exclusive information. And it was one thing less for me to keep tabs on. I could afford to be grateful. Preparing my defence was taking up more time than I could have imagined possible a couple of months ago. I saw myself, with Linden's help, recovering the finds in a blaze of glory, the chairman shaking my hand and offering me a pay rise and full reinstatement which I would decline because of a better offer from a more prestigious museum. Then reality stepped in and I saw myself dismissed and retraining as a teacher just to keep Caesar and me fed and a roof over our heads. I could teach history or art history, I thought gloomily after Linden had left, and while I waited for Hilary to join me for lunch.

The news she brought did nothing to lighten my mood, even though it didn't seem to affect me directly.

'I don't suppose you've been listening to the radio,' she said while we waited for our food to be brought, a mushroom stroganoff for Hilary and spaghetti Bolognese for me.

'I've been with Jack Linden most of the morning. He's been showing me other artefacts like ours. I hope I can take what you're going to tell me. There seems to have been rather a surplus of doom and gloom lately.'

'Well,' Hilary said, 'it's just that your pier has been damaged by fire.'

'That's a relief. I know it sounds strange but we're used to it, rather like it must have been in the Blitz when people got used to bombs. Piers are very vulnerable to fire. Brighton's always losing theirs; so's Worthing. Ours goes up in smoke every decade or so it seems. When did it happen?' I felt on familiar ground for once, in times I understood, not wandering around in the fog of the Dark Ages. 'I take it no one was hurt.'

'The early hours of this morning, I think. There was a night watchman but he seems to have suffered more from the shock of being rescued by helicopter rather than anything physical. But I'm glad you asked.'

'I'm sorry. I know I'm being rather crass about this. I suppose I'm just relieved that no one can blame me.'

'The suspension and all that is getting to you, Alex, isn't it?'

'I suppose it's because I know I'm not above criticism. I should have reported the objects as soon as we found them. I shouldn't have tried to hang on to them, then none of it would have happened. Has Linden told you what he thinks the inscriptions are?'

'No.'

'He says they're instructions for the soul after death on how to get into heaven, only of course they didn't call it heaven.'

'Do you believe in an afterlife, Alex?'

'I wish I could but I can't help thinking this is all we've got. After Lucy died I wanted to believe, as people do.' I hadn't spoken of Lucy before but Hilary didn't ask who I meant. She seemed to know or just to accept without question. But her silence wasn't awkward. 'I'd better start thinking about a train,' I said. 'Caesar will be complaining.'

This time she said: 'Who's Caesar?'

'My familiar or my alter ego. After Lucy I thought of finding a new home for him but somehow he wouldn't let me. Maybe it's time you two met.'

'He might resent me. After all he's had you to himself all this time. Is he a dog or a cat? "Caesar" doesn't give much away.'

'He thinks he's human of course but he's cat-shaped. Will you come?'

'If Caesar approves.'

As the train rattled through east London along the line of the Thames towards the sea, I felt a sudden wave of inexplicable happiness wash over me that even survived the emptiness of the house until I heard Caesar's flick-flap of the cat door. 'You'll have to be good if she comes. No sulking.' I ran my hand, as he liked, the length of his arching black back to the very tip of his tail.

The lightened mood perished in the morning. I was due to meet the union's solicitor to discuss my case so I had an incentive to get up early as if I was going to work as usual, and listen to the news while I showered and made toast. Once a week Doris, Mrs Shepherd, widow, came in to clean and restore order. She preferred to have the house to herself and the next day I would find my portable radio tuned to strange stations it never got from me.

This morning when I switched on it was Radio Essex that came at me out of the little chrome Roberts. The fire at the end of our pier was hot news still. It had consumed a length of one hundred and thirty feet a mile out to sea, destroying the pier railway station, a pub, a restaurant, a souvenir shop and the lavatory block. One of our brave fire fighters was explaining how the tide being out had made it much harder to get the blaze under control. The flames had leapt forty feet into the air, melting the plastic pipe that runs the length of the pier, carrying water against such an emergency. My chairman had managed to get himself quoted as saying that the pier would rise like a phoenix from the ashes but not for at least two years.

Then the newscaster broke into the flow of the recording. 'A statement just issued by the police and fire service confirms that firemen sifting through the charred remains of the pier to try to discover the cause of the fire, have found a body.' The chief fire officer was put on from a radio car. The badly burned corpse had been hidden under fallen timbers. It appeared to be that of a child between the age of nine and twelve. Police were appealing for information about missing children. Suddenly the fire wasn't just an accident or a piece of history that could be restored. Someone, a child, was dead.

Pressed for more details, the officer said it was early days, too soon to judge whether the child had started the fire, died in it or was dead already. He appealed to the public to help and gave a telephone number for information. Then the station switched without a hiccup to the start of the Christmas sales.

What had a child been doing there alone in the dark? Runaway? For a dare? Some people liked to believe the pier was haunted. Sometimes, it was said, drug dealers used it when the tide was in to drop off supplies by boat. Had the child, a boy I was sure, been cold and lit a fire? Or scared and trying to make a light? Why hadn't he just run away, back down the untouched length of the pier, three quarters of a mile of safety that hadn't burnt? Was he scared to meet the firemen and police hurrying out to the blaze? If it was his fault, was he afraid he would be forced to admit it and charged with arson? Maybe no one would ever know. But suddenly what had been no more than a passing end of the pier *son et lumière* had become a titbit for the national tabloids, another nine days' excuse for a ritual outpouring of righteous indignation, for an airing of our blame culture. I put on my jacket and went out to discuss my own mistakes with the union lawyer.

After the meeting at which I'd been promised at least reinstatement ('How could you have known? You acted in good faith in putting the objects on display for the public benefit.'), I walked down through the town to take a look at the pier. The famous gardens were in their winter dress of bright polyanthus and pansies and I remembered how Lucy had disliked the lack of subtlety. 'Institutional planting' she had called it. And all at once I wanted to howl the tears of a frustrated toddler, the tears I hadn't shed before. I cuffed them away trying to pretend it was the salt wind off the sea. The tide was in today but dull and muddied under a dismal sky and the waves sucked at the legs of the pier with a cold swirl that seemed to come from the brine-filled lungs of the drowned.

The entrance to the pier was roped off, with a policeman on duty and a notice stating the obvious. I flashed him my official pass and ducked under the ropes. As I made my way forward to the pier head I could see that the hoses had caused more damage than the fire. If anyone asked me I could say I was making a preliminary assessment of the cost of restoration. After all I was the town's paid expert on Victoriana. The chances were I'd be asked about the refurbishment. It wouldn't hurt to be able to tell the inquiry that I'd gone on doing my job, showing concern, even while suspended.

There were more barriers cordoning off the charred end of the pier and a couple of firemen carefully moving blackened timbers aside and pausing to make notes. The smell of smoke and burnt wood still hung heavy in the air. I produced my pass again. 'Alex Kish,' I said. 'I'm responsible for the museum. I thought I'd just take a look, get some idea of the size of the problem before someone asks me about period restoration. Do you know what started it?'

'We know now it was deliberate,' the one who seemed to be the senior said. 'There was a sort of iron fire basket on a tripod that could have set it off. That's our thinking at the moment.'

'A tramp trying to keep warm,' I suggested.

'More like an addict cooking up a fix,' said the younger one, 'with a portable grate.'

I stared out over the wet slate sea and felt again the strange sensation of being watched, but it was probably only the cold breeze that had sprung up and was fingering my collar, starting the ghost of a shudder down my spine. 'Where was the body found?'

'With the fire basket over there. Part of the roof had collapsed onto him.'

'It was a boy then?'

'Oh yes. Well you wouldn't expect a girl to be out here on her own at that time of night. That was a lad's trick. Anyway forensics have confirmed it.'

'It's certainly a mess,' I said looking around. 'I'd better come back another day with a camera. See if anything can be salvaged. What about the structure itself?'

'That seems to be sound. All steel, you see, and we got the fire under control before it could generate enough heat to start melting the supports. The track's buckled of course.' I could see the twisted rails that had writhed out of their beds and snaked across the deck. I turned and picked my way back towards the beach where the tide was beginning to turn, inching back to expose the famous mudflats whose exhalations had once been thought a cure for whooping cough and croup.

Back home I switched on my computer to check my emails. There was one from Hilary. 'Thought this might interest you. How did your meeting go? My best to Caesar. Hilary.'

I filed it away to attachments and opened it up. There were two parts: text and picture. Carefully working away at a block of sandy soil taken from the king's grave, the conservation team had uncovered something they had identified as an iron lamp. I turned to the picture.

It showed a deeply encrusted but just recognisable shape: a bowl on three or four legs.

Just then the phone rang. It was an excited Jack Linden. 'Have you seen Hilary's latest find?'

'I'm just looking at it now. They seem to think it's a lamp, about AD 600, like the king.'

'To me it looks like a descendant of the Zoroastrian fire holder, the one the king is standing before in the carving on the tomb of Darius a few miles from Persepolis.'

'Do they have three or four legs, these fire holders?'

'They stand on a solid base with a slender shaft topped by a hollowed out stone, which forms a bowl to hold the fire that's never allowed to go out.'

I felt a curious sense of relief. 'But the lamp or whatever it is is quite different: a bowl on a legged stand.'

'Yes, I know. But there was a version that the king took with him when travelling. Obviously he couldn't take his stone hearth but he had to pray to it, or rather the fire, five times a day.'

'Is that where Muhammad got his five prayers a day?'

'Maybe. Anyway the fire would be transferred to a metal bowl and carried with him. It must have been stood on something which made it the same height as the fire back home. The king prayed standing up. So a stand was the obvious solution. Three legs makes the most stable holder, and the Zoroastrians were very keen on things in threes.'

'Trinities?'

'Something like that.'

'Have you ever seen one of these standing fires, in an inscription for instance?'

I heard him hesitate. 'No. But it's a workable hypothesis.'

All this talk of correspondences had set my mind running, a dog after a bone, and maybe it was just harebrained but I heard the senior fire officer saying: 'There was a sort of iron fire basket on a tripod that might have set it off.'

And then I heard myself asking aloud: 'But why fire? Was it seen as a sort of domestic god like the Roman "lares and penates," hearth and home?'

'For the Persians it was the symbol of righteousness, of ultimate purity, and fire permeates all of creation, giving it warmth and life.'

But I could only see charred timbers and heat-twisted rails and somewhere beneath them a boy's soot-blackened body and smoke-shrivelled skin.

Then Darius, King of Kings, by the will of Ahura Mazda, God of Gods, commanded a bridge to be built over the Bosphorus at its narrowest point, halfway to Byzantium, so that he might cross from Asia into Europe to the lands of the Thracians and the Scythians as far as to the Danube. And this bridge was designed by Mandrocles of Samos, an Ionian, who took boats and placed them side by side until the bridge reached the far shore, for which he was loaded with many presents by King Darius. He had the bridge painted in all the stages of its construction, which picture he presented to the temple of the goddess Hera. Then Darius commanded the Ionian fleet, which people were his subjects, to sail into the Black Sea and up the Danube to where the river divides and there build another bridge for the army.

The king having viewed the Black Sea caused two marble columns to be erected at the bridge with inscriptions in Greek and Assyrian showing all the peoples who were with him in that army of 700,000 men.

The Thracians are the most numerous people in the world but they are divided into many tribes. If they were united they could overcome any army for they are fierce warriors who value this class above all others, and live by war and plunder. They worship Ares, Artemis and most of all Dionysus who some say went down into the underworld to restore his mother Semele to life. Here too, men say, Orpheus was born who sang of the mysteries of Dionysus the god who drives his followers mad, and in that frenzy, it is said, the Bacchantes, the women of Thrace, tore Orpheus limb from limb because he would not leave grieving for his wife and join in their rites.

Then leaving his genereal, Megabazus, to subdue Thrace and guard the Hellespont, King Darius set sail again for Asia. And this Megabazus was of all the generals the one most valued by Darius. And always with the Persian armies their magi went too and discoursed with the priests and philosophers of the conquered peoples, and, with the magicians among the Scythians from the north, who profess to foretell the future and work miracles such as raising the dead.

Jack Linden was on the phone to me early next morning. 'What's this in the newspapers, Alex?'

'I haven't had a chance to read them yet, Jack.'

'Sorry. I got used to getting up early in the Middle East before the sun was too hot. It's about this fire of yours and the dead boy.'

That woke me up. 'Old news Jack. I was down there yesterday. I don't see what there is new to say.'

'You didn't see the toys then?'

'What toys?'

'According to the paper they found some toys with the kid.'

'I'll read the article and call you back. It must be something that happened after I'd left.'

I was thinking of the two fire officers continuing their meticulous sift through the ashes. I picked up the paper from the doormat, unfolded it and there it was: front-page news now. Fire Officer Weston giving his story of the strange finds: an old-fashioned, cone-shaped spinning top, a set of five jacks and a ball, a jointed action man doll and other objects too charred to be recognised. It conjured up a sad image of a lonely child hiding out at the end of the pier with his favourite toys for company. I dialled Jack.

'Well?' he said.

'Poor kid. He must have had a hellhole of a home to be living rough like that.'

'But don't you see?' His voice was growing increasingly irritated. Whatever the exam was, I was failing this viva miserably.

'Tell me.'

'The toys of Dionysus, that the Titans lured him away with in order to kill him.'

I didn't understand what he was saying but I wasn't going to let him know that. Not just yet.

'Oh, come off it, Jack. They're just a kid's toys; the things he would take with him if he did a runner, small enough to carry in his pockets.'

'What boy plays with a spinning top these days? And the mirror? Why would a boy want a mirror?'

'To light a fire.' I was becoming irritated in my turn. 'Anyway what mirror? My paper says nothing about a mirror.'

'*The Times* does.'

Like most other Americans he still thought of *The Times* as the custodian of truth and objectivity, a print version of the BBC.

'Okay. Well even if you're right I don't see what it means.'

'It means, as my Irish grandmother might say: there's more to this than meets the eye. And they still don't know how the fire started or whether the child was already dead. What do your legal guys call it: "suspicious circumstances"? I'll say.'

I wasn't convinced. I thought he had been wrong about the fire basket and now I thought that in his determination to find a mystery, the classic 'ritual uses' of a certain school of archaeology, he was way off the mark, seeing conspiracy in a simple runaway. But I knew it was no good arguing. Maybe all those years digging in the sun had affected him or too long among the mysterious alphabets and symbols of ancient beliefs. We agreed to meet soon and keep each other up to date with anything we might find out.

'No sign of our missing objects?' I asked before putting the receiver down.

'Not a whisper. But it's early days, though I have to warn you the recovery rate for such things is minimal. But I expect the police have already told you that. The literally thousands of artefacts from the Baghdad museum that went AWOL after the war have never surfaced. Virtually a whole civilisation gone into oblivion along with the rape of dozens of archaeological sites, places I worked in, torn apart. A monument to human folly.'

'"Look on my works ye mighty and despair," as the poet said.'

He had lost me again but once more I didn't say so. I wasn't sure what I felt, when the papers were full of the dead and maimed, about the loss of inanimate stone, crystal, gold, pots and weapons, things that don't bleed. Or so I thought.

'I'm worried about Jack.' Hilary and I were having a quick drink in the Pier Hotel, to give me some Dutch courage before I took her home to meet Caesar. 'He's making what I think are very tenuous connections and then jumping to rather bizarre conclusions.'

'How do you mean?' We were fighting our way through a disgustingly typical pub lunch of soggy jacket potato over-stuffed with cheddar and coleslaw.

'I'm sorry about the food.'

'Don't worry, I'm used to it. At least this is hot.'

The day was bitterly cold with an arctic wind off the sea that the forecast had warned might bring flurries of snow. 'He thought the lamp you restored from the grave was like some ancient fire altar. That was the first odd thing. Then he thought the toys that were found with the boy's body after the pier fire were the toys of Dionysus. I think that's what he said. He's seeing mysteries everywhere and if he starts saying so in public, or to the press, we'll have hordes of nutters converging on the town.'

'I'd like to have a quick look at the pier before we go to your house,' Hilary said tactfully. 'Would that be a nuisance?'

So I found myself back at the cordoned-off entrance, only there were no police on duty now. Instead, flowers and offerings of toys had been heaped up by the barrier.

'We never used to do this sort of thing.' Even to myself I sounded like a grumpy old fogey.

'Maybe we didn't need to; there were other ways to express a feeling of community. I remember my mother saying that when she was young if somebody in the street had died everyone drew their curtains or blinds at the time of the funeral as a mark of respect.'

'Straw up stret,' I said. 'In Victorian times the cobbles under the horses' hooves were muffled with a layer of straw for a funeral.' I was glad to be able to contribute a bit of information from my own specialism but I didn't know why I had to keep my end up among these experts on ancient civilisations, and felt shut out of the camaraderie there seemed to be between Jack and Hilary. Somehow they made my own work seem frivolous, irrelevant.

'Look,' Hilary said pointing to a group of toys on their own apart from the flowers, plastic soldiers and racing cars. 'Aren't those the things that were described in the newspaper? You would have thought that the police would have wanted to hold on to them for forensic tests.'

'Surely those are new,' I said going closer. 'They're not burnt or damaged as they would be if they were the originals.'

'I suppose somebody thought it would be comforting for the boy's spirit.'

'But what's that in the middle, that rod that has a skein of wool round it and something stuck on the top?'

'It's a whole fennel,' Hilary said. 'Now that really is weird. It reminds me of a Halloween pumpkin head on a pole with a face cut in it.'

'No doubt Jack could give us an equally weird explanation.'

'Perhaps we should ask him. Can you remember all the things in this group?' She looked up at me. Her face was pinched and she shivered slightly.

'Come on. Let me take you to my house and warm you up.' I took her arm and turned away from the pier.

Caesar behaved impeccably, allowing himself to be stroked, and brushing his black sinuous length against her legs as she sat on the sofa. I had gone to town on a choice of tea and a lemon drizzle cake from the local organic shop. I wished the fire was a real one but the mock logs glowed with their electric flicker and their emanation of convenience comfort.

'Goodbye Caesar,' Hilary said as she got up to leave. He stared up at her from his cushion in front of the fire, with wide amber eyes, and purred gently. 'I can't have a cat in my block of flats. But pets are supposed to be good for you, calming.'

'Caesar says you can come and stroke him any time.'

Hilary opened the passenger door when we reached the station car park. I got out too and locked up. 'It's alright, Alex. I can find my way to the right platform,' she laughed.

I came round to her side of the Volkswagen to where she was standing in the light of a street lamp. Suddenly, without thinking, I leant forward and kissed her mouth. She put up a hand to touch the side of my face. 'I was beginning to think you'd never do that.' We kissed again.

'I'll ring you later to make sure you're safely home.'

Back in my own home, with Caesar out for a post-prandial prowl of the neighbouring gardens, and a whisky and dry ginger satisfyingly within reach, I began to think about the toys we had seen. Hilary's explanation of a benign wish to comfort a dead boy's spirit seemed too kindly a theory. Jack Linden was the obvious person to ask but I was afraid he would only jump to some bizarre conclusion again and we would be back in the morass of sinister ancient rituals that I found completely out of place in our cosy seaside, suburban context.

Ringing Hilary as I had promised (or was it threatened?) when I thought she must have made it home, I asked: 'Do you think we should tell anyone about those toys?'

'What could we say? That we thought they were rather peculiar? Wouldn't people think we were, peculiar, I mean? And who would we tell? The police? Jack might have some thoughts but I imagine you must have already discarded that idea. I think we just have to wait and see.'

'I was thinking of the last time we did that. It nearly cost me my job. Will have, even now, if the hearing goes against me. But then I think of my chairman's face if I tried to involve him in some tale of mysterious rituals. He'd probably have me sectioned not just sacked. So I guess you're right. We'll have to wait and see.'

By the time the phone rang again the next morning, I had firmly convinced myself that silence was our best course. It was Jack.

'Well?'

'What's up, Jack?'

'The toys.'

'What about them?'

'Why didn't you tell me? You must have seen them too.'

'Tell you what?'

'That there were more toys of Dionysus.'

I gave in. 'How did you find out?'

He laughed. 'I spotted them in a newspaper photograph. The little group on its own, with that grotesque attempt at a narthex and bull-roarer so I came down early to take a look.'

'A what?'

'A narthex. The fennel head on a stick as carried by the priests of Dionysus and, even earlier, Ahura Mazda.'

'And the other thing?'

'The bull-roarer. Quite a clever substitute: a football rattle. Same principle: whirling something round to make a loud noise. Lots of cults have used those, from every part of the world: Australia, Africa, Greece.'

'What do you think it means?'

'We have a trickster who knows what he's doing.'

'But what's it all for?'

'Somebody either likes to play games or, kindest interpretation, to join in mourning for a child. Maybe a modern day Orphic. Some sort of religious freak.'

'What do you think we should do? Hilary and I wondered whether we should tell anyone.'

'I don't think there's enough, or rather anything concrete, to tell anyone else without being suspected of being a freak oneself.'

'That's what we decided.'

'We have to wait and see. If it's not just a harmless bit of whimsy something will turn up that will tell us more. Or the whole thing will just fade away. Anyway I'm still on your patch, in a pub on the sea front. Very chilly it all looks too. Why don't you join me? Then you can show me the original site where the grave was found.'

My case was due to be heard at the end of the week.

'Do I have to attend?' I asked my union representative.

'Not necessary. We'll be arguing on technicalities and legalities. How probable is it that you could anticipate those bits being stolen when the rest of the stuff had been sitting there safely in their glass cases for a couple of days? The police found evidence of a forced entry by an upper skylight. A professional job that was aborted for some reason after the burglar had only had time to tackle that one case. We've got your statement, yours and the other members of staff. There's no question of anyone inside being involved, least of all you. I'm totally confident. The only question is: do you want reinstatement or compensation?'

'Reinstatement,' I said without thinking and then wondered if that was true. But anyway it was too late to go back on it.

In spite of his reassurances I spent a nervous morning. At 12.30 the telephone rang. 'We've just broken. I think the chairman wanted his lunch. You're back!'

'When can I go in?'

'Tomorrow if you like. Or you can have a week to sort your affairs. Not culpable. Recommendation to upgrade security which means the council will have to spend some money. Cheers.' And he was off.

It was strange to be walking in through the door of the museum the next morning.

'Oh, Mr Kish,' Phoebe hurried towards me, 'we're all so glad to see you back. I've put a little plant pot on your desk as a welcome.'

I managed to thank her and say yes it was nice for me too, surprised at the threat of tears that sprang up in my throat and behind my eyes. A few early miniature daffodils lit up the December gloom of my office. Or were they narcissi. And what had I read somewhere about Narcissus? I took down the *Encyclopaedia of Myth and Legend* I had bought when all this first began. And then I put it back. I wouldn't look him up. I'd been too much alone all these weeks, thinking, brooding. Now I had to get stuck in to something practical. Soon the chairman was on the line.

'Good to have you back. You do understand we had to go through the accepted procedures. I'll be in touch about the security upgrade.'

Silently I thought that now there was nothing worth stealing. Perhaps I should have opted for compensation, taken the money and run. But, when I asked her, Hilary was adamant that for the sake of the future I had to take up my old job again. If I were unemployed I would be looked at suspiciously every time I went after something new, and how long until the compensation ran out? To become a teacher I'd need at least a year's retraining with no guarantee of an easier job at the end of it. More like a mob of ungovernable teenagers on the most run-down estate in Barking.

Post had continued to come in while I'd been away. Some of it Lisa had dealt with but there was a little stack of unopened envelopes. I began to go through them, tossing some of the contents into the shredder and putting others aside. Hilary rang in the middle of it.

'How does it feel to be back?'

'Strange. But I suppose I'll get used to it. Do you fancy an official junket?'

'Depends what it is.'

'We're unveiling the first piece of town sculpture since that of Queen Victoria for her Golden Jubilee. The mayor's going to pull the cord that opens the curtains or whatever and then there's a civic reception. I ought to show my face to prove I'm not still in the doghouse but it would be a lot easier if you were with me.'

'Of course I'll come if I can. When is it?'

'That's the snag. It's very early in the morning for some reason, sunrise on midwinter day, the shortest day – however you care to think of it.' I hesitated. 'I wondered if you'd like to stay the night before. At my place I mean.'

I heard her pause before answering and I could imagine her straight look as she said very steadily: 'I don't think we're quite ready for that, Alex. You don't really know very much about me yet. Anyway the sun doesn't get up until about eight. There are plenty of early trains.'

I felt a mixture of disappointment and relief. 'Okay. I can pick you up at the station at about 7.15. That should give us time to get to Canvey Point where the ceremony is. I hope you can spend the rest of the day with me.'

'I'll take one of my days off. I've got some in hand.'

When I got in that evening Caesar was waiting for me to open the tin of cat food at once and fork the unappealing brown mess into his dish. He had got used to having me around all day and wasn't pleased with the resumption of my old routine. I felt curiously drained. It had been hard work pretending everything was back to normal, as if I had never been away. Lethargically I checked the television schedules to see if there was anything that caught my eye. As I flipped from channel to channel I was suddenly transfixed by a programme on BBC4. A concert of words and music from St John's Smith Square in London for St Lucy's Day. I hadn't even known there was a St Lucy. I found the weekly magazine guide and began to read the accompanying puff. The concert was in aid of the partially sighted because her name meant light or, more grisly thought, she had torn out her eyes rather than be forced into marriage, like the beautiful Asian girls one sometimes saw in newspaper photographs who killed themselves to avoid unknown bridegrooms chosen by their parents.

Wordsworth's *Lucy Poems*, it said, in a new setting.

*She lived unknown and few could know*
*When Lucy ceased to be;*
*But she is in her grave, and, oh*
*The difference to me!*

It could have been an epitaph for my own Lucy. And suddenly I was choking on a great sob for all the unknown lives gone into their graves, and a rush of guilt that I hadn't loved her enough, known what she wanted, saw into what we call the heart, given her more of myself. It was as if all my life I'd been frozen inside and that when she died that coldness had become a rigid block of ice that was only now beginning to crack under some unacknowledged strain. Or could it be a new warmth? Caesar rubbed himself against my legs and sat down to wash the traces of dinner from around his muzzle with a delicate questing paw, and looking down at his vulnerability, I felt a new sob rising. He trusted me and I could crush him with a blow. Had my coldness crushed Lucy? We had never discussed how we felt about each other or about much else except our relative jobs and colleagues and the daily practicalities of our lives. From time to time I had gone off with a map on a cycling tour while she in turn had gone to visit her aging parents in Ipswich. Sometimes we took a walking week in the Lake District or Scotland. Was I weeping internally for her or for myself? Or for both of us? There was a blindness of the heart that Lucy hadn't been able to cure even if she had tried. And that itself held a question I couldn't answer. No wonder Hilary had sensed that I wasn't ready for intimacy, that like Kay in the faery story I still had a splinter of ice in my heart.

Would I have gone down into the dark to bring back my lost wife like Orpheus? Even with a magic harp, lute or Papageno's pipes that could neutralise death? Could I ever love anyone enough? Could they love me enough to follow me up into the light? Or would my doubts always cause me to look back and push them down into the shadows again while I went on alone, to be torn to bits by the very emotions I'd suppressed?

It was still pitch black when I picked Hilary up at Southend Station. She kissed me lightly on the cheek. 'What a time to hold a junket. It had better be spectacular.'

'Thank you for coming. I'm rather dreading the whole thing and very relieved not to be responsible for any of it. I hope you're well wrapped up. We have to stand around waiting for the sunrise or something. Then it's champagne breakfast in a marquee.'

As we drove along the promenade against the morning rush hour traffic, a smear of grey began to show itself out over the sea.

'Where exactly are we going?' Hilary asked.

'Canvey Point, the tip of the island, only of course it isn't an island, only a promontory. We're just crossing over Leigh Beck. If it was light enough you could see Hadleigh Castle. Now we've turned back towards the sea.' Lights appeared ahead, leading forward to a car park where we were beckoned on by an attendant and waved into a space. Doors slammed as people spilled out, pulling on gloves and huddling down inside their coat collars. A sign pointed us towards the exhibition. We breasted a sand dune and came to a halt on a natural rise from the shore that provided a perfect raked theatre before the estuary mudflats, that now began to gleam here and there as the misty grey light was caught on the surface of little rock pools. Suddenly the sky was washed blue with small clouds floating in it that began to blush an almost indecent pink. Against this theatrical backdrop we could see a tall structure raised on a plinth and obscured by a dark curtain. The light was turning golden, the pink and blue being driven out. Beyond the tall mysterious shape the sea still showed a flat gunmetal grey, quite still, as if the tide was held on a cusp between ebb and flow.

'Look,' Hilary said pointing behind us. A perfectly round white moon hung in that still blue region of sky looking towards the sunrise. And then, as if to a triumphal chorus, the sun itself lifted a bright rim over the horizon making a path of light across the sea towards the installation. As it reached the structure silhouetted against it, the curtains were drawn back on both sides to reveal a huge transparent egg through which the light streamed, picking out a dark core at its centre.

There was a gasp from the crowd and then what seemed a commotion breaking out at the front where the dignitaries were. 'Can you see what it is? I'm not tall enough,' Hilary said.

'It seems to have a human shape at the centre.'

A young man beside me said. 'There's something wrong. That isn't how it's meant to be.'

'How do you know?'

'I'm one of Reg North's students. I helped him with the installation. There's meant to be another egg in the middle that's opalescent, and then another darker inside that. Like Russian dolls.'

'Come on,' I pulled at Hilary's arm. 'I'm going down there. Hang on to me.'

I pushed through the crowd that was now noisy with reaction and speculation.

'It's not a real child; it can't be,' I heard a woman saying.

'They get up to anything these days. Bloody obscene I call it, and we're paying for it.'

The word 'child' seemed to run through the crowd in a chilled whisper like a breaking wave.

We reached the front at the foot of the plinth. The mayor and my chairman seemed struck dumb. I looked up at the huge egg with what looked like the body of a child floating in the middle, lit now by the full disc of a blazing winter sun. The boy was naked except for some kind of necklace that caught the light as if on fire, his arms outstretched in welcome, the childish penis contracted into a scarfed acorn of flesh. Someone, I thought must be the artist, was shouting.

'Cover it up. Pull the bloody curtain.'

'We can't. It opens automatically. It's light sensitive to the sunrise.'

'Christ! Then get rid of the bloody people.'

A man I recognised as one of our local police inspectors stepped forward. 'I've sent for reinforcements to deal with the crowd. Now, sir, what's your explanation?'

'How the fuck do I know? It was alright when I left it yesterday.'

'So you're saying it's been tampered with? How was it supposed to be? After all we've seen this sort of thing before. With animals for instance; a cow and a shark wasn't it? It looks to me like a dead child in there, in which case we're dealing with murder. Wasn't there a case of human foetuses being used in some way for so-called art?'

'Look. That isn't the kind of thing I do. I'm out to make something beautiful not just to shock.'

'I'll have to ask you to come to the station to make a statement of course. Meanwhile we need to remove the body. How do we get in there, sir?'

'The same way whoever tampered with it got in.'

'And what would that be, sir?'

'How should I know? I suppose they must have melted the weld that holds the two halves together. With a blowtorch. There must have been more than one of them. The two halves are quite heavy. I had the help of several students when I put it up. Anyway we don't know that what's in there isn't just a model, a dummy.'

'I'm afraid that won't do, sir. It's quite clear to me what we're dealing with here. Do you know of anyone who might have wanted to get back at you in this way?'

'Everyone's got enemies but I can't think of anyone who would do this. You need to know what you're doing for a start. I think it's more likely to be some kind of sick joke by someone who hates installation art.'

Suddenly the inspector made up his mind. 'There's nothing to be done here. Constable, call up the traffic department. They can send one of their car-removal transporters.'

I looked up again at the floating child, suspended now with a halo of sun around his head and thought of Apollo and Ra. He seemed to be almost smiling. At least his face was composed, tranquil.

The artist had disappeared round the side of the plinth. When he came back he was clearly excited. 'It's not mine. I thought it was and somebody had got at it. But it isn't. It's a substitute.'

'How do you know, sir? You seemed pretty certain before.'

'I was upset. And I didn't imagine that anyone could have put something in its place but looking at it more calmly I can see that no one could have altered mine without smashing the whole thing. It was all of a piece, like an old-fashioned marble with a barley sugar design running through it. This is just a glass shell with something floating in it. Like a glass coffin.'

'Nevertheless, sir, I must insist you come with me to make a statement. Help us with our enquiries. After all you're the only one who knows how and where such an object can be made. And we can try to trace your own piece of work.'

This seemed to further calm Reg North. 'Can I leave you for a moment?' I said to Hilary. 'I'll just have a word with my chairman and then we'll go and get breakfast. I imagine the champagne reception is off.'

I walked over to where the mayor and the chairman were standing together. The transporter had arrived quickly and a team was dismantling the piece under the supervision of the artist who now seemed keen to help.

'I'm sorry about this, Mr Tarrant. Very disappointing,' I said.

'And a bloody waste of money. Why us? Why this town? Nothing's gone right since we found that grave. That king or whatever seems to haunt us like some malign influence. First the robbery, then the fire on the pier, now this.'

'If there's anything I can do to help,' I heard myself offering.

'At least they're taking the bloody thing away. But I can see the enquiry dragging on for weeks. Unless the police can get some sort of a lead. That artist North isn't off my list of suspects, I can tell you. Could be some sort of getting back at authority. What do you think, Kish? Is it a real child in there?' The chairman used surnames as if we were at some long defunct public school.

'We can only hope not.'

'You can deal with the police, Kish. You've got more experience and more patience than I have. I'd only lose my temper. Keep me up to speed on it. Meanwhile we go on as normally as possible.'

'I doubt if the press will let us do that,' the mayor spoke for the first time. 'I need a drink. Let's see if they haven't taken all the champagne away yet.'

Hilary and I drove slowly back into town, following the transporter where the egg shape now lay on its flatbed shrouded by blue plastic sheeting.

'There's a little café I know on the front where they do a really hearty breakfast. That should warm us up.' The cold seemed to have lodged somewhere in my gut and was radiating icicles through my bones. 'You must be frozen. I'm sorry I got you into this.'

'You weren't to know. And anyway I wouldn't have missed it. It's a pretty routine existence in conservation, no matter what people may think. Weeks of work for often a rather unspectacular result. Whereas who knows where this might be going?'

As I pushed open the café door I was surprised to see Jean and Harry Bates waving from a table. I waved back.

'Some of our local amateurs: they're the ones who found the grave. Fortunately their table's full so we can be on our own without giving offence. You pick a spot and I'll just go over and have a polite word.'

There were two others at the Bates's table, a man and a woman in late middle age that I thought I'd seen at some of our lectures. The four of them had an air of intense but suppressed excitement like children with a secret.

'Hallo, Alex,' Jean said. 'We're glad you've come in. Harry's got something to show you. Go on, Harry.'

'You'll have to come round here,' Harry said, 'and look over my shoulder.'

Obediently I moved to stand behind him. He was holding a state-of-the-art digital camera, at least four millimetre mega pixels. He pressed a button. The egg sprang onto the little screen. 'Look at this,' he said, focusing on a close-up of the floating boy. The image loomed larger, the screen homing in finally on the thing gleaming at the boy's throat. A small bright square of golden light. 'Now look at this.' Another golden square filled the frame, etched with precise markings. 'Now look at this again.'

The first bright object took its place but now I could see it was covered with similar marks.

'Tell me what I'm looking at,' I said.

'This one,' Harry flicked on the second picture, 'is the square amulet you found in the buckle from the grave, and this,' he brought up the first one again, 'is the pendant round the boy's neck. They're the same. Except that I think the boy is wearing only a part, not the whole thing.'

'One leaf?'

'That's it.'

I felt a shiver run through me as if someone had poured icy water down my spine. In his clumsy way the chairman had been right. We were being haunted. The mayor had been right too. The press the next morning had a field day with child sacrifice and pictures of the 'floating boy'. I waited for Jack Linden's call.

✳

*Putative Restoration of a Missing Part of the Derveni Papyrus, discovered in a charred condition on a Thracian funeral pyre by workmen digging a road from Thessalonika to Kavala, January 15th, 16th 1962. The pyre also contained male human remains, weapons and horse accoutrements and was clearly that of a noble warrior. The extant scroll however begins with Zeus, having seized power, swallowing the severed genitals of his grandfather Uranus in order to recreate the entire universe from within his own belly. An attempt has therefore been made to reconstruct what must have been the beginning, describing creation according to the Orphic theogony with the help of the late Professor Guthrie, Fellow of Peterhouse and his groundbreaking* Orpheus and Greek Religion.

*'First was Enduring Time whom the Greeks call Chronos. Out of Chronos are born Aither or Air and Chaos and Erebos, the yawning gulf and darkness over all. In Aither Chronos fashioned the Cosmic Egg, which split in two to form the heavens and earth, and as it split there sprang from it the winged Phanes in a blaze of light, the beautiful one, creator of the sun and moon and of the men of the Golden Age. And of himself he bore a daughter, Night or wisdom, whom he took to himself. And the Greeks know him as Dionysus or Eros.'*

*If this is accepted as at least plausible then it will be immediately clear that the Orphic seems to owe much to the earlier Iranian theogony, a conclusion which gains considerable strength when we consider the occupation of Thrace by the Persians and that Hesiod himself, through his father, came from Lydia (another satrap of the Persian Empire), and whose own creation myth has many similar elements.*

**Paper delivered to the Symposium on The Influence of Middle Eastern and Classical Beliefs on Later Monotheisms**

**Universidad de Huelva, June 2003**

*

But it was the chairman who rang me first. The press had continued their feeding frenzy. Normally we don't take all the national papers at the museum. There's no need. Today I sent Phoebe out to pick up the lot as soon as I opened my own daily rag.

'Have you seen the papers, Kish?' The chairman believed in going straight to the point. 'I've had local councillors on to me already, suggesting it's our fault for wasting residents' money on dodgy modern art.'

As he spoke I was running through successive headlines from the pile in front of me. As usual those in red were the most hysterical in their prurient, self-righteous voyeurism. I saw where our local broadcasters had picked up their ideas. It was a chance that wasn't to be missed to make political capital out of a grisly event and knock the council's cultural budget at the same time. 'It's the effect on the town,' he went on, 'that has to be my concern. No one will want to come here.'

'I think you might find just the opposite.'

'A lot of ghouls. No, we want this cleared up as soon as possible We've got just over three months before the start of the season. Have you spoken to the police yet? What do they think?'

'I was just about to ring them,' I lied, 'but you got me first.'

'I'll get off the line then. Keep me up to speed, Alex.'

Who should I ring? I looked up our usual liaison officer and dialled the number. 'Inspector Hobbs? It's Alex Kish from the museum. I thought I should make contact, or rather the chairman thinks so. I hope that isn't a nuisance.' I knew the notion of local political interest would do the trick.

'We'd like you to come in, sir, and discuss it with us. There seem to be some factors that might be more in your field than ours. Incidentally we've called in the Met. Had to. We think this goes much farther than our patch. Certainly the victims weren't from round here. That much we know.'

'Of course. I'll come whenever you say. Our chairman is worried about the town's image. He's anxious the thing should be out of the public mind by Easter.'

I heard the inspector give a short satirical laugh. 'He'll be lucky. So will we.'

The next call was Jack. 'What took you so long?' I said, determined to seize the initiative.

'You've been engaged for hours.'

'I know: the chairman, the police. You're lucky to have got in now. So what's your theory, Jack?'

'Hang on. What about: "Sorry, Jack, you were right"?'

'Sorry, Jack, you were right. So? I have to go and talk to the police. The locals have called in the Met, probably Interpol, or whatever it's called these days, by now. Anything you can suggest I can feed through if…'

'If you don't think it's too nutty?'

'We don't want to lose their confidence. So what can you tell me?'

'I've seen a reference to a Persian lord who was suspended in a crystal coffin so that the sun's rays would light him up.'

'Okay. Let's leave that out for the moment. This is something even the police don't know yet.' I quickly filled him in about the gold leaf, seeming to be from our amulet, round the boy's neck. 'From what you told me before that could be inscribed with instructions on how to behave after death.'

'That's what I could read. But that was only one facet because of the way the sheet was folded in four. The others may have, will have, different bits of text.'

'If I emailed you a photograph of this leaf could you tell if it's what you saw before?'

'I can try. Depends on the definition in the photograph.'

'I think it's a different bit but as you know I don't read Greek.'

'I'll see what I can come up with.'

It would be good to go to the police with something they didn't know, something I could contribute as an expert, even if only at second hand.

Jack's answer came quickly. 'It's Greek, alright. But there's something weird. I thought I'd seen it before and then I remembered. It's in a book on the Derveni papyrus.'

'What's that?'

'It's something the Greeks found when they were building a road.'

'Which Greeks? When are we talking about?'

'In the sixties, as far as I recall. Anyway the whole text was published in 2005. There'd been a gap because the academic who'd ended up with it didn't want to let go. Then a samizdat version began to circulate and finally the whole thing went public.

'How does this fit in with our text round the boy's neck?'

'It's part of it and, as I said at first, it's an Orphic text.'

'Instructions for the dead?'

'Not this one. This bit is all about creation. Zeus swallowing "the glorious firstborn of the egg". It isn't exactly the same but it's close enough for me to recognise where it comes from. There's a later, fuller version of the creation story according to Orpheus in something called *The Rhapsodies* in English.'

'Where do we go from there?'

'That I don't know. I'll have to dig around some more. But what's clear is that someone is mixed up in this who knows the whole field, maybe even better than I do. Didn't I say that if there was more to this than just a game being played with the toys of Dionysus, that something else would happen to confirm it? Well this is it.'

'What do I say to the police?'

'You'll have to play it by ear, tell them what you can without them thinking we've all completely lost it. Crazy professors: that sort of thing.'

As I made my way to the police station that afternoon I felt less and less sure. All I had to offer was some mad conspiracy theory, maybe involving ancient cults. I was shown into an interview room, and left kicking my heels for ten minutes by the clock on the wall, time enough to begin to feel that I was the criminal. I became convinced that I was being observed and tried to sit looking relaxed and dignified, resisting the impulse to keep shifting on the hard chair or crossing or uncrossing my legs. Finally the door opened and Inspector Hobbs came in, followed by a uniformed policeman, and a man I judged to be in his forties, with short black curly hair and very blue eyes.

'Sorry to keep you waiting, Mr Kish. This is Detective Chief Inspector Hildreth of the Met and our own Constable Jenkins.'

I stood up to shake hands with the man from the Met while the constable positioned himself at the table beside some kind of recording equipment.

'Peter Hildreth but I'm usually called Hilo,' the detective said. The voice was strong with a north of Watford accent I couldn't identify. Brought up on the south suburban fringes of London I was bad at differentiating anything other than refined estuary or cockney.

'You don't mind if we take a record of this do you, sir?' Hobbs asked.

'No, no, go ahead.' We all sat down.

'Gerald here says you run the local museum.'

'I'm the director,' I said rather stiffly. 'My chairman has given me the job of liaising with the police.'

'But why, if you don't mind me asking, does he, or you, come into it? Don't get me wrong. I'm not doubting your legitimate interest. I'm just trying to understand the set-up.'

'It's our responsibility. His because his committee commissioned the sculpture under their tourism brief which includes entertainment, culture, town improvement, anything that might be thought to bring the punters in. But also,' I was choosing my words carefully, 'because there seem to be certain unusual elements to recent events connected with our discovery of the Prince's grave which make it my concern.'

Hildreth nodded. 'Ah yes. I read about that in the press. Archaeology, armchair archaeology, is by way of being a hobby of mine. So you think there's some connection between what happened yesterday and that grave?'

I took a deep breath and tried to speak as calmly and factually as possible. 'An amulet was found in the grave and was subsequently stolen from the museum. It consisted of a thin sheet of gold inscribed with a Greek text and folded up very small to the size of a matchbox. Part of that was round the neck of the child in the glass egg.'

Hobbs shifted in his seat. 'What you don't know, Mr Kish, is that a similar thing was found with the remains of the body burnt in the pier fire. We didn't tell the public because we didn't see it had any significance and anyway it'd been so badly warped by the heat as to be unrecognisable, at least to us, then, but from what you say now, I'm in no doubt it's the same kind of thing.'

'So it looks like we have two similar killings and therefore a serial killer. Let's see what other similarities there are. Both young boys for a start.' Hildreth counted the points off on a well-manicured hand. 'Both in bizarre circumstances. The boy on the pier didn't go there of his own accord and start a fire playing with matches. He was taken there, possibly, probably, already dead.'

'The boys weren't local,' Hobbs said. 'We've no reported missing persons of their description. Anyway if there had been there would have been a national manhunt. We would all have known about it. Essex people don't take things quietly, especially anything to do with children.'

I realised the local police would have their own problems. Negligence or incompetence accusations would start to fly and I knew how that felt. I wondered how much I could add to the list and still keep a reputation for credibility with these two hard-headed enforcers of the law. I decided to keep quiet unless asked a direct question. I wasn't let off the hook for long.

'Anything to add, Mr Kish?' Hildreth asked. I had decided in my own mind that he was a black Celt with all that implied of imagination, what I remembered from somewhere as 'the lovely gift of the gab,' not at all the stereotype PC Plod. I felt he sensed I was holding something back with an almost traditionally feminine intuition or even a touch of the magician but with no whiff of charlatan that I could detect.

'The bizarre circumstances you listed both show elements of some ancient cult.'

'Which is?'

'I'm not sure because I'm not an expert. It's not my field.'

'Speculation?'

'At this stage, yes.'

'Let me know if you come up with anything more concrete. What's happened twice can happen again and I imagine none of us want that. The public will want to know why we're faffing about.'

I was dismissed. I wanted to ask what they would do next 'to pursue their inquiries' but supposed that would be classified information. Should I have told them about the real expert, sicked them on to Jack? I'd held back and I didn't quite know why, except that I had the impression that he wasn't comfortable being publicly quizzed or handling that kind of interrogation.

And I was right. 'I hope you managed to keep me out of it,' he said later when I rang to fill him in on my interview with the police. 'Officialdom makes me nervous.'

'It's okay. I didn't need to involve you. But I don't know if I can keep you out forever unless I pretend that what you tell me I thought of for myself.'

'That's fine by me.'

'It may not work. Remember you were quoted in the press.'

'I know. I just hope everyone else has forgotten or doesn't make the connection.'

I had to wonder why he was so averse to publicity when most people, including archaeologists, can't wait to be picked out by the media spotlight.

'What are you doing for Christmas?' I asked Hilary as the fatal day loomed closer.

'Beth will be home and we'll probably go to my sister's.'

'Beth?'

'My daughter at uni in Durham. Honestly, Alex, your face! You didn't think I was still a virgin, did you? I warned you that you know nothing about me.'

Up until now I had existed in a kind of time capsule, a bubble of the present in my head. I realised I had asked her nothing and in turn told her almost nothing. And now I didn't know how to begin. Beth must be about nineteen. What had happened to her father? Obviously he wasn't around.

'Beth's father and I split up when she was ten. He lives in the States. She goes to stay with him from time to time. He's quite a distinguished anthropologist in his own field.'

I felt a rush of envy, or was it jealousy, of this unknown man who had just come into my life as fertile husband and no doubt brilliant academic.

'What will you do?' Hilary asked.

'I might see if Jack Linden wants to get out of London for a couple of days. I don't get the impression he's overburdened with friends and family.'

'What will Caesar say to that?' she laughed.

'He'll have to mind his manners if he wants any turkey.'

'Who'll do the cooking?'

'I will. I've got rather good at it since I've been on my own. I've had to.'

Jack seemed delighted at the invitation. 'I never know quite what to do with myself when the city empties and everything's closed, libraries, museums and so on. Thanks, Alex, thanks a lot.'

'Bracing walks along the front,' I said. 'Bring warm clothes.'

'And I'll bring some booze. What's yours?'

'Anything except gin.' It sounded as if we were auditioning for a buddy movie.

'I thought you and Hilary…'

'She's got family obligations.'

I let the police simmer for a couple of days then, before everything closed down for the holiday, I rang the mobile number Hildreth had given me.

'Hilo.'

'It's Alex Kish,' I said, 'from the museum. I wondered if there were any developments.'

'We've ascertained that the first boy was Asian, or rather Asiatic, Chinese in fact. The second is more difficult. From the DNA we think Eastern European.' The Northern twang to his voice was more distinctive on the telephone, even against the background of other voices and the grind of London traffic.

'And the egg?'

'We've interviewed the manufacturers. They thought the artist had changed his mind and ordered a slightly different version.'

'Where did they send it?'

'It was collected, signed for with an illegible signature.'

'And the real one? Have you found that?'

'Not yet. Why are you asking, Alex?'

'Someone will have to pay for it. I can't see the artist, Reg North, footing the bill, or the makers. It looks like a hole in my budget, and the council's, and nothing to show for it. What chance do you think there is of getting it back? It's not an easy thing to conceal. Too big.'

'The artist thinks it's been smashed up and recycled. He's pretty depressed about the whole thing. We offered him the other one when we've finished with it but he says it's tainted.'

'How did the boy die?'

'Drugged and suffocated while asleep.'

That was why he had looked so calm and peaceful.

'Let's hope we can all have a quiet Christmas,' Hildreth said, 'but I wouldn't bet on it.'

I had wondered how Jack and I would get along on our own together for two whole days but in the end it was surprisingly easy. We went for cold rambles along the front and out to Canvey so that I could show him where the second boy had appeared in the egg.

'Do you know why the artist chose that shape?' he asked as we stood beside the empty plinth.

'He said something on local radio about it being the perfect sculptural form, and signifying hope and rebirth.'

'That's how it's always been seen; why so many religions have adopted it as part of their mythology. The Iranians give each other symbolic eggs at the start of their new year in spring, roughly corresponding to our Easter. Nothing to do with a Christian crucifixion except that that's another rebirth through a death. And our Easter eggs must go back to that same Indo-European root, along with the chicks and the bunnies who are really those magic animals, Mad March hares.'

'So the answer to that old riddle about what came first the chicken or the egg is the cosmic egg.'

'You could say that,' Jack laughed and then was silent a moment. 'What does your policeman think is going on?'

'If he knows he isn't saying. I haven't told him too much because as we agreed it sounds so fanciful but I did tell him about the gold leaf round the boy's neck and it turns out that the boy on the pier had one too. He is, or was, Chinese, they think.'

'When will you tell him the rest?'

'What could I say? That we think there's somebody with a knowledge of ancient beliefs who's killing boys in bizarre circumstances. He knows that already.'

'We can't just sit around waiting for the next death.'

'You think there will be another?'

'There were four gold leaves, Alex. I mean the sheet was folded into four. Two have been detached and used. That means there are two more to go.'

'I don't see what we can do about it. It's a job for the police. It does explain why there was no sign of the stolen pieces being offered for sale on the internet. Someone had a use for them. They must have been taken with exactly this in mind.'

Hilary rang on Christmas morning. 'We're just setting off for my sister's; back after Boxing Day. How are you two boys making out? Have you solved all the problems yet?'

'Tomorrow,' I said. Hearing her voice like that on Christmas morning was a message that there was something between us; I wasn't forgotten.

'Perhaps when the holiday's over you'd like to come and see where I work. Then you could take in the rest of the king's treasure.'

'I would, very much.' I knew I was responding stupidly, like a nervous teenager although of course they're not nervous in the way we were back in the seventies. It was almost a relief when she rang off and I could stop making a fool of myself.

The rest of Jack's stay passed quietly. Master Chef would have been proud of my turkey with all the trimmings and both Jack and Caesar tucked in to a flattering share. Caesar behaved immaculately, making up to Jack's leg as he sat in the armchair, demanding to be fussed over until Jack gave in and stroked him.

'He knows you're harmless,' I laughed, 'or else he's just a tart. I thought Hilary had won his heart.'

Jack had brought wine as well as whisky with him and in the evening we sat companionably in front of the artificial flame of the gas fire, rather, I suddenly thought, like an old married queer couple.

'It must be easy for the few remaining Zoroastrians,' Jack said, rolling the wine around his glass, 'to carry the sacred fire around with them nowadays. Just a little Calor gas bottle and stove. I wonder if they do?'

'How long since you were in the Middle East?'

'For any length of time? Not since the early eighties. I've paid various flying visits but I haven't been able to work there. Fortunately I've got some private money or I'd be trying to get a job with you or Hilary.'

'Would you ever go back to the States?'

'I have a house there at Ann Arbour that I rent out. But I'm too much at odds with the administration's foreign policy. However, decrepitude might force me back as it's done with the old lion, Vidal, who's spent most of his life in Europe worrying the sheep from a distance as long as he could. I miss those places badly. The countries, the people, the work, the night skies where the stars are so bright they seem to be falling down to earth. So many lost civilisations while we were still in diapers: Egypt, Babylon, the Hittites, Persians, Greeks. The Romans were only yesterday.'

'So our little bits of Saxon tat were last night. I don't know where that leaves my Victorians.'

He laughed. 'About half an hour ago.'

'And the present?'

'Fleeting minutes made up of even more fleeting seconds. You know Omar Khyam: "the moving finger writes and having writ/Moves on".'

'So what's the answer?'

'Khyam's was to get drunk. Like the kids today. Only he knew he was drowning the sorrows of the human condition. Theirs is the pursuit of pleasure, just something to do... I don't know. Let's have another bottle and we can toast Khyam'

'Who was he?' Jack had lost me again.

'Persian poet. Twelfth century. When Europe was having its first renaissance. There's a brilliant, because entirely convincing as a poem, nineteenth-century translation into English by Edward Fitzgerald. I learnt chunks of it when I was a kid and used to chant it aloud in my room. No wonder my father, who was a strict Methodist, was convinced I'd go to the bad.'

'If he lived in the twelfth century he must have been a Muslim. I thought they didn't drink.'

'They did then. The Puritanism came later as it did for Christianity. Shiraz,' he picked up the bottle of red wine, 'is a Persian name, after the place where some of their finest grapes were grown.'

'Here's to… what did you say his name was?'

'Omar Khyam'

'Here's to Omar then. Jack, how come you know so much about so many things? For you all knowledge seems to hang together. Am I right?'

'I guess I do see it that way. What a French existentialist philosopher called the nousphere, an envelope of knowledge like an intellectual atmosphere. The original of the worldwide web that has now given it the dubious benefit of a physical manifestation. Click the mouse, press the button and hey presto, you've rubbed Al Adin's lamp and let the genie out of the bottle. Now we're starting to wonder how to get him back in again. I had the best education you could buy in the States at that time. I was a great disappointment to my Pa because the only sports that interested me were swimming and cross-country running, fairly solitary. Then I got the chance as a student to join a dig in Mesopotamia during the long vacation and I was hooked. Everything seemed to fit together. One civilisation giving way to another; the evolution of writing and technical know-how, rather than how I'd been taught; a few battles and conquests, our war of independence, our civil war, our Great Depression. We Americans don't have a natural sense of history so when it does hit us we get it bad from having no built-in immunity. I got the whole works: the rise and fall of empires, religions, because I saw that was civilisation's cradle I'd landed in. History I could hold in my hand in a bit of bone or a pottery shard. It was like falling in love.'

I drove Jack to the station after Boxing Day. The museum was closed until the beginning of January but we always took the opportunity to do some housekeeping while the public was away, including the annual inventory to make sure none of our artefacts had gone astray. I had to come up with something novel that would draw the summer tourists in and please the chairman. I'd also set myself a course of reading and research, so that I could try to make some sense of the events we had become involved in. Bede's *History* and the *Anglo Saxon Chronicle* had been ticked off from the top of my list but now I had begun to stretch out farther back into the past and across the continents to see if I could catch the panoramic view that had so dazzled Jack. Echoes came back to me from my university days as if from a distant galaxy. So much I must have studied then had become submerged, an Atlantis sunk under waves of the everyday, of management, finance, admin, until the passion I had once felt, that had driven me to my career, had been lost and I might as well have been selling real estate or clerking in an office.

I had become immersed in, drowned by the appearance of things and forgotten the people who made them, the myriad multicoloured lives, the hands and brains of their creators, the belief that had shaped them so that they weren't just artefacts, divorced from a way of thinking, even though they were often rich and shapely in themselves. Standing in the empty museum, looking around me at the parade of civilisations, I almost laughed out loud at myself and the belated epiphany I was having on my Damascus road, sparked off by Jack's account of his own youthful awakening in the land of the Phoenicians, among the tumbled columns half buried in sand or in rose-red Petra, Babylon's hanging gardens, the library at Alexandria, the old seven wonders of the world, and then on through our own latter days, seeing it as one unfolding narrative, tracking down to the last shot that was only another beginning.

I felt myself going under again but now it was time 'like an ever rolling stream' that was bearing me away, as I clutched at bits of flotsam going past, remembered scenes: the school hall in assembly with a thousand voices thundering out the morning hymn, and even those who could barely read the words moving their lips in order not to be spotted by the head's darting eyes, and then a form outing to Colchester museum with its spears, shield bosses, horse gear that might have belonged to our first rebel, Boudicca and old Latham who taught us history reciting at some inattentive boy: 'Those who cannot remember the past are condemned to repeat it, Wilkins,' as he handed back a red scored exam paper.

'History is more or less bunk.' Discuss. 'The only history that is worth a damn is what we make today.' I opened the office safe, took out the inventory and went down to the storeroom to check out hidden treasures not on display. What could have been an annual chore was something I found stimulating, that gave me ideas for exhibitions, new angles, even, if there was room in the budget, new acquisitions. After a couple of hours I closed the book and went up to the little kitchen where the staff made their cups of tea and coffee.

Armed with a steaming mug and a feeling of satisfaction that nothing more than the contents of the prince's buckle had gone adrift in the last year, and with some idea of 'I do Like to be Beside the Seaside' as the theme for a summer exhibition, the history of the ice-cream cone or the bathing costume, something light but themed through like a stick of rock, I went back to the office and dialled Hilary's number.

'Has Jack gone?'

'I put him on the train this morning. I'm in the office doing the annual stock-taking.'

'That sounds like fun. Very festive.'

'And you?'

'Beth's gone to stay with a friend, having done her daughterly duty. At least she's over the Boxing Day panto age which is a bit of a relief. But it's probably only been displaced by sex, drugs and booze: a mother's worst fear. How did it go with Jack?'

'I did sometimes wonder if we were rehearsing for a buddy movie.'

'Why don't you have a trip to London? We could go to the theatre or something. It doesn't have to be the panto. Bring your toothbrush.'

'Tomorrow a possibility?' I hoped she couldn't hear my heart hammering.

'Why not? Come to the museum. We're not open yet either. You know where it is. I'm in the basement at the back: Conservation. They keep us away from the masses. If you come about one, we'll go out and find some lunch.'

Next morning I put out two extra dishes for Caesar who watched me balefully from the arm of his favourite chair, left a note exhorting Mrs Shepherd to feed him some more from the tins in the fridge and the rattling packet of dried nodules, not forgetting to refill the saucer of special cat milk, and set off to drive to the station. What to pack had been a problem, as well as what bag. Hilary's throwaway remark about the toothbrush might have been just that, meaning everything or nothing. I didn't want my expectations, hopes, to be too obvious in case I was wildly misinterpreting or she had simply changed her mind overnight. So I took as little as was decently possible. Should I put in a packet of Featherlite? I hadn't any in the house; it had been so long since I'd needed or even wanted them. At the station, leaving my car in the car park I found the nearest chemist's just in case. As the train rattled its way through the seaside, rural and finally urban Essex, I tried to think of other things in order not to disgrace myself in front of my fellow travellers.

At Liverpool Street I took the District line going West and arrived at the Barbican, after only two stops, much too early. I would have to walk about a bit to waste some time. Surprisingly when I stepped out into Charterhouse Street, it was a fine though cold winter morning of hazy sunshine. The streets were empty and everywhere shuttered for the holiday, even the little cafés and sandwich bars I passed, the only relief in the cliff façades of office blocks, were darkly shut up. Somewhere to my right was the Charterhouse, once a Carthusian monastery. I was walking along the city boundary, on the edge of the Square Mile with the warehouses of Smithfield Market on my left. Taking a quick look at the map I had brought in my pocket, and glad there was no one around to see my tourist's ignorance, I turned down a street between the handsome mid-Victorian brick buildings of the market halls that had once disguised their bloody trade.

The air should have been full of the cries of martyred men and animals. Dissidents had burned here; Wat Tyler had been beheaded for leading the first poll tax revolt; cattle pole-axed in their millions over the years, but it was silent. Not even a car went by. In the distance I could see a bundle huddled beside a wall that, as I passed, resolved itself into the shape of a man and his dog which looked up at me defensively as his owner slept on, daring me to interfere.

Continuing south down Little Britain I passed St Bartholomew's and turned left along Newgate Street towards St Paul's. Suddenly coming into view between the office skyscrapers, its dome and towers seemed to float upwards in the opal light. A quick look at my watch showed me I had wasted enough time and was now in danger of being late. Leaving the shimmering stone of the great carbuncle on its baroque pedestal, I hurried north up Aldersgate Street.

Ahead was the dark tunnel entrance to the Barbican. Briefly I wondered why I'd never been to the Museum of London before that one visit to see our finds, in what seemed a lifetime ago, and perhaps, in a sense, was, when Hilary was still just the Head of Conservation. After all London were our overseers, providing research and backup our own funds wouldn't run to, including the rescue dig that had started all this with Harry Bates falling into the prince's grave. Sometimes I almost wished that he hadn't, that I'd been left to vegetate in my own quiet way. Now I was aware that I was breathing heavily from a sensation of, not exactly fear but apprehension as I hurried along between the tall blocks.

All this area must have been a maze of streets flattened by the Blitz, and rebuilt as an arts and residential area in the late seventies, judging by the aspirationally ugly architecture that had been meant to signify a clean modern future where culture was for every man, a pedestrianised, slabbed village on stilts, with airy walkways open to the elements, that should have given an illusion of light and space. As I half remembered, the sign for the museum pointed me up wide shallow steps to an upper level, a cathedral-sized west face in plate glass, steel and concrete. The revolving door poured me into a vast atrium filled with rippling light from the winter sun like a huge aquarium where many-coloured posters swam instead of exotic fish. It all had that quality of a dream, an unreality that made me think I must have been in some kind of daze or semi-catatonic state on my last visit, or like the sudden apprehension of déjà vu: I have been here before. Perhaps Hilary wasn't real either.

Last time she had met me in the atrium. Now I had to seek her out. 'I'm afraid we're closed until next week.' An attendant had appeared from behind an exhibition screen showing a recent find below the crypt of St Martin-in-the-Fields, a sarcophagus that might contain the bones of the soldier martyr Martin himself and might even rewrite the accepted history of the collapse of Roman London as a capital city of the empire.

'I'm looking for Hilary Caistor in Conservation.'

'Do you have an appointment?'

'Yes.'

'I'll ring through and see if she's in. Could I have your name please.'

'Alex Kish.'

'Just one moment.' He's watching me carefully while he dials, just in case I suddenly run amok, produce a gun, set off a bomb, make a wild dash among the exhibits. 'I have a Mr Kish here. That's fine. I'll send him along.' He puts back the receiver. 'We have to be so careful. Last week we had someone claiming his ethnic group was underrepresented and waving what turned out to be a water pistol. He wanted the Iron Age stuff labelled in Cornish or Breton on the grounds that they were Celts.'

'I know the feeling. I'm the curator at Southend. We get our weirdoes even there. Where do I go?'

Hilary's door had her nameplate on it, Dr H. Caistor, which was a little intimidating. I knocked. Suddenly the door opened. We stood for a second looking at each other and then spontaneously and simultaneously kissed.

'Did you bring your toothbrush?'

'I did.'

'Then you can come in.'

## 327 BC Bucephala on the Hydaspes

*Here died Bucephalus, beloved of the Lord Alexander, which city was named after him, for that he had carried his master across the world in journeying and in battle since his master first tamed him. For he was brought to King Philip as an unbroken colt whom none could mount or break although many tried. Then the king commanded him to be returned to Philonicus Of Thessaly, who had sent the beast, but the young prince stepping forward said first he would try him. Then was a wager made between father and son, for the price of the horse, that the prince could not subdue him. But Alexander had observed that the horse started at his own shadow when it danced before him. Therefore, turning him about so that the sun was in his eyes he gentled him with his hands and voice until the horse would let him mount. Then the horse began to gallop and Alexander let him have his head until he had done and the prince was able to turn him at the end of his career and bring him quietly about.*

*And Alexander, I believe, understood the nature of the horse as his own that he could not be forced but only persuaded by gentle means and for this reason King Philip, his father, appointed the philosopher Aristotle to be his tutor who was ever known as the prince's governor because he was of too noble birth to bear the title of schoolmaster or tutor. He schooled the prince for seven years before he returned to Athens full of honours.*

*Yet in the matter of the mysteries of Orpheus Aristotle who regarded them as mere superstition and charlatanry was unable to persuade the prince and some men said that it was because his mother, Olympias of the Island of Samothrace was possessed with the spirit of Orpheus and the divine madness of Dionysus such as inspires the women of Thrace and that in the dances to the god she carried many small snakes about her that twined in the ivy she wore, and around the little javelins that the dancers carried in their hands, that all the men were afraid to approach her.*

*So when his father was dead and Alexander became King of Macedon and the Athenians, he set out to conquer Asia, for Darius III had assembled a great army against him to protect his empire. Alexander was chosen general of all the Greeks* and many omens of victory were shown him by the gods such as the wooden statue of Orpheus which sweat miraculously when he came to the city of Lebethres. And wherever he went Bucephalus went with him. Yet in the first great battle after he had crossed the Hellespont the prince did not ride him but another that was killed under him. After this great victory over the Persians he subdued all the lands round about. And hence, as all the world knows, he continued with his conquests even into Egypt where he founded Alexandria, and thus through Mesopotamia, Media and Persia even up to the Caspian Sea, and there in the land of the barbarians and monsters, called Hyrcania, Bucephalus was captured as he was being led along. Enraged the King sent a herald to say that he would raze all their towns and kill every man, woman and child if his horse was not returned safe and whole to him. Yet when they did so he was overcome with joy and sent them a ransom for his horse.

Now marching ever west he came at last to the borders of India, having conquered all in his path. And here he did battle at the River Hydaspes with King Poros, a mighty king with many elephants in his army, and even so Alexander conquered him. Yet his victory was not so sweet for here, as I have told you, Bucephalus died, not of the wounds for which he was being treated, but worn out with age and journeying. And he was about fourteen years old.

After this last great battle the Macedonian troops would go no further into India and Alexander was forced to lead them back through Asia, settling his new kingdoms as he went. In his lands that were formerly those of the Persians he adopted their dress and customs in order to be more acceptable to the people, and to their soothsayers and magi, even wearing the Phrygian cap in which they depict the young god Mithras. And on this journey he became more and more fearful and distrustful of the gods, the priest, magi and oracles. Reaching Babylon after four years, he was taken with a fever of which after twenty-seven days he died in his thirty-second year. And it is certain that after the death of Bucephalus the king declined in spirit, feasting and drinking too much and fearful of the future that some would take all from him. And so it was.

Fragment of a lost work by Eratosthenes of Alexandria c. 220 BC

When we made love that first time it was the fumbled messy affair of people thinking it was too important to be just sex but that all the same they should try to get it right. It wasn't that I was in too much of a hurry but it had been a long time and because I was unsure of my performance it was all over too soon. The next morning after a night together with the rhythms of sleep and breathing, the warmth of two bodies familiarly beside each other we made love again.

'Mm. That was nice,' Hilary said. 'I'll make some tea.'

'Tell me about Beth's father,' I said over my steaming cup. I hadn't had tea in bed since Lucy. It isn't much fun on your own.

'We were married very young; met at university. When I got pregnant and then had Beth he was teaching. I was bored at home, and he was surrounded by adoring students. The inevitable happened. I had the choice: either call it a day and start again or try to live with a serial philanderer who didn't really want me anymore. I think it was a relief to him when I said I thought we should give up trying to make a go of it and moved out with Beth. I'd always thought I'd be a teacher too. I'd managed to finish my doctorate. But somehow after this I didn't fancy it. I applied for the museum service. It seemed more stable, humdrum if you like.'

'Tell me about it. But then your job is more exciting than mine. You get all that sexy dead stuff. I get whether the toilets are clean for thirty children to visit. It can't have been easy with a small child.'

'You'll have to meet her soon, that's if we're going on like this.'

'Do you want to?'

'Do you?'

'Yes, yes I do. Very much, if you do.' I hesitated. 'Perhaps she won't like me, take to me I mean.'

'You were worried that Caesar wouldn't like me and that turned out fine. Anyway she's already curious. She's probably telling her friend

Julie right now: "Mum's got a boyfriend. Isn't that cool," or whatever the in-word is now.'

Hilary's flat was at the top of a tall block in the Barbican itself: 'so that I can walk to work.' The huge windows looked out on a sea of sky where from time to time gulls wheeled shrieking their anguished cries of drowned sailors or were carried up on thermals, like bits of blown charred rag against the light.

'What time do you have to go?'

'I ought to get back this afternoon.'

'Come and see what we've done with your prince. Then we can have some lunch.'

So we went back to the high atrium of the museum and then down into the dimmed light of a basement room, lined with drawers and cupboards, and glass display cases standing here and there, interspersed with shrouded shadowy statuary as if we had descended to a sunken city, the cursed and drowned bones of Semmerwater, where: *By king's tower and queen's bower // The fishes come and go.*

Hilary pulled back a screen. 'We did a reconstruction for fun and to see if it would be possible to put the whole tomb on display for the public. We haven't quite decided yet.'

We were looking into the timber-lined tomb as if peering into a life-size maquette. There lay the king or prince with all his comforts and symbols of power about him in death. 'Do you know any more about who he was?'

'Not precisely but we managed to get some DNA from a tooth, the only one, and he was definitely a Saxon.'

'Not even an Angle or a Kentish Jute?'

Hilary laughed. 'I don't think we can get into that sort of granularity yet. All they can say is he's certainly not a Roman Briton. My money is still on Saegebert. But of course we have to show proper academic caution.'

The walls were hung with gleaming copper bowls, a flagon, a cauldron. Blue glass drinking cups threw back a cold sapphire gleam. His sword and shield lay at right angles to the wooden bed the king rested on, opposite a pair of crossed drinking horns. Reconstructions of the lyre and the folding stool were placed at his right hand and his head.

The gold coins lay one above and one below the waist and two small gold crosses were placed on his forehead. The body itself was so life-like in that dim light that I almost thought I saw it breathe as if at any moment it might stand up and resume its princely life.

'That bag has a set of Anglo-Saxon draughtsmen in it. The flagon is from Byzantium, so is that silver spoon. One coin is from Paris; the other we're not sure about. We think the bowl and the flagon are from the Eastern Mediterranean, probably Coptic, and the crosses perhaps Italian. Very multicultured, your prince.'

And there too was the gold buckle on a leather belt at his waist. 'Any more surprises?'

'Not like we found in the buckle. But the whole thing still surprises me: that it could have lain there for over twelve hundred years undis-turbed and unknown.'

'Was he definitely a Christian?'

'It's a strange mixture: a burial that manages to be both Christian and yet pagan, as if those in charge of it couldn't quite make up their minds so they hedged their bets. Like our reconstruction; a mixture of real and fake.'

'It all looks amazingly real to me. I definitely think you should show it. Of course I would love to have it all back.'

'Time for lunch, I think,' Hilary said, 'before you're tempted to run off with something.'

The house seemed extra cold and empty when I got back until I switched on the fire's fake flames and, as if he'd been waiting for me, Caesar came flip-flopping in through his door. As usual I wanted him to tell me where he'd been. Maybe one day some urban wildlife Atten-borough will hang a mini video camera round a cat's neck and film that mysterious life lived beyond our grasp.

Overnight my own life had taken a seismic shift into very deep waters. We had more or less committed ourselves and each other to something that we couldn't foresee, something I wasn't good at and neither, I suspected, was Hilary. For different reasons we'd both had to narrow our lives to the immediately predictable, to getting up each day, knowing exactly what we had to do. I wanted to ring her as soon as I got back, to say... what? Instead I told myself I would go to the museum in the morning and pick up the stock-taking where I'd left off. After all I wasn't a teenager. So why did I feel like one, like the one I'd once been for a brief time before the everyday closed irrevocably around me?

By next morning I was desperate. I rang her mobile.

'I was beginning to think you were one of the fuck-and-run brigade,' Hilary said. 'Anyway I couldn't sleep so I read till quite late and I came across something that reminded me of how the second boy was set up. Apparently a Persian warlord about the first millennium BC called Gunbad-i-Kabus was buried, if you can call it that, suspended in a coffin of rock crystal so that a shaft of light would come through and light up the body. Do you think they knew about that?'

'If they did we're dealing with a very well informed set of weirdoes, someone well up in history and archaeology.'

'Someone like Jack?'

'I suppose so.' And I remembered queasily how he had spoken of it himself.

'Then there's a chance he knows them or they know about him.'

'We keep saying "they" but we don't know there's more than one person involved.'

'Logistically, if you look at the complexity of the set-ups, I think it has to be more than one, even if there's a directing hand.'

We were on safe ground, not talking about ourselves or the future, but holding hands and stepping carefully from tussock to tussock through the emotional quagmire, in that English way I had absorbed with my mother's milk. Suddenly I had a picture of the Chinese cockle pickers, the illegal immigrants left to drown in the quicksand of Morecombe Bay as the tide rushed in. I felt myself going down, grit filling my nose and mouth and silting up my eyes. The police had said the first boy was Asiatic. Or was it the second? Either way I couldn't go down that road, a favourite expression of Lisa's, when she thought I was being negative about a problem she would then solve with a: 'How about if we were to, like…?'

'Have you heard from Jack?'

'Not since I put him on the train.'

'Neither have I. Maybe he's gone away on a dig somewhere.'

'Wouldn't he have said something while he was with me?'

'Perhaps. But I've known him disappear before, be off the map when I've wanted to consult him about something.'

I felt a chill of unease akin to the sensation I had had alone that night with the finds in our own little exhibition that we had grandiosely called 'the king's room'. It was as if someone was watching and we were the exhibits.

Each time the phone rang I expected to hear from Jack so at first I didn't recognise the voice saying my name when I picked up the handset later that day. 'Mr Alex Kish?'

'Yes?'

'Detective Chief Inspector Hildreth.'

'Oh. Happy New Year,' I said stupidly and then wondered why.

'I believe you're a friend of a Professor Jack Linden.'

'Yes, yes I am. Is anything wrong?'

'We just need to get in touch with him. Do you have an address?'

'I can give you that certainly.' It crossed my mind that the police might want to consult Jack as an expert as we had done. I read out his address from my personal organiser. 'I haven't heard from him for a few days so he might be away. If I do, should I mention that you would like to talk to him?'

'No, no thanks. We'll do our own legwork when we're ready. But I'd be glad if you could drop in for a chat too. Tomorrow at three suit you?'

'Of course. We haven't opened yet after the holiday so I'm fairly free.'

'Good. We'll see you then.'

The town decorations were still up but the chains of light swinging in a cold wind from the grey edgy sea looked exhausted and forlorn. The party was over. The millennium that had begun with such optimism in a glittering firework of hope and energy, of relief that the bloody twentieth century was behind us, had been eclipsed almost at once by the choking fumes of despair as the juggernaut rolled out again in all its trappings of torn flesh and bloodied wounds.

'How long have you known Professor Linden?' Hildreth's next question took me by surprise.

'Not long. A few months.'

'And where did you meet?'

'Dr Caistor introduced us.'

'Dr Caistor? How do you spell that?'

I spelled out Hilary's name. 'And where would I find him?'

'She works at the Museum of London.'

'And what was the purpose of your meeting?'

'Jack's an expert on Middle Eastern civilisations. Dr Caistor thought he might be able to help with some finds we'd made locally.'

'And did he?'

'He deciphered the symbols and the scripts and set them in their historical context. It's all a bit above me, I'm afraid. Not my period.'

'And after?'

'After the objects were stolen he tried to track them down on the antiques black market.'

'And when did you last speak to him?'

'Boxing Day, when I dropped him off at the station.'

'Which station was that?'

'Here. He'd been staying with me over Christmas.'

'I see. And what did you talk about?'

'The Middle East and his time there. The American attitude to history. He feels very badly about the war. Really I don't see where all this is leading.'

'Bear with me a bit longer, Mr Kish. You say he was looking for your stolen property on the antiques black market. Would that be using the internet?'

'I imagine so.'

'You see we've been informed that he's been accessing child pornography sites.'

I felt my gorge rise as if he had calmly kicked me in the gut, and suddenly I saw the drift of all his questions and that I might be suspect too. Jack had stayed at my house, perhaps even in my bed. How long had I known him? What had we talked about? Maybe he thought that we had sat there watching porn videos together. What had I said to Hilary about feeling as if I was in a buddy movie? How do you prove there's nothing suspicious without beginning to stammer guiltily? If I said, 'the night before last I was in bed with a mature woman,' would he or anyone else except Hilary believe me? And anyway what did it prove? There were known precedents for predatory, even murderous, couples: Brady and Hindley, the Wests. Ian Huntley had a live-in partner. What better cover than to appear an ordinary straight tax-paying citizen?

I was like the proverbial drowning man with all his life passing before him, only it was my future I saw unreeling, not my past. I could be judged unfit to be around children which would mean the end of my job.

'As far as I know they were illegal antique dealing sites: nothing to do with children or pornography.'

'We were contacted by colleagues in the States. They'd been doing a sweep, drawing up lists. Your Professor was on one. We've managed to close down any UK-based sites but they have a much bigger problem over there, and in Russia, for different reasons. They keep us informed of any UK residents that turn up. So then we go after them.'

His voice was very calm, and the tone a chilling matter-of-fact that seemed to leave no room for doubt. I was numb with fear and disbelief like those nightmares where you're paralysed, unable to move or ward off the horror advancing towards you. 'I'm sure there's some simple explanation, mistaken identity, something of that sort.'

'Well we shall find out. Meanwhile if you could drop by tomorrow at three...'

Was it just paranoia or did I detect an unspoken: 'Or else...?', barely disguised by the friendly Northern burr, an order not an invitation?

My first instinct was to ring Hilary, mentally crossing my fingers, against all my principles, that she would answer.

'You don't seem surprised,' I said when I'd told her what Hildreth had said.

'I think I can see what he was up to.'

'So you think it's true.'

'I think it's possible, given the nature of what's happened, that Jack might have been looking for any signs, just as he looked for evidence of the objects coming onto the black market.'

'So how do I play it tomorrow?'

'Don't let him panic you. After all we don't know and lots of quite innocent people are accused of all sorts of crimes they had nothing to do with.'

'Should I try to get hold of Jack, warn him?'

'No, they might have a phone tap on him and then you would look complicit.'

As long as I could hear her voice I could stay calm but as soon as I put the phone down, I was aware of my own vulnerability threatening to choke me. I got out the car and drove down to the front where I could struggle against the knife wind that flayed my face, and stare out across the leaden sea laced with white spume crests and with the dark crescents of gulls mewling above, and imagine the wave after wave of invaders that the millennia had brought, from those earliest hominids, heavy browed and thick necked, stepping tentatively across the land bridge, only to be overwhelmed by the first of the Ice Ages, to the latest incomers in flight from poverty or violence, and among them somewhere my unknown father.

It was a relief to find Caesar waiting when I got back. Somehow the evening passed with enough whisky and dry ginger to keep me under for the night and then it was morning. Now I had to get through the day. I decided the best idea was to busy myself at the museum until it was time for my interview with Hildreth.

'Thank you for coming in, Mr Kish. We won't keep you long. We've tracked down Professor Linden. He was looking for an old colleague in Oxford. We've had to caution him. He says he was investigating whether the dead boys' pictures might have turned up on the internet.'

'We wondered about that.'

'We…?'

'Dr Caistor and I.'

'A dangerous game if so. People should leave that sort of thing to the police. It still constitutes an illegal access so we had to bring him in and obviously we shall continue to monitor the situation. So you believe that was his motive?'

'Yes, yes I do.'

'Would you know how to access such sites, Mr Kish?'

'I wouldn't even know how to begin. Presumably it's not something you can ask a search engine to find.' I felt myself on the verge of a nervous giggle.

'Presumably not. Well I don't think we need to keep you any longer. We may need to talk to you again ...' He let the rest of the sentence hang unspoken in the air.

Unable to face going back to the office, I drove straight home. I needed to talk to Hilary but first there was a message from Jack asking me to ring him. I hesitated. It wasn't a conversation I looked forward to. Had I betrayed him in some way? I dimly remembered a Chinese story about Confucius's reply to the question whether a man should hide his son knowing he was a murderer. 'He should hide him.' And then wasn't there something about 'betraying my friend or betraying my country'? But Jack wasn't a murderer and neither had he betrayed anyone or anything as far as I knew. I had to ask myself if I was the traitor. I'd given Hildreth his address even though I hadn't realised that might be a mistake and I'd said I didn't know how to access certain sites which could imply something about those who could.

'Jack. It's Alex.'

'Hi there. You got my call?'

'I tried you before. The police asked me to go in.'

'Me too. Did they tell you what it was about?'

'Yes, they did. I'm sorry: I may have dropped you in it. I gave them your address.'

'Oh, they knew that already. I'm registered as a foreign resident here on a visa. I think they were just checking up on you. What else did they say?'

'That you'd been looking at dodgy sites on the internet.'

'And what did you say?'

'Hilary and I both thought it might be something to do with the happenings here and so I told them.'

'Thanks, Alex. They let me go with a caution. I think we should meet. All three, if you and Hilary can make it. There's stuff I need to talk to you about.'

So the next day I found myself being whisked up to Hilary's flat high above the city without the feeling of excited anticipation I had expected on my next visit but instead a hollow sickness wherever the pit of my stomach was supposed to be, deep inside.

Hilary had given us all a drink to loosen our tongues but even so it was hard to know how to begin.

Finally after enquiries about Hilary's holiday and praise for her apartment and its furnishings, Jack said:

'There's something I have to tell you guys that your busybody cop doesn't know about yet but he soon will if he digs into the records back in the States, and it may, I realise, affect your own attitude.' He paused and then went on: 'I was sacked from my last project in the Middle East: that's why I'm here. After the revolution in Iran cut off ties with the West our team moved to Egypt while we waited to see whether we'd be able to resume work at our old site. Apart from Crete, Egypt is the oldest territory for archaeological exploration; exploitation some would call it. Anyway because of that, a culture of exclusiveness has built up, an elitism that says ours, Egyptology, is the real thing. This is the cradle of civilisation, we're the scholars who explain it to the world, and the rest of you are just treasure hunters and amateurs. One of their team took it very hard, became obsessed in fact with trying to prove our work was about as valid as any of the old Pitt-Rivers hands. So when, quite by chance, I stumbled on a previously unknown tomb with a particularly interesting hieroglyphic text, this guy transferred his obsession to me and was determined to bring me down and take over my site.'

He paused again and drained his glass with a quick gulp. Hilary refilled it without asking. 'Thanks. A dig is very labour intensive, especially in countries where you don't have the use of technology as you do in Europe or the States. A lot of kids hang round the sites looking for odd jobs to pick up some money. The older ones work as labourers, digging and shifting the soil. In the sun their skin glows like copper just as you see in the papyri and the wall paintings. They are a beautiful people, fine boned and featured. There was a boy called Fareed who ran errands for me, fetching drinks, changing the film in my camera, handing me the tools I needed: that sort of stuff. Then he started asking to be shown how to use the trowel and the brush, and the English words for things. Finally he picked up an English language journal one day and asked me to teach him to read. It seemed a good idea. We take so much out of these countries. We use them for our own research and academic advancement, and then for cultural tourism. Of course they need all this. But then we go home. Somewhere else becomes the fashionable place to visit this year and they're back where they were, unless they strike oil, literally that is.

'So I took on teaching him to read and some elementary field archaeology. And suddenly I found I was involved, looking forward to seeing him each morning, moved by the way his gestures were so graceful, by his big smile when he saw me. What I didn't know was that all this was being observed. When I was accused of abusing the boy, even though we both denied that anything had happened, which was true, I felt guilty as hell. It was almost a relief when I was suspended because the accusation had made me acknowledge to myself that I was in deeper than I'd known. The organisers gave me the option of resigning from the project or facing a criminal charge.'

'How old was Fareed?' Hilary asked.

'About thirteen, he thought. People don't take so much account of ages and birthdays in other cultures, and they grow up more quickly. Girls of thirteen or even twelve can marry. What we would consider children are young adults in many other countries. His father was dead and he thought of himself as the man of the family.'

'But they're still at an impressionable age, easily swayed by people they look up to?'

'Wanting to please them? Even more so I'd say. I knew that if I'd wanted I could easily have had boys. Sex tourism isn't new. Think of EM Forster, and all those English artists, writers, intellectuals who went off to North Africa every year, Morocco, Tunisia, to get their kicks. But that wasn't what I wanted.'

'You'd fallen in love,' Hilary said.

'What's that line by Kingsley Amis: "Love never lets you go." When I got back here I found I couldn't forget him. I kept replaying everything in my head. And then I went looking for answers. That's how I found out about the internet but of course that wasn't what I wanted either.'

I'd been silent all this time, leaving Hilary to ask the questions and trying to take my cue about what I should think from her. Now I said: 'How do you feel about it, about the boy, since we've got involved in all this strange business?'

'It's brought it all back of course. I watched a replay of that old movie *Death in Venice* the other night and I was sickened, as you're meant to be, at the end by Aschenbach's attempts at youthfulness, the dribble of hair dye and smudged cosmetics but at the same time I understood his obsession. I know my own vulnerability. I also know that I can never get a teaching post, that somewhere my name is probably on a list of undesirables. It makes the title 'Professor' meaningless so I don't quite know why I hang on to it.'

'And did you find anything before the police stepped in?'

'I found some pretty nasty stuff, snuff movies and so on but nothing that seemed to relate to what's happened your way.'

## A Roman Soldier Writes Home AD 52

*And here in these wild Northern parts of Thracia which we have annexed that our borders might be made safe against the barbarians, there are as many and strange religions as at home, such as those who worship the Egyptian Isis or follow Dionysius and his priest Orpheus who made many hymns to his lord in which he set down the way to follow if a man would go to the Blessed Isles after his death, which is the thing all men seek by whatever name they call it. And I carry with me always the instructions set down in immortal gold for my own safe passage when the time should come.*

*But as well as these ancient gods hidden in the shadow of time, there are many sects among the Jews who are great merchants here. Hither this year came one Saul, a Jew but a Roman citizen and therefore having great freedom to travel, work and preach his new religion as I heard. But the Jews not having him, he turned to any who would listen and has persuaded some to follow his god, Jesus, who promises resurrection as others do. His following is chiefly among the poor who are deceived into worshipping this new god and neglecting their duty towards the Divine Claudius and the due ceremonies of the state and our gods.*

*And this Saul taught that their god Jesus would return to judge the world and would lead the believers up to the sky and the others he would cast into Hades, so that some of them have ceased to work, daily expecting their god to appear.*

*But as for the soldiers, we primarily follow the Lord Mithras, the warrior, bringer of light who sprang from the primal egg at the command of Ormuz, the mightiest, and are received into his mysteries, which binds us together when we must fight side by side, each relying on his comrade. May the Lord Mithras be with me wherever in the Empire I may serve.*

I didn't stay over at Hilary's flat that night. I think we both felt it wouldn't work. A sword doesn't have to be made of steel to lie between lovers. And we didn't talk about what Jack had told us. When I put my arms around her to say goodnight, I felt not desire but intimacy, a shared comforting.

It was different in the morning. 'What do you think we ought to do?'

'I'm certainly not going to shop him to Hildreth.'

'I'm glad you said that. I don't see what we can do except wait. Jack didn't find anything. It all seems to have gone quiet. Presumably Hildreth would have told you if they'd identified the boys or if anyone had come forward with any information.'

'Perhaps I should ask him directly?'

'Perhaps you should,' she said. So I rang him.

'We're, as the media believe we say, pursuing our enquiries, Mr Kish, but without much progress. These were foreigners so no one's coming forward. The body in the pier fire we were able to identify as probably Chinese, but even his mother wouldn't have recognised him if we'd circulated his photograph to their authorities and the DNA doesn't help with precise identification. There are over a billion people in China. As for the other body, we are able to circulate these details but as yet there's nothing. Do you have anything to tell us, anything more from your professor friend?'

'No, no. It's just that we were wondering...'

'There's a terminology for these things, Mr Kish. At the moment Professor Linden is simply classed as a downloader. It's an offence in itself, of course, but in my experience such people aren't necessarily dangerous. I mean they don't always go on to do anything, like going into chat rooms, trying to set up meetings. Is your friend a collector?'

'A collector?'

'We often find paedophiles collect things – daleks, models, toys, photographs etc. Obsessive behaviour you see.'

'Not as far as I know but I don't know him very well. I've never visited where he lives.'

'We have. We didn't spot anything. But then if as you say, it was all in the course of helping the police with their enquiries there wouldn't be, would there?'

'I'm sure that's what it was.' I hoped I sounded convinced, and convincing. But when I put the phone down, my hand was shaking.

'Hildreth doesn't seem to know any more,' I reported to Hilary. 'He seems to be waiting for someone to make a wrong move.'

'Like Jack?'

'It's hard to tell. He was also anxious to give the impression, to reassure me even, that Jack wasn't necessarily dangerous. Or he might have been trying to lull me into a false sense of everything being alright in order to trip me up. But maybe I'm just getting paranoid.'

If I was looking for sympathy, I wasn't going to get it from Hilary. Ignoring my bid she said, 'Didn't your inspector friend say Jack had been to see a colleague in Oxford? I wonder who that was and what it was about?'

'This time you can do the asking.'

'Perhaps he'd like a tour of my museum. We've got a special collection on show at the moment that might interest him: what the Brits were up to while the Middle Eastern peoples were inventing writing and everything else. I'll give him a call and see if I can arrange it. Can you get away easily? Could you meet us for lunch?'

'It's one of the few advantages of being the boss.'

By the time I joined them in the Barbican restaurant they were chatting like old friends. It was Jack himself who brought up the real reason for our meeting.'

'I've heard no more from the police, have you?'

'Hildreth called me in the other day,' I said.

'Uhuh. What did he want?'

'He asked me if you collected daleks.'

'Daleks?'

'Toys, photographs. He has some theory that people who download certain kinds of material are often collectors.'

'Wow!' Jack laughed. 'I'd better get rid of… let me see… Do Mesopotamian figurines count?'

'Depends how many you've got. He said you'd been to see somebody in Oxford.' Even as I said it I was aware of my own use of the half lie and how easy it was to fall into.

'Did he say who?'

'Just a colleague.'

He laughed again. 'That's what I told him. I went to try and track down the guy who got me fired. Unfinished business, I suppose. I'd found out that he was teaching in Oxford, St Julian's Hall.'

'And did you find him?' Hilary asked.

'We had a brief encounter in his room. We didn't come to blows; luckily, for both of us, I think. He said he'd been expecting me.'

'So he knew you were here?'

'I think he's known more about me than I've known about him all along.'

'And does he have a name?' Hilary asked, anticipating my next question.

'James, Jim Stalbridge.'

Hilary looked at her watch. 'I must get back to my work. What will you two do?'

'I've got some stuff on order at the British Library,' Jack said. So there was nothing for me to do but to take myself back to Liverpool Street Station and home, trying to resist the pall of gloom that was settling on me. We seemed to be tainted by events only half understood and not yet complete, 'unfinished business' as Jack had said. Yet nothing had really happened for several weeks. Perhaps it was all over.

In the morning I felt more cheerful. At the office early I began to sketch out the 'History of the Seaside Holiday' exhibition for the summer. 'Oh I do like to be beside the seaside.' And then the phone rang.

'Alex, I thought I ought to tell you there's been another incident. Someone must have broken into our place last night. It's horrible, grotesque. The cleaner who found it had to be sent home in shock. We've had to close the museum of course and the police are here.'

'Is it another boy?'

'It was.'

Then it was Hildreth on the line. 'I've suppose you've heard, Mr Kish? Bad news travels fast.'

'Dr Caistor has just rung me.'

'I'm on my way but I'd like you there as soon as possible. Similarities. It looks like the same hand but if so he's moved his patch.'

'I don't know if I can get away.'

'I'm sorry but you're involved and so is Dr Caistor now. You can't simply refuse to help us. This isn't our usual sort of thing, this mix of history and religion or ancient cults with murder. And the boy was dressed up with another bit of your gold leaf. That puts you right in the centre of things.'

I suddenly realised my reluctance could make me a possible suspect. 'I'll have to square it with my staff.'

'You do that.'

So for the second day running I was on the train to Liverpool Street, taking the now familiar route to St Paul's and hurrying up Aldersgate Street to arrive only a few minutes after Hildreth who had been driven up in an unmarked police car. I took the escalator from street level and scurried across the walkway in a sudden shower, past the monument to John Wesley and the great bronze figure of a horse between two round shields or wheels. 'Boudicca?' my mind asked itself as the automatic doors slid open and I stated my name and business to a watchful policeman.

'You'll find the Detective Chief Inspector over there, sir.'

A little knot of people was gathered beside the central reception desk: Hilary and Hildreth with, I suppose, an assistant at his elbow, a Lewis to his Morse, a man I didn't recognise in a striped shirt and tie, and Jack Linden.

'This is our director,' Hilary introduced the striped shirt.

'Nothing's been touched, I hope,' Hildreth said.

'Everything's exactly as it was found.'

'Let's get started then.'

Hilary led the way to the right of the atrium under a sign marked 'Galleries'. We passed through 'Britain before London', the horns and tusks of long dead mammals, mammoths, oryx, rhinoceros jutting at us out of their glass coffins, the rictus grin of a lemur's skull, small as a cat's, staring from its empty eye sockets, and then the row upon row of weapons and tools, painfully hammered from rock, knapped and polished beyond necessity into art. Down the millennia we went, carving and weaving, baking pots, flighting arrows, making temples for gods until we passed into Roman London, conquest and the building of the first city.

Hilary quickened the pace. Hundreds of years passed. I caught sight of a label, the Temple of Mithras, a stone boy in a soft pointed cap that wouldn't have been out of place on the piste, and then we turned a corner. I was aware of a strange incongruous sound and we all stopped to stare at the scene in front of us.

For it was a deliberately contrived scene. The label above, the museum's own sign, read 'The End of Roman London'. There on open display were the fallen remains of temples, walls, and monumental buildings: a fluted drum that had once held up a Basilican roof, a stone soldier with a long oval shield, the bottom halves of two statues of the mother goddesses, their pleated skirts and sandaled feet, and over this broken masonry of a lost civilisation was draped the headless body of a boy. Between his open legs lay a small statue of a youth, naked except for a cloak, also missing his head, lower right leg and left foot.

To the right on a kind of plinth made of a shattered column rested what must be the head of the dead boy, mouth open with the strange noise seeming to come from it. A little square of gold leaf was bound round his forehead. I had no doubt what it was.

'What's the noise?' Hildreth asked.

'I imagine it's meant to be singing. Some sort of battery driven device I think we'll find,' Jack said.

'I'm almost sure I recognise it,' Hilary said, 'even though it's very garbled. The thing must be running down but I believe it's something we used to sing at school:

*'Orpheus with his lute made trees*
*And the mountain tops that freeze*
*Bow their heads when he did sing...'*

'That's it,' Jack said. 'It's Orpheus after he'd been torn to pieces by the Bacchae. His head, still singing, floated down the river with his lyre and then over the sea to Lesbos.'

Now I could see that the boy's body was gashed in places as if by the claws of a lion or a bear.

'Okay,' said Hildreth to his sidekick. 'Call in the forensics and the rest of the boys. Put up the scene of crime screens. Is there somewhere we can talk?' he asked the director.

'My office,' the director said

'Now then,' Hildreth began when we were all seated, 'what's all this about? Stones and bones I can cope with but fairy tales are beyond me. Who's this Orpheus?'

'He's a character from Greek myth,' Jack said. 'A priest and poet kind of, who might, just might have really existed.'

'So we're talking about a long time ago.'

'Two and a half thousand years at least.'

'And how do you think he fits in.'

'He was a teacher of a mystery religion of death and the afterlife. His story is that he was such a great poet, in those days, poetry was sung or chanted not written down, but anyway he could calm the wind and waves with his song and any kind of wild or human thing. When his wife was carried off to the underworld he went after her and charmed the king of darkness to let her go, on the condition that she would follow him up and he didn't look back.'

'So?'

'He looked back and she sank from his sight. Then he was killed himself by a pack of frenzied women, some say because he wouldn't look at another woman after Eurydice. His followers were male; women weren't welcome in the cult. There's a lot more...'

'I think that gives me the picture. So what have we got? Whoever did this knows as much as you. Some sort of specialist?'

'Not necessarily,' Hilary said. 'Parts of his story are well known. At least two operas, lots of paintings, and to anyone who had myths read to them as a child or studied the classics or English literature.'

'There was no blood from the wounds,' Hildreth said. 'The pathology people will tell us but it looks as if he was dead before they were made. More like ritual markings. Post-mortem mutilation. Kinky. But then so is this whole thing. It certainly looks like the same hand or hands.'

'And then there's the gold square from our find; just like the other two,' I said.

'That's right, and that clinches it.' Hildreth leant back in his chair with a kind of satisfaction as if the whole messy business was clear and solved. 'He's changed the venue but only by fifty miles and all the other hallmarks are the same. But why move this time to London?'

'Because the original finds are all here,' I heard myself saying, 'the grave goods of the Prittlewell Prince.'

'How does he know that?'

'It was in the press. If he's been following all this he'll know, especially if he took the things from our museum in the first place.'

Suddenly Hilary put her hands over her face. 'We're talking about this as if these children weren't dead.'

'It's the only way to get at the truth. It's not that I don't care: I've got two kids myself,' Hildreth said. 'But you have to think clearly, try to understand what's going on, not be confused by your own emotions. Now, we have to let forensics do their job, then see what we've got. That's all we can do here for now. Thank you all for coming in.'

'When will we be able to open to the public again?' Hilary's director asked.

'Not for several days at least, I'm afraid, sir. I'll be in touch. Of course we'll make it as quick as we can. We want the answers as soon as possible but we don't want to miss anything through too much haste. This guy is playing with us but it's a deadly sort of game.'

As we got up to leave the director called Hilary back.

'I'll be in touch,' I said, and Jack and I made our way to the entrance, past the policeman on guard. Hildreth had returned to the Roman gallery and the scene of the crime. I didn't feel in the mood for lengthy post-mortems so I said goodbye to Jack and walked quickly down Aldersgate Street to start my journey home. I felt numb, almost dead and in some kind of limbo myself. My mind refused to take on what I had just seen or to try to make sense of it. Hildreth was right. We were the victims of a deadly game where we didn't know the rules. No, that was wrong. The boys were the victims. We were just what the press would no doubt call 'helpless bystanders'. Yet I felt it was more than that. Whoever it was had involved us by putting the stolen objects from the Prittlewell grave on the boys' bodies, he or they, knew something at least about us. Perhaps we were being watched. To Hildreth it was just a job but we were being subtly drawn into the game.

The chairman rang the next day when the news hit the media. 'A terrible thing, Kish. Thank God it wasn't in our baileywick this time. Do you know what's happening up there?'

'I was at the museum yesterday. The police called me in to see whether I could help them decide if the three deaths were linked.'

'I suppose they've had to close to the public, just as we did. Anyway let's hope it means the end of our troubles.'

'I wouldn't bank on it,' I said, irritated by his naked relief. 'After all a part of one of our missing artefacts was found on the boy, just like the others.'

'That wasn't in the papers.'

'I imagine the police didn't want it broadcast.'

'And neither do we. It looks bad for us. I don't think you should put it about.'

'I don't intend to. I just thought you ought to be informed.'

'Quite so. Quite so.'

Hildreth was the next to call. 'We've had an email from some of our colleagues overseas, sending us some pictures from a new site they've tracked down. I'm afraid you would recognise them at once: the boy in the egg, and this latest one.'

'So Professor Linden was right.'

'It looks like it. It's from a site called Nursery Crimes. How do they think these things up, Mr Kish?'

'What's your theory Chief Inspector?'

'It's an obsession that sees what obsesses it everywhere it looks, in everything it hears. That's my theory. A kind of pathology. I wonder what your professor friend would say?'

My immediate thought was that I didn't know and didn't want to speculate, even for myself, but aloud I said, 'I didn't think that's quite his field.'

'Maybe not. I'll let you know when we've more information. Whoever they are they're very well organised to get these pictures up so quickly. The site's been closed down of course but they can't trace the perpetrators because it was being piggy-backed on a perfectly legal site of children's literature.'

I thought of the Opies' great work on street and playground games, the last knockings of Victoriana, that I had come across in my own studies:

> 'Here comes a chopper to chop off your head
> Chip chop, chip chop. The last man's head.'

Even so, I wasn't prepared for the inspector's next call the following morning before I left for work.

'It seems I can't get along without you, Alex.' The sudden use of my first name was alarming in itself as well as the early call at home. 'Could you come in and see me.'

'What, now?'

'Yes, I'm afraid so. I've moved back to the Yard since the action shifted to London. There's a little café round the corner, Bettina's. Meet me there as soon as you can. I take it you've got a mobile. Ring me when you get there and I'll come and join you. You know where the Yard is?'

'I've never been there but I've passed it in the bus coming from Trafalgar Square.'

'Victoria Street. St James's Park Tube station. As quick as you can make it.'

I rang Lisa to let her know I was wanted by the police and wouldn't be in the museum until later, if at all.

'I hope they don't lock you up. We need you back,' she joked.

'So do I.'

The air outside the station when I stepped into a mild, moist London morning, was heavy with the fumes of combusting fuel, the thick diesel stink of buses and taxis and the more acrid burn of petrol. A sign pointed to the park where I caught the brief flash of early crocus, yellow, deep purple, and pale lilac. I turned away, following the finger that pointed towards New Scotland Yard, a building anonymous as any other office block without a whiff of Baker Street, the Clink or Bow Street Runners. How did I know that even those not in uniform, heading to or from the station, were police? But I did. Something in the confident walk, an ooze of camaraderie as if they'd been studying themselves on the television screen, and were auditioning for a part in *The Bill*.

Bettina's, when I pushed the door open was filled with more of the same, male and female. I found the only free table and rang Hildreth. 'Sit tight. I'm there in five minutes.'

As he pushed his way across the space between us some faces looked up in recognition, then went back to their intense conversations.

'Come on, we can't talk in this din.'

I followed him out into the street again and through the elegant glass doors of St Ermin's Hotel. 'That's better. I'll get them to bring us some coffee. They know me here.'

He disappeared among the potted palms, redolent of a setting for *Poirot*. 'Now,' he said, settling himself into an armchair, 'this isn't very pleasant, Alex. I need you to identify a body. Have you done this sort of thing before?'

'No, never.'

'There's a bit of urgency of course. I know who it is but I need an independent identification and the only one I could think of was you. So as soon as we've had our coffee, we'll get on with it if that's all right with you.'

'So is it male or female?' I asked, my gut churning with fear.

'It's male. I've got a car waiting.'

He drove us expertly south through the old suburbs of Lambeth, past the Old Vic and the Imperial War Museum, between the elegant town houses of Camberwell and up Denmark Hill to King's College Hospital.

Less than an hour later I was staring down at the bloodied and battered face of Jack Linden.

'I could have asked Dr Caistor of course but I thought she might find it all too upsetting.'

'How did he die? Where?'

'It's a toss up at the moment between his being run over or beaten to death, or both. As to where… he was found on a piece of waste ground behind the Vauxhall Tavern.'

'South of the river?'

'That's right. That's why they brought him here.'

'What was he doing there? That wasn't where he lived. I thought he had a flat in Hammersmith somewhere.'

'So he did. I see you don't know. This is a pub frequented by gents of a certain sexual persuasion. Has been for years. Others come and go but the Vauxhall's almost an institution, a national monument, you could say.'

I thought of the thousand lamps of the old Vauxhall Pleasure Gardens, closed down by the Victorians as a venue for vice of various kinds, the pale faces of prostitutes of all ages, and all sexes, under the flickering torches or yellow hissing gas mantles, a scene Degas might have painted.

'If he was found on a piece of waste ground how could he have been run over, unless by a motorbike?'

'A good question.' Hildreth dropped the sheet back over Jack's face. 'Will you tell Dr Caistor or shall I?'

'I will,' I said but my stomach lurched at the thought of trying to find the right words, partly because I didn't know how I felt myself. I seemed to be quite numb, unable to take in what Hildreth had just told me. I presumed he had meant that Jack's body had been found behind a gay pub. But that wasn't Jack's scene or so he had implied.

In the end I rang Hilary and asked her if she was free for lunch.

'What is it, Alex? Your voice sounds strange.'

'There is something we have to talk about. Are you free?'

'Where are you?'

'I'm in London. Hildreth wanted to see me.'

'Can you be at the Wheatsheaf in half an hour? We might be able to beat the lunchtime scrum.'

I was the first to arrive. I found a corner table and sat playing with my whisky and water while I turned over various ways to break the news. As she crossed the bar towards me I felt a sinking wave of sadness that this couldn't just be an ordinary meeting of hopeful lovers. 'What will you drink?'

'Just a mineral water. I'd better not breathe alcohol all over the director this afternoon.' And then when she had poured the foaming bubbles into her glass: 'Now tell me.'

'It's about Jack.'

'They've arrested him again.'

'No, not that. It's worse. Much worse. I'm afraid he's been killed.'

Hilary put down the glass and covered her face as she had at the thought of the dead boys. I wanted to put my arms round her but the bar was filling up and the place was too public. Then she clasped her hands in front of her and rested her chin on her palms. Suddenly I wanted to kiss her.

'Do they know how?'

'They're not sure. It's too soon.'

'He rang me two days ago and said he was going to see the man in Oxford again. What was his name?'

'Jim Stalbridge?'

'Yes, that was it. He thought he was on to something. I suppose I should tell the inspector.'

'I don't know. Let's think about it. I don't know why I somehow feel it might be a betrayal of Jack or even a false lead that might set them off on the wrong trail.'

'Poor Jack. I wonder what he was trying to find out. Why he didn't just tell the police if he suspected something?'

'Perhaps he was afraid they wouldn't believe him, that they would think he was trying to cover up his own involvement with the boys, that they still suspected him of something.'

'Can you come back to my place tonight, Alex. I don't think I want to be alone.'

So that night we did make love, but afterwards I saw that her face was wet with tears as she turned her head away from me.

＊

Translated from the Welsh. After AD 79

Then the Roman general Agricola returned to govern Britain and set out to complete
the conquest of our island. Before him Frontinus had beaten down the warlike Silures
in the south and west and now Agricola turned north to the lands of the Ordovices,
and the holy island of Mona. We keeping to the mountains for a time held him off
until, putting himself at the head of his army, although the summer was nearly over, he
led his men against us into the hills. High on the hilltops we raised up our ramparts,
our spears over our heads, our faces over the shield rims. Useless the chariot in those
mountains and rocky valleys. Terrible the slaughter. After, ravens grew red from the
blood of warriors.

Then those who remained withdrew to the Holy Island of Mona where the priests
made sacrifice in the sacred groves. We kept watch for ships crossing the Hibernian
waters that would bring the Roman army. But they did not appear those sails across
the horizon, the prows biting the water. None came. Then we rejoiced in feasting and
drinking not knowing the cunning of their general. For Agricola caused those of his
men trained in breasting the waters holding their swords and shields above their heads,
with their horses following after, to cross the narrow waters, naked except for their
arms. Surprise was our undoing. Yet some fought on protecting the sacred groves until
all the warriors and all the priests were put to the slaughter for the Romans believed
they were the source of our anger and rebellion.

Then the governor built many forts to subdue the tribes and leaving us conquered
turned his attention to the north so that once again we were free to worship our own
gods, the Mothers and the Horned One, the hunter. But also men began to sacrifice to
the gods of the Romans, and others from beyond the seas, fearing that our own gods of
grove and river had forsaken the land or had lost their power to protect us.

We hadn't discussed Jack's death the night before but in the morning it couldn't be put off any longer.

'Do you think he was lying to us?' Hilary asked.

It seemed strange to be considering such things over marmite toast.

'How do you mean?'

'Well, about his sexuality. He told us he wasn't interested in the kind of place where he was found but perhaps he thought we wouldn't approve of gay cruising, that we'd drop him if we thought that. So he pretended to be, not straight but at least celibate, not practising.'

'Would you have dropped him?'

'Of course not. But I didn't get the feeling that he had many friends, did you? He might have thought … Oh I don't know.'

'He said he'd tried that sort of thing and it wasn't what he wanted – like someone straight who's turned off by the thought of going with prostitutes.'

'But if what you want is forbidden you might settle for second or third best.'

'I don't suppose we'll ever know.'

'I wouldn't bet on it. Not with Hildreth still looking for answers.'

'Somehow I hope he doesn't find them, or anyway not that answer. I liked Jack.'

I thought that I did want to know, wanted to know if he'd lied to us and if any of it fitted into the jigsaw puzzle of the deaths of the three boys.

It wasn't long before I found out something at least. A call from Hildreth was waiting for me at the office. As soon as I could I rang him, after I'd made sure Doris Shepherd was available to go and feed Caesar.

'Your friend wasn't killed where he was found,' Hildreth said. 'He was done over elsewhere and the body dumped there, presumably to make it look like a queer killing. They stripped him of everything, apart from his clothes, just to add the suggestion of robbery for more confusion. We've no means of knowing where he was killed unless we can find a witness but it's hard to get people to come forward and admit they were in such a place at round about three in the morning. It looks from one or two signs in his flat that he went out to meet someone. Do you know any of his friends? Anyone he might go out to see?'

'He didn't say much about his present life. More about his past, working abroad, or his subject.'

'No mention of any family?'

'None.' It crossed my mind to mention Jim Stalbridge, the man he had visited in Oxford but for some reason I held back.

'Should I have?' I asked Hilary later.

'I don't know. You could have put him on to somebody perfectly innocent. I imagine the inspector hangs on like a bulldog if he gets his teeth into someone or something.'

'Suppose I went and looked him up to see what I think, whether he knows anything.'

'If he does you could be at risk yourself.'

'Not in broad daylight. I feel we owe it to Jack and Hildreth doesn't seem to have any leads.'

'When will you go?'

'Tomorrow. I can take some time off.'

'I wish I could come with you but I can't get away. You will be careful, Alex. No heroics please.'

Secretly I was flattered that Hilary thought I might be capable of something rash. First though I had to find an address. I opened up St Julian's website: Professor James Stalbridge with a photograph I could download. Then I tried the Oxford area phonebook and there he was again, alive and well and living in Westmoor Road, north Oxford. It was as if I was meant to find him. Now I had no choice in my own mind, but to go and search. I knew Oxford from summer courses; Westmoor Road was in the respectable part where dons kept their families in tall grey houses and assembled on Sunday mornings at St Philip and St James for old style matins, if I wasn't too out of date and they'd swapped the organ for the guitar or bongo drums.

I felt a childish excitement as I set off up the A127, the old arterial road to London for pre-Second World War outings 'beside the seaside' to join the M25 snaking round north London before turning west on the M40, and eventually down another old London Road, over Magdalen Bridge into the city centre, past St John's College and out on the Woodstock Road, where I pulled in to study my city map.

The excitement had faded on the long drive. Now I was here what should I say or do? I wished Hilary had been able to come with me. The whole enterprise of private detective Alex Kish seemed not just a bad idea but rather silly. I sat there behind the wheel and watched the ragged shapes of rooks thrown up against a grey sky and wished I was a bird. Then I remembered Jack's bloodied face, switched on the engine and drove slowly to the turnoff for Westmoor Road, cruising gently along it to read the house numbers, looking for twenty-eight with its stacks of doorbells. I pulled in again a little further along where I could watch the comings and goings through the front gate.

I sat there for about half an hour, covertly inspecting the cyclists and a few walkers, mainly women with dogs and pushchairs on their way to the Parks. Then suddenly there he was turning the corner, a little hunched inside his overcoat but unmistakable from the website photograph, slightly shaggy moustache, plump face with two wings of bushy hair sprouting from a bald patch stretching back from his forehead. I got out of the car and walked towards him.

The words came out as if they had been well rehearsed. 'I'm a friend of Jack Linden's. I think we should talk.'

He stood quite still for a moment like someone who might suddenly take flight and then his shoulders sagged and he put out his hand. 'Jim Stalbridge, Come on up. I'll make us some coffee.'

I followed him up to the third floor. The stair carpet had been flattened by a procession of feet over the years and the air was slightly stale from the cooking I supposed went on behind closed doors. Inside though, Stalbridge's flat was airy with high ceilings and light from a big sash window.

'Have a seat. It won't take long.'

I sat down in a dark blue, buttoned armchair and looked about. I could hear him clattering cups and spoons in the kitchen. There were hundreds of books, mostly relating to Egyptian archaeology as far as I could see, and a collection of figurines, jackal and hawk headed gods, a portrait of a beautiful golden skinned, olive-eyed boy painted on a wooden panel, and a miniature chariot with a rider but no horse.

On a table by the window I could see a newspaper. I stood up quietly and walked across the room. A short column had been ringed in black: an account of the finding of Jack's body. And then: 'The body has been identified as that of visiting American professor Jack Linden. Police are treating the death as murder.' So he knew. I went quietly back to my armchair.

'I see you know about Jack,' I began when Stalbridge had handed me a thick mug of coffee with 'University of Cairo' written on it.

'Tell me what happened,' Stalbridge said.

'He was found behind a gay pub in south London early on Tuesday morning, seemingly beaten to death and robbed.'

'Seemingly?'

'The police don't believe it was a queer bashing. They think he was killed somewhere else and dumped there. They think he went to meet someone. Do you have any idea who that might be?'

Stalbridge slowly shook his head. 'None. We hadn't kept up until he dropped in on me the other day. I didn't find out why he'd called out of the blue like that. We had a bit of a row and he left. I've no idea who his friends or acquaintances might be.'

'But you knew he was here, in this country.'

'These things get around. Academic gossip. I hadn't seen him since Egypt.'

'Were you instrumental in getting him sacked.'

'He told you that? Jack wasn't an Egypt scholar. That wasn't his field. He just got lucky. But he wouldn't have known what to do with what he'd found. Couldn't even read the hieroglyphs on the front walls. The project managers knew it needed an expert. They asked me to take over.'

'But you didn't stay?'

'I finished the excavation and wrote it all up in the report. We put the stuff on show for everyone who wanted to come. Then I was offered this fellowship. I could see how the whole Middle East was going: a bonfire waiting for the match. Then it spilled over into Egypt with foreign nationals being targeted. Kidnappings, bombings. It was time to go. I'd had a good run. You have to know when it's the right time to quit.'

He seemed affable and convincing so why wasn't I more convinced? I felt he was holding something back and had cleverly steered me away from the matter of Jack's death. I'd learnt nothing from my attempt at amateur sleuthing. Not even enough to pass on to the experts, Hildreth and his team. Again I regretted Hilary's absence. She might have been able to get more out of Stalbridge.

My coffee mug was empty. I tried to think of another opening, another excuse for sitting there.

'If you think I can help do get in touch. Here's my card.'

He stood up and fetched a printed slip from a terracotta pot on an old-style sideboard in dark oak. As he handed it to me I made one desperate bid. 'What did you and Jack Linden row about?'

'He thought I got him sacked because I was asked to take over his part of the site.'

'And you didn't?'

'Jack was indiscreet. He didn't hide his liking for some of the boys, the Egyptian labourers. That sort of thing doesn't go down well in some quarters. Our work was supported by a Christian college from the Bible Belt in the States. They were hoping we could find another Nag Hammadi or some Dead Sea scrolls to support some of their theories and beliefs. I didn't care where the money came from as long as I could get on with the excavation.'

'Did you find anything they wanted? Did Linden?'

'There was some Coptic stuff in with the dynastic material. Someone must have buried it thinking it would be safe that way. A small copper bronze cauldron with a papyrus inside it. The papyrus went missing before it could be deciphered. So the sponsors never knew if it had been worth their while. I expect it'll end up on the black market for antiquities. Someone will probably offer it for sale somewhere, like the Gospel of Thomas codex.'

'Was the cauldron anything like the one that turned up in the grave of the Prittlewell Prince?'

Stalbridge looked up sharply. For the first time his affability dropped away. 'How do you know about that?'

'I'm the curator of the local museum. Two of our local volunteers found the grave. Alex Kish.' I put out my hand.

Stalbridge looked quickly at his watch. 'Is that the time? I'm sorry, I'm due back for a tutorial in half an hour. We'll have to go on with this another time. I'd like to hear more about the finds at Prittlewell. Sorry to rush you out. I'll give you a call if I may.'

'Please do.' I was being ushered abruptly towards the door. Stalbridge locked it behind us and followed me down the stairs.

'Can I give you a lift. My car's over there.'

'Thanks but my doctor says I should walk as much as possible. Good for the heart. I'll cut through the Parks. I'll be in touch.' He turned and walked briskly away while I went back to my car. I let him turn the corner before starting the engine.

As I drove back I became even more convinced that my first instinct of unease had been right. Stalbridge knew more, was more deeply involved than he was admitting. But I still didn't have enough to give to the police. I imagined myself under Hildreth's cool eye stuttering out something about Stalbridge being disturbed with my knowing about the Prittlewell finds. Perhaps it had been dishonest to lead him on without letting him know who I was. But why hadn't he asked me straightaway? Why had he let himself be led on? It suggested an arrogant confidence in his own immunity. Or perhaps I was wrong and he really had run out of time.

Hilary was no more reassuring. 'Not much to build on,' she said. 'I don't see where we go from here.'

'I'm sure he was lying. I'm convinced he knew Jack better than he admitted.'

'That doesn't necessarily implicate him in his death.'

'I know I can't prove anything, it's just…'

'Feminine intuition?'

'Well I never had anything against that and now the psychologists are saying it works better than conscious reasoning. Hildreth would no doubt call it imagination.'

She laughed. 'What's the next step? The police seem to have

finished with us here. They've said we can reopen. They think it took more than one person to set the whole thing up. The boy died, was killed elsewhere. There must have been some inside help to get in without setting off the security. They're checking everyone who's left recently or any casuals we might have had in.'

'I don't know what we can do next. I don't seem to be very good at sleuthing. All I've got is so slight, a suspicion. I can't go to the police with that. They might think I was trying to hide something else. After all isn't it often the first person to help the police who turns out to be the murderer, like at Soham.'

'Don't,' Hilary said.

I decided it was time to change the subject. 'What are you doing at the weekend?'

'Beth and I are going to stay with my brother.'

I felt defeated. My only living relative that I knew of, was a distant cousin I had no contact with, apart from a Christmas card, though, for all I knew, Budapest might be teeming with half brothers and sisters and their offspring. Once I'd leafed through a Hungarian dictionary, wondering whether I ought to try and learn my father's language but it looked so alien that I gave up. Only from a glossary of names at the back I discovered that in Budapest I would be Sandor and liked the sound of it, tougher, more positive, I thought than Alex.

Suddenly I missed Jack. I was being forced to look at my life of work and home to Caesar rather as an insect must experience its own emerging from a pupa to dry its wings and peer about before take-off over this new world. Even the spring which had seemed to promise so much at the beginning of February was now on hold under a bitter wind bringing showers of sleet, cold enough to chill to the bone but without the purity of snow.

Well, on Saturday morning I could work and then ... It was too soon to go back to Oxford and try to pin down Stalbridge again. I would go to the British Museum and see whether among its engraved faces and sculptured dead, intuition would help me out since everyone's reason, mine included, didn't seem to be coming up with anything. I would just wander from room to room in the hope that the lightning would strike and I could leap from my bath shouting 'Eureka'.

Even going up Smirke's great wing of grey stone steps I could see that Saturday afternoon wasn't the best time to come if you were hoping for a revelation among the crowds from, it seemed, every nation on earth thronging in and out.

Still I was there now and I hadn't anything else to do. 'No man is an island', I remembered as I was absorbed into the crowd, and yet we were all islands, floating islands, contiguous maybe, an endless string of atolls, lapped round by solitude, a fleet of canoes or coracles frenetically paddling towards some shore before squalls sank us or the currents drove us back.

A continuous stream of people was heading for the Egyptian galleries. The mummies were always the most popular with children, except for the dinosaurs at the National History Museum. Fleetingly I wished we had a couple of really popular draws. Where should I go for my road to Damascus experience? There was a special exhibition: 'The Forgotten Empire'. If it was forgotten maybe fewer people would want to remember it. I went to the ticket desk and then through a great stone arch of winged figures Smirke might have copied for the museum itself, into a narrow corridor, lined on one side with exhibits taking us back in time to forgotten emperors Cyrus, Darius, Xerxes, to the first known Aryan Empire that once stretched from the Danube to the Indus, and from the Oxus to the Nile, so the wall map told me. Briefly I wondered if Hitler would have admitted them to his pantheon. There was the first known writing in an Indo-European language, the immutable laws of the Medes and Persians, and a list of the Tributes sent from all the conquered territories to the capital Persepolis, including a marble statue of Penelope from Greece and five hundred boys to be eunuchs whom a magnanimous emperor had sent back. There too was the meticulous script of the seal of the Emperor Cyrus allowing the Jews to return from their captivity in Babylon after he had conquered it. But the thing that touched me most was two gold coins, no bigger than buttons, like the coins we had found in the prince's grave. There was an answer here if only I could grasp it. And then ahead as I turned a corner I saw what I thought was the figure of Stalbridge bending over a glass case.

I stepped back at once. What was he doing here? But then why shouldn't he be? Perhaps I was mistaken. I chanced a quick look around the corner. No mistake. There was the shaggy moustache, the wings of bushy hair. Why was he in this exhibition and not among the mummies that were his field of expertise? Perhaps he was just bored with them, had seen them too often. Or maybe he was looking for a new twist to his career now that Iran was so much in the news, laying claim to that old empire as its legitimate sphere of influence re-conquering Babylon – Iraq by faith and stealth. It would certainly be a way to liven up a dull lecture on Middle Eastern politics.

I peered round my corner again. He seemed to be sketching something in the case, presumably because in most museums you aren't allowed to take photographs: we all want to sell our own souvenir merchandise of bling, T-shirt and postcard. I saw him look from his notebook down into the case and back again at the page. Then he shut the notebook, put it, together with the pen, into the briefcase he was carrying and walked away. Once he was safely round the next corner I moved to see what he had been copying. It was a golden symbol, a winged disk that looked as if it was a figure, the whole thing reminding me of the Holy Spirit descending as a dove in a Renaissance painting of the Annunciation. The label identified it as a classic Persian representation of Phanes, the creator. It told me nothing.

I hurried after Stalbridge but he had disappeared. Perhaps he had simply left the exhibition but when I went outside into the main hall there was no sign of him. The crowds were even denser now as if all the tourists in London were converging on this one space.

What were we trying to give them, those of us engaged in this enterprise of preserving and presenting history. A sense of the past, of it all being the same yet different? A way of understanding the present? We have been here before. War, technology, art, religion, everything we call culture. The DNA of history, a double helix of genetic programming and external pressures to produce the variations through time. And that's what we mostly see. The momentary manifestation in a new toy or a new conflict, not what shapes it and us.

Saul was overwhelmed with joy when he fell off his horse. Mine was a bleak vision though, seeing us as rats on a tread wheel, doomed to pursue the same meaningless path, a bloody determinism. How was it still possible to reconcile the concept of free will with such knowledge?

I'd never looked at what I did in this way before. I'd got up and gone to work, put in a good day, made decisions, kept the organisation running smoothly without considering what it was all for, whether it had any purpose beyond satisfying the public curiosity, giving us a chance to feel superior to our quaint ancestors, and providing teachers with a break, somewhere to go on a wet afternoon. Perhaps it was mere self indulgence, a waste of precious time, to look for purpose, meaning, beyond the thing itself, the doing of it. Like asking for a Creator to justify the existence of butterfly or flower, rather than simply their own being. Suddenly I was considering all the questions usually posed and resolved in adolescence. Next thing I'd be throwing up my job and taking a gap year to backpack round the world before it was too late, if it wasn't already. Looking down the hall of sculptured forms and carved masonry I suddenly saw the murdered boy from the Museum of London stretched out on a plank at the end of a row as if fallen asleep but when I moved towards him I saw it was only one of the stone figures reclining face down with an arm under his head. It was time to go home, away from such hauntings.

That evening I rang to see if Hilary was back from her weekend away with Beth, to fill her in on my latest sighting of Stalbridge but got only the voicemail. Tomorrow I must put it all out of my mind and concentrate on planning the summer exhibition which should open after Easter, only weeks away. I must set Lisa hunting down saucy postcards, bathing machines and costumes, antique ice-cream carts and pier concert posters. The board of governors, even the chairman had seemed quite enthusiastic about the project, voting me a small increase in budget. 'Something light-hearted, Kish. That's the ticket,' the chairman had said, 'after all we've been through.'

It was Hilary's turn to ring me. 'Did you have a good time?' I asked.

'It was good for Beth to see her cousins but my brother and I have never had much in common, excepts our parents. I know he thinks I should have married again and he's never understood the fascination of the job, bringing things and ways of life back to the light. He's an accountant. He finds what I do rather disgusting – cleaning up bones and bits of broken pot. His worst moment was when I told him we were working on a plague pit. I bet he searched his armpits for pustules after our lunch date. So what did you get up to?'

I told her about seeing Stalbridge but not about my pitiful attempt at enlightenment, as I now saw it.

'What was he copying?'

'A sort of winged disk. The caption said Phanes.'

There was a pause and then Hilary said: 'I think that was the creative principle that first sprang out of the primal egg and was swallowed by Ormuz. The Greeks took it into a version of their mythologies, with Zeus swallowing Protogonus and giving birth to the universe. Something the same turns up with the Gnostics in their theories of creation via Plato. Sometimes there's a female principle in there too: the creator-mother, Night or Thought or, for some of the Gnostics, Sophia, Wisdom. Sorry about the lecture. Isn't that part of our job? Anyway, it all makes Darwin sound comfortingly simple.

Some people still accept explanations like it: the spirit of god moving on the face of the primal waters and so on. Maybe the Big Bang is just another theory to try to make sense of the inexplicable. Maybe we'll never know. We still have to put the milk bottles out and recycle the tins and papers.'

'You're a pragmatist.'

Hilary laughed. 'In my job, when you're dealing with the dead all the time, it seems safer.'

'When can I see you?'

'Why don't you come to supper tomorrow?'

This time we fell on each other ferociously as soon as Hilary had shut the door of her flat behind us and she turned to face me. Later with our first hunger satisfied we ate the supper of pasta and salad that she had prepared, and then to bed, my arm under her head resting on my shoulder until we moved apart in sleep, but still wrapped around each other, companionable as an old married couple.

In the morning over a quick breakfast of tea and toast, before I went off to catch the Tube for Liverpool Street and work, she said: 'What happens next? Will you tell Hildreth?'

'About seeing Stalbridge? I keep imagining myself ringing him up and then I don't know what I would say. It's all so nebulous. If Jack were still alive I feel he would know what to do.'

'We're like the babes in the wood having to fend for ourselves and hoping not to fall into the clutches of the wicked witch.' Hilary laughed. 'A bit pathetic at our age and job seniority. I suppose we're out of our depth because, like most people, we've never had to deal with anything so far beyond our usual experience.'

When I came out of our miniaturised Victoria Station the sun was shining and I imagined I caught a whiff of the sea. Instead of going directly into the museum I crossed the roundabout, turned down the High Street, and over the cliff, down to the esplanade towards the entrance to the pier and the distantly glinting water, the narrow passage for incomers to cross, whether hostile or benign or merely desperate. Last night with Hilary had made me uneasy about my lone state. Perhaps I should look for a transfer to London? But I loved the town that had nurtured me in my career, its history, its mix of royal bathing and works outing, and I loved the sea that today was lying glassily relaxed but in winter could become a heaving beast hurling itself against the town's defences. Should I ask Hilary to marry me? We'd never discussed permanence, apart from that one moment right at the beginning when she'd asked me if this was more than a one-night stand. Yet somehow I shied away from the question, sensing that perhaps she did too. I turned back towards my office and the 'old toad' of work.

A small padded manila envelope lay on the top of the pile of officially franked letters asking for my attention or a quick trip to the shredder. It was addressed in handwriting and marked 'personal'. I never received such post at the office; indeed like most people in the email age I hardly received post at all that wasn't charity or sales flyers. I picked it up. The thought of a letter bomb passed through my mind but the envelope felt too light and there were no obvious wires sticking out of the stapled flap. But then such devices must be more sophisticated these days, and what about things like anthrax spores or polonium which must have just this appearance of weightlessness.

Suddenly it all seemed silly, the result of a media-induced paranoia that kept us trembling and reaching in our pockets for the price of the latest horror story. We were losing mankind's necessary resilience to the fact of death that was part of the individual and collective survival kit. I remembered the words of a traveller I had read somewhere, writing home in the seventeenth century for news of the pregnant wife he had left behind: 'I know not whether I be increased by a child or diminished by a wife.' Now somebody would have sent him a text message. I opened the top drawer of my desk and took out a paper knife to prise up the staples.

Inside was a single sheet of handwritten paper. I unfolded it to read:

> *Some people who are inclined to play rough have remarked your visit to me in Oxford and that you seemed to have been following me the other day in the BM although I did not myself see you. They have expressed curiosity about your interest. I have told them that we have mutual friends through our field of study. It seemed to satisfy them but I thought you should know!*
>
> *By the way I also thought you should have this which I came across for sale on the internet.*

The spidery signature confirmed that the note was from Stalbridge, I upended the envelope and shook it. A small round object wrapped in tissue paper fell into my palm. Even before I uncovered it I knew what it was. The medallion from the Prittlewell Prince's buckle lay there burning in my hand like a stigma.

I put it down carefully on my desk. It seemed like a reproach, another haunting. My instinct was to ring Stalbridge and ask him for more details of how he had found it, and whether the gold plate or any part of it had been with it. One leaf was still unaccounted for after all.

If only there were some rite of divination I could use to get it to give up its secret, to tell its story of who had taken it and whose hands it had passed through. Suddenly I understood how our ancestors must have felt, confronted with mysteries that they couldn't unravel, how they would have stood peering down at the bloody innards of a sacrifice looking for understanding or opened a holy text at random and stabbed at a verse blindfold, searching for guidance, or thrown the sacred wands to see what pattern they would make in the dust. Now we had the unpicking of the human genome to tell us our fate but we were still crossing our fingers and reading our luck in the stars like an emotional appendix, a useless relic that could fester and infect us with a destructive septicaemia.

Jack had said that this small, innocuous-seeming, round of metal held the symbols of four religions, cults or sects, however you liked to call them. The wearer hedging his bets. Again I felt the impulse to ring Stalbridge and ask him what he knew about it, what he thought it all meant and what Jack had really wanted when he called on him in Oxford. But from my own experience of his evasiveness I knew he would tell me nothing. Perhaps he had sent me a clue in the medallion and expected me to tease it out. Perhaps it was just an excuse to warn me about the people 'who play rough'. Or something he wanted to get rid of himself, a haunting he needed to exorcise.

There were no answers. The amulet was mute or if it spoke it was in a whisper I couldn't catch, the sound of the sea in a shell. I wrapped it in its shroud of tissue paper again and locked it in the safe. Then I rang Hildreth, not because I had decided to tell him about Stalbridge but simply to be doing something and in the hope that he might have some news.

'Ah, Alex, I was going to ring you. Not that there's much to tell, more questions than answers. We know how they got into Dr Caistor's museum. Contract cleaners for the windows. Started early to be finished before the public arrived, so they said. Obviously sussed out the security, how to knock out the alarm system and then in through the roof. But someone must have been there too during the day as a visitor, we think, and picked the spot to place the body. Unfortunately CCTV doesn't show anyone behaving suspiciously among the hundreds who went through in the days before.

The boy was from somewhere in Eastern Europe or even as far away as the Middle East. Dead before he was put there, like the others. Not more than twenty-four hours. Rigor would have had to be over to arrange the body as it was. But decomposition had barely set in so forensics are pretty clear about the timing. So far they're all foreign. No one knows about them. No one comes forward to claim them. Lost boys, you might say.'

Aren't we all, I thought, in one way or the other. 'I went to see Stalbridge,' I said.

'Stalbridge?'

'Jack Linden's sometime colleague he visited in Oxford.'

'And did you find anything? Like why did your professor pay him a visit.'

'Nothing. He talked about Jack and how they worked together in Egypt, but that was all.'

'You have to be careful going off on your own like that, Alex. You could alert a suspect or even just muddy the waters for us.'

'Yes, I see that. It's just I felt I owed it to Jack. Nothing seemed to be happening. No answers as to why he was killed. Do you still think it wasn't just a queer bashing, being in the wrong place at the wrong time?'

'No, we don't think it was that. But that's all I can tell you because we've got no further ourselves. We believe, I believe, all these happenings are connected but we don't know how. Anyway let me know next time if you feel like going off on your own, and I'll tell you whether I think it's a good idea.'

My wrist was being well and truly slapped though in a very gentle way. Yet it was clear that the police weren't getting anywhere either. I hadn't mentioned Stalbridge's letter with its bizarre enclosure, partly because I would have been forced to give it up as possible evidence. So I was still withholding information; this time hard facts not just speculation. I wondered what Hilary would advise when, if, I told her.

I'd allowed myself to be distracted by Jack's unsolved death. 'Get back to the day job,' I told myself. The chairman had said he wanted something light for the summer exhibition, 'to lift people's spirits': candy floss and striped deckchairs. But all I could think of was the dark underbelly of Victorian life, Wilde's stable boys, flower-girl prostitutes, Dickensian alleys, gaslight blaring through a broken mantle, the tattered lungs of consumptive seamstresses.

## Post Adversus Haereses c. AD 180 Lyons

*For they allege that after Joseph of Arimathea had laid the body of the Lord in the tomb prepared for himself then he washed it and closed up the wounds and in the morning came Mary of Magdala and breathed into the Lord the breath that he had given her when he kissed her on the mouth.*

*Others say that Christ did not die but Simon who carried the cross was crucified in his place because God cannot die, being immortal and all spirit. Yet others that the human flesh clothing the Lord perished but the spirit flew up.*

*Those first say too that Joseph of Arimathea, after the Lord was gone away, came to Saul with that Mary and after went to the Cassiterides, and that therefore he was the founder of the Christian church here but the truth is that, when he was very old and on his way to his death, the blessed Ignatius, bishop of Antioch, who had known the Apostles, Peter and Paul, stopped at Smyrna where he was met by St Polycarp, then a young man. And it seems to me most certain that from thereabouts the word was carried to the West, following the example of St Paul to the places where the Greeks had settled or Greek Jews, and thence to the Greeks of Massilia, so that in the persecution of the Emperor, Marcus Aurelius, there were already some forty-eight persons here who died for their Lord, including their bishop Pothinus, to whom I have succeeded. And I too was born in Smyrna and hold the memory of St Polycarp ever in my heart. So I say with the Apostle Paul 'If Christ is not risen our faith is in vain.'*

*I warn you therefore, beloved, against those heretics who would lead you astray with their false gospels and thegonies that claim a divine mother, sometimes called Sophia, as the source of creation and of the Christ, who is not, they say falsely, the Lord born of Mary but only enters into him at baptism. And these teachings come in part from the heathen philosophers who lived before the Lord and did not know him or from the stories of the gods of the pagans.*

*And so our people suffer because they are forced to worship these gods or perish by decree of the emperors, who claim to be god themselves, or to eat the meat that has been sacrificed to idols. Then the people cry out against them when they see them refuse saying: 'Give us back our gods who preserve us, not just this Jesus who, you teach, died like a felon on the cross.'*

*The names of the false teachers are Cerinthus, Basilides, Valentinus whom the Romans refused to make a bishop, Ptolemaeus and many others who write and teach contrary to the evidence of the true church, not in the name of the Lord and his truth but for their own glory, making congregations of followers under their own names. But the truth will be revealed when he comes in his glory. So my brethren hold fast and the gates of hell shall not prevail against you nor any suffering cause you to falter.*

There was a note from Doris Shepherd on the kitchen table when I went through to make myself some tea.

'Caesar hadn't ate much so I left it.'

I stared down at the desiccated plates of food I had put out for him yesterday morning. A numb sickness punched me in the stomach. Usually he would be waiting when I came back; reproachful, demanding attention before I could be forgiven. Today the house was silent, empty. I went to the foot of the stairs and called. Often, when I was out, he slept on my bed. Perhaps he was ill. I climbed to the top landing but my bedroom was empty. I went down and opened the back door calling into the garden. Sometimes he waited for me on the strip of front lawn but I would have seen him as I came in.

The back gardens were his stalking ground. The house fronted onto a busy road and he was afraid of traffic, usually going no further than the front porch or the few feet of grass inside the gate. I called again. Often he would come clambering over the fence with a little cry of recognition, but of chastisement too. A blackbird sang briefly. Then a gull wheeled overhead with a long ululating cry. I turned back indoors.

All evening I waited for the sound of the cat flap dropping back into place, with only half an ear for the television or the phone. He hadn't stayed away like this since he was a kitten and had fallen through the open skylight of a neighbour's greenhouse. I saw him savaged by the pit bull a few doors away and lying under a bush, broken and bleeding, and blamed myself for going straight to work instead of coming home first.

In the end, after too much whisky, I fell asleep in front of the screen to wake thickly and stagger to bed trying to believe he would be back in the morning but daylight came and no Caesar.

I wanted to howl and yet part of my mind knew this would be

condemned as a totally disproportionate response by most people. I tried to think of the dead boys, the welter of grief and pain, an envelope of violence and despair blanketing the earth with its burden of living creatures but my own pain was too sharp. Was there something wrong with me that I could feel like this for a non-human animal when the suffering of my own species could leave me unmoved? Men, especially, aren't supposed to feel like this or not to admit to it, even to themselves.

I rang the RSPCA, the police and Caesar's vet. Then I set up a poster on the computer with his picture and printed off twenty copies. At the last moment I added: *Reward*. Where I live the houses are constantly changing owner so that there were few friendly neighbours I could call on and ask them to search garden sheds and greenhouses.

Looking at Caesar's black-and-white photograph I realised there was nothing to distinguish him in most people's eyes from any other black-and-white cat. Once you leave out colour and size, the other animals appear deceptively homogenous within their type and species. An Alsatian is an Alsatian first, an individual second and often only perceived to be so by the doting owner, looking for difference within similarity. Whereas, we wear our hearts on our faces unless we're trying to hide something.

The trees were in fresh green leaf or sprinkled with small white flowers clinging like wet confetti. Soon the petals would fall and the pavement be deep in their post-wedding drift. Tacking up the posters at head height on their bark I suddenly hoped the trees didn't feel the pins going in but I couldn't think of any other way of doing it. There was nothing more I could do but before I set off to the museum I had to share my ache with somebody. I rang Hilary.

'Where are you?' she asked when I said her name. 'What's happened?'

'I'm just going to work. Caesar's missing. He wasn't here when I got back and he didn't come in this morning. He hadn't eaten anything either so that means he's been gone two days. I've rung everybody and put up posters. I can't think what else to do.'

'You've done everything you can. We just have to hope someone finds him. I'm so sorry, Alex.'

'Do you think I'm – well wet to be so...? I just want to howl.'

'Of course not. It shows you're human. But don't be alone. Go to work and try not to think about it.'

Of course she was right. But the moment would come when I had to go home again, hoping to find him here and dreading the disappointment of the empty house. Trying not to think of him shut in somewhere without food or water, or worse, I took the bus down into town. The ornate façade of what had once been the library, and was now the museum, endowed by Andrew Carnegie, was solid and comforting in its late Victorian dress, echoed all over the country, of red brick and carved stone trimmings.

There was an unfamiliar envelope among the usual pile of circulars and official communications on my desk. Wary of the unknown I picked it up and weighed it in the palm of my head. By now I could recognise Stalbridge's writing and the address wasn't in his script. The envelope was a plain long white A3 one, slightly stiff suggesting a folded sheet of A4 with a small lump in the middle. There must be an enclosure. And suddenly I didn't care if I died, was blown to bits or poisoned. I was tired of being suspicious, afraid. I tore open the envelope, putting a forefinger under the loose end of the flap and ripping along the seam. At least it would be quick. Nothing happened. I found, in spite of my brave or foolhardy action, I'd been holding my breath and let it out in a gusty sigh. Then I took out a single sheet of white paper folded into three. A small mound of black fur fell onto the table. When I opened the sheet I found a single sentence in that device of anonymous letter writers that's such a cliché, words cut from newsprint:

*Let's see if he's clever enough to find his way home.*

So I had been right to be apprehensive. Caesar hadn't just run off on an adventure or been shut in. He'd been catnapped. Even as I thought it I knew that wasn't the right word. Stolen, made off with, kidnapped. There was no other word for it. It was meant to be a warning. It told me I was being watched, that they knew my comings and goings and even those of my cat. It had to be the people Stalbridge had described as liking 'to play rough', who had seen me at his house in Oxford and concluded, wrongly, that I had been following him at the British Museum.

How far had they taken him? How could he possibly find his way back from wherever, over unknown territory, perhaps having to cross twenty roads, Caesar who was so easily frightened by traffic? If they'd killed him as a warning, and sent me the black fur as proof, it would have been easier to resign myself. But they had known me well enough or made a fortunate guess that this not knowing was more painful and therefore, in their terms, a more effective warning. Reason told me I would never see him again but there was still the worm of hope and the fear that he might be suffering, at the very least terrified.

Should I involve Hildreth now? I'd already asked the local police about strays and they'd put me on to a cat rescue organisation. But Hildreth was a different matter. I imagined myself saying: 'I've lost my cat,' and his complete bewilderment and then contempt. I wasn't even sure about telling Hilary. She might think I'd lost it completely if I suggested he'd been kidnapped. There seemed nothing I could do but ring the vet and the cat rescue people and say I thought he had been driven off in some car or van by mistake and ask them to keep an eye out for a black-and-white cat, possibly missing some fur. I emailed them his picture.

'We've got one in but it's got more white than yours and anyway she's a female. We'll keep looking. Let us know if he comes back. Not everyone bothers and it clutters up the records. By the way there's been a lot of pet napping recently. Have you thought of that? You wouldn't think there'd be a market when so many animals are just abandoned but there you are.'

Her matter-of-factness was reassuring. She didn't think I was wet or mad. She still had hope. I could imagine her easily from her voice: greying, perhaps a retired schoolteacher, firm but kind, used to the idiosyncrasies of pet owners but more concerned for the animals themselves, probably saying to an assistant: 'Why can't people look after their pets properly?'

My next but one caller, after a difficult conversation with the chairman wanting to know whether the jolly seaside exhibition would be ready on time as if it was Wembley Stadium and he was the Queen cutting the ribbon, was Hildreth himself almost as if he could read my thoughts.

'Ah, Alex. I'm coming down to your neck of the woods. Can you meet me for a trip up the coast? There's been a development. I'd like your input.'

Perhaps this was my chance to tell him about Caesar and Stalbridge's 'people who play rough'. 'I was going to phone you anyway about something... I don't, didn't know how important it is,' I said to give myself an opening.

'We can talk in the car. I'll pick you up... let me see: it's ten thirty now, around twelve thirty, at work.'

'How long will we be away? I need to tell my staff.'

'It's hard to say. I'll probably stay on and send you back in the car. We're going to Bradwell. To some chapel by the sea. There's been another body found. It looks like the same lot.'

No, my mind said, leave me out. I don't want to be involved but I knew it was useless. I would go with Hildreth and be made party to more violence and death. Now I couldn't tell him about Caesar, not without a lot of editing.

'Does Dr Caistor know?'

'Not yet.'

'Shall I tell her?'

'You do that. It'll come better from you. I don't pretend to have a gentle touch.'

'Look,' I said, 'are you sure you need me? It's out of your way to come here first.'

'You're my talisman, Alex. You have to see this through.'

I hoped he couldn't hear me sigh. 'Okay. But I'll meet you there. Same time: twelve thirty.'

'Don't be late.'

'Is it another boy?' Hilary asked.

'I suppose so. He didn't say. Just that it looked like the same lot.'

'Jack must have been involved in some way.'

'We'll never know that for sure.'

'I don't want to believe it.'

'I know. Neither do I. I'll ring you as soon as I'm back. My chairman won't like this. It's much too close to home again.'

So I set out up the A127 towards London, passing the prince's grave site and the end of my own road. Had Caesar come home yet? I couldn't stop to find out. Leaving the old London arterial I turned north through Rayleigh to cross the River Crouch at Battlesbridge, and then drove north-east towards the Blackwater and the sea. By now I knew Bede's history almost by heart and the *Anglo Saxon Chronicle* since the prince had so clearly become part of my life, so that even I knew that this is an old landscape stamped with the footprints of the dead Saxons and Vikings battling it out at Maldon.

*Minds shall be stronger, hearts shall be bolder*
*Courage shall be more, as our strength grows less ...*

The exhortation of Byrtnoth, the Saxon commander, as his remaining warriors rallied round him for a last stand, could have inspired a Henry V or a Churchill. This time though it hadn't been enough. They were all cut down.

Now I was driving through the saltings of the Essex marshes where Mehalah was drowned by her lover in the bestselling romance by the local vicar, Sabine Baring Gould, collector of folksongs, author of such religious hits as *Onward Christian Soldiers* and *Through the Night of Doubt and Sorrow*, and contemporary of Thomas Hardy, an Essex Tess of the D'Urbervilles. 'One of your lot,' Hilary would say. Bradwell is on a hunched back of land between the Blackwater and the cold North Sea, a place of wheeling gulls and solitude, apart from the pilgrims and picnickers.

The entrance for the car park was blocked by a police barrier, manned on either side by officers in luminous yellow jackets. I pulled up and wound down my window as one of them stepped forward.

'The chapel is closed to the public, sir.'

'Yes, I know. Chief Inspector Hildreth asked me to meet him here.'

'I see.' He thought for a moment, staring hard at my face as if he could see through to my black heart and lying tongue. 'Do you have some ID with you sir?'

'Driving licence?'

'That would help.'

I fished in the glove compartment and handed over the green form in its plastic jacket.

'Alex Kish?'

'That's right.' The other officer had been busy on his mobile phone. Now he came over.

'Alex Kish?' The first one said.

'That tallies with the number plate.'

'Detective Chief Inspector Hildreth hasn't arrived yet. I suggest you pull over there in the car park and someone will let you know when he's ready for you.'

'Thank you, officer.' He handed back my driving licence.

'I expect the traffic is bad getting out of London,' I said, feeling some need to prove I was a normal, rational citizen. Then I drove carefully to a corner of the car park where they could keep an eye on me from the barrier and switched the engine off. It wouldn't be seemly to play the radio I decided, so I got out the leaflets on the chapel that I had picked up from our display shelves, which included material on all the local places of interest tourists and natives might want to visit: Colchester Castle, Thaxted Windmill, Ingatestone Hall: the tangible fabric of Essex history.

The two leaflets weren't glossy affairs but single folded A4 sheets, with black-and-white prints and line drawings, giving the history of the chapel, proudly called 'the first cathedral in England,' and its founder, St Cedd, who had built it in 654 during the second attempt, this time by the Irish, to christianise the heathen Saxons. Cedd had sailed down from Lindisfarne where he had been schooled by St Aidan, who in turn had been taught by St Columba on Iona.

Cedd had looked for the wildest place he could find to found his mission church and had used the remains of a Roman fort built to defend the Saxon shore as, legend said, St Antony, reputedly the first hermit, had done in Egypt. A line of saints stretched back from Essex to the North African deserts and the sphinx's smile.

I remembered paintings of the temptations of St Antony, of the haggard face of a man beset with demons in every shape and size, embodying all the conceivable weaknesses human flesh is prone to. Nowadays he would probably be diagnosed as schizophrenic, suffering from multiple delusions, rather than an epileptic like Paul. But he had started a worldwide movement of monastic retreat that Cedd had still tried to follow, thousands of miles away and over three hundred years later, not just for his own spiritual satisfaction but, through the men and women he gathered around him, a mini-welfare state, a community of education, health care, food and safety until corruption and violence overwhelmed it.

Now his chapel lay between the abandoned nuclear power station and the wildlife preservation area of Dengie to the south, home to a million migrant seabirds.

'Dirty mags, Alex?' Hildreth stuck his head through the window I had left wound down to reassure his colleagues.

'Descriptions of the chapel and its founder.'

'You can tell me as we walk. I gather it's quite a hike.'

'This was the Roman road to the fort before the church was built,' I said, airing my newly acquired knowledge.

'You're not religious are you, Alex?'

'No. Why? Are you?'

'I was brought up a Catholic but the wife and I lapsed after our two kids were born. We thought that was enough. They sent me through some pictures on the computer before I left. That's why I had to ask.'

'Cedd used the tiles and stones from the fort and straddled the old wall with his new building. Hence the name, St Peter-on-the-wall. Apparently it's much the same, that is the nave is, as when he left it to go and found another monastery in Yorkshire where he died.'

'You've been here before?'

'Once, a long time ago.'

After about a half-mile walk, we came out from behind a hedge beside the path. A meadow of wild flowers and grasses waved between us and a small grey stone building with little windows like arrow slits set high up in its single storey. Beyond, the water glinted, very still, waiting. At high tide, the leaflet said, two thirds of the old fort is covered by the sea. I wondered briefly how it would manage the rise in sea level as the ice caps melted.

A uniformed policeman stood by the door. Behind the chapel the sky was a high, luminous, pale opal as if there was nothing beyond but the edge of the world.

'They won't like having to carry the stuff all the way from the car park,' Hildreth said motioning to the guard to open the door. 'Come on.'

Inside was a heavy curtain he pushed roughly aside. There was a pause while Hildreth felt around for a switch. The small windows high up in the rafters let in very little light. The smell of damp stone, slightly acid, mingling with a salty tone, as if the essence of the sea was trapped within the walls, gave me a sense of being entombed in a stone coffin. As my eyes grew more used to the gloom I could see a few patches of coloured light at the far end that must be a bigger window with stained glass. Then the light went on.

'Good god!'

'You see why I had to ask if you were religious.'

At the far end on an altar, a single stone slab resting on three stone pillars, a boy's body was propped upright fastened to a wooden cross, quite naked except for a chaplet of glossy leaves round his head. Holly, my mind supplied unconsciously.

'You see what I mean?'

I followed Hildreth as he walked towards the figure.

'Who found it?'

'Some woman who came in to do the flowers. There's a service tomorrow. I haven't, of course, spoken to her yet, she's in shock, but I doubt if there's much she can tell us. What do you think?'

'I don't know what to say.' I stared at the strange scene, shocked to find myself unable to be horrified. Perhaps so many carved or painted crucifixions had dulled the senses after nearly two millennia but I could only see a macabre beauty in the still childishly soft skin, the closed bud of the penis drooping to one side like a wilting unopened peony, echoing the head slumped towards the left shoulder with the pointed chin resting on the jutting ridge of pale collar bone above the rack of ribs. And then the light from high up in the roof was caught on the small square of metal at the boy's throat.

'You're right of course: it is the same.'

'It could be a copycat.'

'No,' I said pointing at the figure, 'there's the lost piece from our stolen amulet.'

'That's it. The signature this kind of killer so often can't resist. Except that until now they've been dead beforehand. We shan't know about this one until forensics have a go at it. Come on, there's nothing more we can do at the moment and I have to let the team get started. Let's find a pub. This place gives me the creeps.'

And yet, I remembered, when I had been here before it was filled with light, flowers, music, living people. It had seen death many times before when the Vikings ravaged this coast, then as a chapel of ease. Its tower had been a beacon for ships, then it became a barn. Through all the mutations it had kept a secret life of its own as if it had been waiting for this moment, a passion play in stone.

Hildreth pulled back the curtain and we stepped out into the grey afternoon. I was glad of the sudden gust of wind and walked on ahead while he stopped to talk to the policemen.

'The rest of the team has arrived. Where can we find a pub? All that cold and damp has made me want to pee.'

'There's a village...'

'Now,' he said when we were safely settled with drinks and sandwiches from the bar, 'what's it all about?'

'Why do you think I know any more than you?'

'Because it started on your patch and it's something to do with your field – history, museums...'

'Jack Linden would have been more use to you.'

'Ay, but he's dead, and that may be part of it. All I've got is you and what facts we can piece together. I feel, I know, in this case, facts alone aren't enough. I need to know why, what's behind it, what it means, if it has a meaning, before I can go after whoever's doing it.'

'I don't know what you want.'

'Fair enough. I'll be more precise. What's all this religious stuff? Explain that to me.'

'I'll try as far as I can understand it myself. Right then. The finds in the amulet that were stolen from us had two parts: a square of gold leaf with writing on it, folded up into four, so it made a smaller square the size of a postage stamp. It was very old. Jack said it was pre-Christian. The writing was Greek. Instructions to the soul on what to do after death.'

'So where does this crucifixion bit come in?'

'The other thing in the amulet was a round disc like a coin. Jack thought it might have been a Roman coin that had been altered. It had the symbols for several religions engraved on it: Mithraism, Orphism, Zoroastrianism and Christianity. Jack said the owner must have been hedging his bets, making sure all possibilities were covered.'

'For good luck?'

'For good luck after death. That's how it ties in with the small gold plate. And it was found in a grave. But there were also two small gold crosses probably laid over his eyes so maybe he, or whoever buried him, thought Christianity gave him the best chance.'

'Okay. I follow you so far. How does it tie in with the killings? I suppose this one's obvious but what about the others?'

'I'm not an expert but Jack thought the first boy on the pier had something to do with Dionysius because of a legend that included the toys that were found with the body.'

'Go on.'

'The second in the glass egg was apparently Mithraism because Mithras was born from the cosmic egg.'

'What's that?'

'Part of an old creation story like God moving on the face of the waters and taking six days to make the world.'

'I think I can just remember that. Go on.'

'The third one was Orpheus because of the severed head still singing.'

'You said the gold square that was stolen was divided into four bits.'

'Yes.'

'And we've had four deaths so is that the end of it? No more bits; no more deaths? But what do the bits mean? Just a signature?'

'You've forgotten the coin, the clue to the deaths,' I said. So why didn't I go on to say: 'I've got it locked in my safe. I'll tell you all about it'? But I didn't. Again I held back. An idea was forming in my mind:

that I would go and see Stalbridge again, confront him with the whole thing.

Suddenly Hildreth said: 'No, we can't assume that. It's too risky. They don't stop like that, this sort of crime. They get a taste for it; they have to go on. Maybe they know what we've worked out and hope we'll drop our guard: if there's really all this religious stuff mixed up in it then we're not just dealing with your ordinary paedo like Brady or Huntley, funny by the way they're both called Ian. No, this is someone, or more than one, very sophisticated, probably contemptuous of your ordinary copper. He doesn't know I've got you for back up.'

Oh yes he does, I thought, but it had passed the point where I could blurt everything out, like not being able to remember some important official's name at a function or a conference and having to pretend because it's too late to ask and admit your failure. And maybe they didn't know, only about my visit to Stalbridge. But then they had watched the house, taken Caesar, maybe even followed me here. I had to assume they knew about Hildreth and our meetings as well, even if it had been only by coincidence that they had seen me at the British Museum when they were really following Stalbridge.

'I don't see that I can be of any more use now,' I said. 'I'd better get back to work.' I was thinking that if the news had already got out the chairman would be on the blower, no doubt holding me personally responsible.

'There's not much I can do either until forensics and the others come up with some results. The days of Sherlock Holmes snooping for clues with his magnifying glass are over. Now it's all teamwork, technology and psychological profiling.' He ran his fingers through the short black curls and heaved himself to his feet, downing the last of his lager. The tough Geordie mask slipped for a moment and I saw the strain on his face. Then he smiled and put out a hand. 'We'll keep in touch, Alex. Let's hope this is the last but we still need to unravel this mess. They mustn't beat us.'

As I had feared, the next morning there was a call from the chairman. 'Have you seen the papers, Kish? What's all this about?'

'What's that, chairman?'

'This, this thing at Bradwell. Too close, it's too close.'

'I'm just opening today's paper. I'll call you back.'

'Soon as you can.' The phone was slammed down.

There it all was. The woman who had gone to do the flowers and found the body, telling her story; the police not commenting 'at this stage of the enquiry'.

Last night when I reached my house after a long crawl through the homebound traffic into Southend, and armed myself with a whisky and dry ginger, I had rung Hilary.

'I wish you were here.'

'So do I. Are they sure it's another one like the others?'

'He had the last piece of the amulet round his neck. That clinches it rather.'

'Yes. Yes, it does. When can we meet?'

And suddenly I thought that if they were really watching maybe she wouldn't be safe either. 'I'll have to hang on here for a bit after today's little outing in case Hildreth blows for me again. I suppose I should feel flattered that he seems to think I can help him. I just wish it would all go away. But you can't refuse a Detective Chief Inspector. He might think I've got something to hide.' Even to me my excuses didn't sound convincing.

'Hell hath no fury like a Chief Inspector scorned.'

'Something like that.' She had made a joke of it but I detected the hurt in her voice. 'I miss you,' I said and it was true but I couldn't explain, and anyway I knew she wouldn't accept an explanation that involved her own safety.

'Do you, Alex?'

It was a painful end to my call and again I wished irrationally that the whole bizarre train of events had never begun but then I might never have got to know Hilary.

I dialled the chairman's number hoping he wouldn't be there.

'Well you took your time. So what's all this about? Is it anything to do with us?'

'Not directly, of course. Bradwell comes under Colchester.'

'It's still Essex. I see what you mean though. People may not make the connection. Bradwell's pretty out of the way; almost in Suffolk. So you think we're in the clear?'

I took a deep breath. 'Not quite. The police think it's the same person, or persons, doing all these things.'

'Murders you mean. Say what you mean, Kish.'

'They're not sure. It's certainly a series of deaths but they're keeping an open mind about murder.'

'You seem to know a lot about what the police are thinking.'

'The inspector in charge asked me to go to Bradwell yesterday.'

'And you went?'

'Yes.'

'So they do think it's something to do with us, otherwise why would they want you?'

'There are certain aspects to do with the historical background that they think are important.' I sounded like a real prick.

'Why don't they just get on and find these people rather than flapping about? I don't approve of one of our staff being involved in this way.'

'I could hardly refuse the police.'

'Oh, I'm not blaming you, Kish. It's just that they should do their own dirty work, what they're paid for. Any more requests of that nature you refer them to me.'

It was a relief when the phone went dead. Now I was in the doghouse with everyone. I just hoped Hildreth wouldn't call on me again, at least not yet. My hand gripping the receiver had gone numb. I felt I was on the edge of something but whether it was a breakthrough or a breakdown I couldn't tell. In one way the chairman was right. The police didn't seem to be making any progress. Was that my fault? Would it provide a vital clue if I set the police on to them? They had shown again that they were capable of anything. They might torch the museum, kidnap Hilary, kill me, without revealing who they were anymore than they had already, and where would be the gain in that? I was afraid; I admitted to myself. It wasn't a heroic or attractive posture but there it was.

A hole had been dug for me: a grave. I had fallen in and now I had to try to claw my way out before someone came and filled it in, burying me forever. I needed to take control of my life, not passively suffer whatever others threw at me. But how?

I could try to get Stalbridge to meet me somewhere, if he could shake off his tail, and ask him outright what he knew. Would he agree? Well, if not I would say I was going to tell the police about his involvement and that would bring both the law and the people who 'played rough' down on him. Where could we meet? Not somewhere public where he could easily be followed. It would have to be private but a place he might reasonably go without rousing their suspicions. If he was a member of the London Library that might do. The chances were that he was, and his followers weren't. And security at the library was very strict with only members being admitted on production of a valid membership card. It wasn't somewhere you could just walk in.

Hildreth had warned me against going it alone but I felt I had no choice. If they were watching me they knew about my involvement with the police so if Hildreth suddenly turned up on Stalbridge's doorstep, with or without an escort everything could be blown apart. I picked up the phone and dialled Stalbridge's number wondering if his line was tapped.

'Professor Stalbridge? I wanted to ask you a few questions about the amulet?'

'Who am I speaking to?'

'I thought we should discuss your kind donation of the Saxon coin to our museum.'

'It's alright. That's Kish, isn't it. The phone's safe as far as I know.'

'I thought we should meet. I need to talk to you. I'm being watched. I'm being threatened.'

'I was afraid that might happen.'

'Are you a member of the London Library?'

'Yes, yes I am.'

'Let's meet there. We can find a quiet book stack for our chat. Even if either of us is followed they can't get in. But try not to be and I will too. When can you make it?'

The doubts set in as soon as I put the phone down. What was I doing against police advice? Why was I starting out on this escapade, like some inept Don Quixote, not a knight in shining armour out of Malory but more the Tennysonian, miminy-piminy Launcelot, singing 'tirra lirra by the river' while endangering the life of someone,

I believed, loved me. I must find a way to shake off any tail that might follow. I would go to work as usual and leave by the back way. I could easily spot anyone lurking about outside the museum in the open avenue leading to our Victoria Station. And Liverpool Street, when I got there, would be busy enough for me to lose a tail even if they'd managed to follow me that far. I had set up this meeting and now I had to go through with it. Stalbridge had a far harder task.

Next morning I set off for work as usual, told Lisa I had to go to London, left by the back door, looked hastily up and down the road and felt a kind of elation when I saw the tree-lined pavement was quite empty. I walked briskly to the station where the last of the commuters were lining up for the London train, bought my ticket and stepped through the automatic doors of the carriage just before they closed. No one got in after me and when I looked out as the train moved away I could see no frustrated figure left on the platform – so far I hoped, so good.

At Liverpool Street I merged into the crowd, only glancing up at the glass walls of the café where Hilary and I had met Jack what seemed so long ago although it was only a matter of weeks. I saw his thin veined hands spooning cappuccino froth into his mouth as if it was a great treat to be savoured. Someone had killed him, presumably Stalbridge's rough friends. They had to be stopped. Maybe I was Sir Galahad after all. Looking back on myself then, I feel only astonishment and shame at such arrogant naivety.

I took the Central line to Holborn, changed onto the Piccadilly, got out at the Circus and trotted along Jermyn Street, past the back side of elegant St James's Church and down to the square. The London Library, for those who don't know it, lies behind a tall thin façade squashed onto the furthest corner of St James's Square. With a quick look round I trotted up the wide stony steps to the glass door. A driver was carrying brown cardboard boxes into one of the embassies, pausing to chat to a doorman in a black-fronted waistcoat. The usual rim of parked cars fringed the little park in the middle. I pushed open the door and presented my membership card, went through into the front hall and, as the rules require, hung up my briefcase and coat on a peg in the open slip of cloakroom, visible to the librarians sitting behind the long counter opposite.

Leaving the computer seating, catalogue boxes and the rank of heavy red leather-bound volumes that looked as if they might have belonged to the founder, Thomas Carlisle, I climbed the mahogany-banistered, broad staircase under the gaze of past scholars, mostly males in mutton chop whiskers and high stiff collars, to the members' room.

Stalbridge was already sitting at one of the tables, reading the latest *Historical Review* but keeping a lookout for me. He got up at once and came to join me on the landing where we could talk.

'Where shall we go?'

'Let's start in the basement then we can work our way up through the floors as people come in.' I led the way back to where an arrow pointed down through a door marked *Periodicals*, along a narrow passage and another door into the room that housed bound back numbers of newspapers, journals and magazines in stacks of metal shelving that have to be rolled back by rotating a ship's wheel before you can get at the papers.

We perched ourselves in a corner, on the one chair for Stalbridge and a hard concrete ledge for me, where we could keep the door in view.

'Thanks for coming,' I said, not knowing quite how to begin. 'Were you followed?'

'I did my best not to be. I'm not very used to this sort of thing.'

'Have you seen the papers?'

'What in particular?'

'The body at Bradwell. I think you know what I mean.'

'Yes, yes, I did see something but I don't see …'

'I think you do.'

'Why do you think … what do you think?'

'That you know more about what's been going on than you've admitted, maybe even to yourself.'

'Sorry, I'm not with you.'

'Oh come on, professor. You know perfectly well I'm talking about a series of, at the very least, bizarre stagings of death scenes.' Inconsequentially I found myself thinking of others: Madame Tussaud's with its guillotine, the execution of Charles I, the death of Nelson, the London Dungeon.

'Why should you think I would take an interest in anything so macabre?'

'Because although the general public doesn't know this, because the press haven't picked it up yet, each boy had a piece of the Prittlewell gold plate from the amulet round his neck, and you gave me the companion to those pieces: the reworked Roman coin, knowing perfectly well where it came from. I've been wondering why you did that. Was it a cry for help? Or were you just playing with a not very bright provincial museum director?'

'No, of course not. It wasn't that. I suppose you were right the first time. I wanted someone else to be involved however peripherally. I was alone. I could have talked to Jack Linden I suppose but then it was too late, and anyway we never got on. Now I can't talk to you because I'm afraid. Only I can say I had nothing to do with the deaths. I never thought, understood that they could be real. I thought they would be dummies.'

'Are you saying you designed the installations?'

'They blackmailed me.'

'How?'

'They played on my collector's addiction. They sold me stolen stuff. First they advertised artefacts on the internet, knowing someone would take the bait. Then they sold me things at low prices, things I'd always wanted but could never afford, reminders of my time in the Middle East, statuettes, a painted late Sarcophagus lid, treasures looted from war zones, until I was hooked and too far in to go to the police. Then they got me to design the scenes. I'd been in charge of the presentation of show finds for a time in Egypt. The first one, the fire on the pier, I'd thought would be a dummy. When I read in the papers…'

'How did they know you could do presentations, installations, to target you in the first place or was it just chance?'

Stalbridge gave me a short bark of laughter. 'They'd looked up my CV on the internet. Then they were very persuasive when they'd got me. I was only asked to do some sketches based on different historical or architectural locations, embodying some socio-cultural material on the subject of funerary rituals. I even found it quite amusing, using my skills.'

'And if you wouldn't do that?'

'I suppose they would have found another way to involve me or someone else to do what I did.'

His head sagged forward and he put his hands up to his face as if to hold it in place. 'I'm so tired.'

'You realise I'll have to go to the police now…'

'Give me a day.' He stood up. 'I'm ill, you can see. I can't tell you any more. I have to go. Just give me a day.'

I stood up too. He was clearly unsteady on his feet. He put out a hand to stop himself falling and I saw that his hand shook as he laid it palm down, against the cold metal frame of the shelving. 'I'll get you a taxi. Can you make it up to the entrance?' I knew I should take his arm to help him but my hand recoiled from touching even the sleeve of his jacket.

Near Durovernum c. AD 316

*So I have placed orders for the mosaic floor of the triclinium in my new villa and it shall show Orpheus returning from the dead with the symbols of Bacchus, Christus and, not to be forgotten, Mithras who all give us hope of another life to come. And the design shall be ringed by dolphins who carry us to the Blessed Isles and in one corner shall be set the Chi Rho to please my wife and her Christian priest who since the visit of the Emperor has found a stronger voice so that our household is sometimes riven with discord when I wish to perform those ancient ceremonies due to the gods of our fathers, and even that due to the Emperor for, although he too has embraced Christianity, he has not forbidden the customary worship of himself as a god and benefactor of the whole empire.*

*I must confess to a liking for those tales of gods and heroes, which I heard in my youth in the words of the poets, as part of the learning of the civilised world, whereas the story of a carpenter's son, crucified as a felon, seems to lack the dignity and beauty of our heritage and is therefore espoused mainly by the plebs and women. My wife's priest is from Gaul and returned with the Christian episcopi who attended their great council there two years ago. Many such came seeking positions among noble families or taking over the former temples of our gods for their own worship with an especial hatred of the worship of Mithras and Isis whom they despise as false creations and their worship mere superstition. Thus their influence grows daily throughout the land especially now that they have imperial authority for their beliefs and actions. They differ from the old ways in that they forbid their followers to take part in the ceremonies hallowed by tradition though we do not forbid them ours but would have all citizens of the Empire show the customary respect. So that if they continue in their way I fear that all the old ways, the very laws by which we live and the words of the poets will be lost to our children forever.*

*And if they say there is only one god after the doctrine of their Jewish ancestors and as many faiths have held before them, and even the philosophers like Plato, and Socrates before him, then I would rather see him in the likeness of Dionysus with a wine cup in his hand or as the beautiful youth desired of both men and women and believe that love is god rather than as the Christians say their god is love while forbidding the pleasures of the flesh and even marriage itself, according to one of their prophets who has taught that abstinence is the state to be desired, so that sometimes I fear that my wife may take to refusing to share her couch with me anymore in the service of her god.*

I knew once I had seen Stalbridge off in a black cab that I had to contact Hildreth but I had agreed to give him a day before speaking to the police. Perhaps he needed time to recover enough to face them. It suited me to prevaricate. I was going to look at best a fool, at worst someone who had withheld possibly vital information and impeded a police investigation into very serious crimes. As Stalbridge's cab drew away I wondered whether among the loiterers in the square there was anyone watching. His sudden collapse had meant I might have been seen in the street with him when I had tried so hard to keep our meeting secret.

Should I warn Hilary? But what more could she do that I was fairly sure she would already be doing as a city dweller: not opening the door to strangers, not coming home late at night alone. I would ask Hildreth whether to warn her when I spoke to him in the morning. But next day, it was Hildreth who got in first. I was still having my breakfast when the phone rang.

'Ah, Alex, I'm glad I've caught you. Were you going into work?'

'Yes, yes I am.'

'I'm afraid you'll have to postpone that. I need you here in Oxford.'

'Why? What's happened?'

'Meet me at Professor Stalbridge's flat as soon as you can. He's dead.'

The line itself died but I stood there holding the buzzing receiver and knew I was deep in trouble, even danger. As I drove towards the legendary dreaming spires I tried to rehearse what I would say but every attempt at an explanation sounded so lame in my head, like a kid caught nicking cheap sweets from the newsagents, that I gave up. I had to wait for Hildreth to speak first. And then? I just hoped some inspiration would come from whatever god of prevaricators and cowards.

There was the usual police presence outside the house when I drew up at Stalbridge's flat, as if I were a walk-on part in some detective series and Morse or Linley or Barnaby, or even Wexford, would be behind the front door. In my present state of guilt-ridden anxiety I rather hoped for Wexford's comforting voice with its unthreatening rustic burr. They were all father figures who would restore order, chastise the wrongdoer, and we watchers could only observe and empathise with the surrogate victims who died in our place for our failings of commission and omission, the done and the undone.

I gave my now usual pass formula, Hildreth's name, and was waved upstairs. The door to what had been Stalbridge's flat was open. Hildreth stood by the fireplace with a long white envelope in his hand, expecting me. The men below must have told him I was on my way up.

'Come in, Alex. You made good time.'

I looked around quickly and was relieved that there was no sign of a body. The room as far as I could see was completely undisturbed, uncannily as I had last seen it and as if Stalbridge might walk in at any minute.

'What happened?'

'He seems to have taken his own life. At least at the moment we see no reason to suspect anyone else was involved. He left this addressed for you. I'd like you to open it now and then we can talk about what this all means.' He held the envelope towards me and I put out my hand to take it as if it might itself be dangerous, a poisoned chalice I was being told to drain.

'How did he die?'

'The usual overdose, washed down with a lot of whisky. The cleaning woman found him this morning but time of death is set at around midnight.'

So often it seemed it was women who went out to clean that were faced with these lonely deaths. They fitted their duplicate key in the lock, called out to see if anyone was in, went through to look for a note and found a body, and an envelope not addressed to them, or just an exhausted still lump, in a bed or slumped over the lavatory seat. There ought to be a society dealing with post-traumatic counselling for the army of cleaners. I opened a corner of the flap sealing the envelope and ran my forefinger along its length. Then I took out a sheet of A4 closely written on both sides in a script as small as on a clay tablet in cuneiform, that I recognised as Stalbridge's.

'Can I look through it first? I don't know his writing very well. It's rather hard to make out.'

'Take your time, Alex. There's no hurry. We've got all day.'

I carried the letter over to the window where the light was better. I had driven down through waterfalls of cloudburst that had my windscreen wipers swinging dementedly. Now the sky was a sullen grey.

*Dear Alex Kish,*

*I am writing this to you because I feel I owe you more of an explanation than I was able to give you earlier today when we met, and because this is my last chance to try to set things right and help, perhaps, to repair some of the damage.*

*I was jealous of Jack Linden on several counts which was why I shopped him to the project managers. I was jealous of his commitment, his idealism. He wasn't out there for status or money but out of a passion for the history of civilisation and a possibly naive belief that we could learn from it, whereas I believe that what history really teaches us is that we've learnt nothing, seem destined to repeat the same mistakes over and over until we finally destroy ourselves, and history indeed comes to an end as Fukyama once suggested, although he meant it rather differently, and anyway has since retracted his own proposition.*

*But I was also jealous of his relationship with Fareed. The boy loved him and he did nothing about it. And I wanted him but he only had eyes for Linden. It became an obsession until I determined that if I couldn't have him no one would. I was afraid that Linden would succumb and at the same time contemptuous of him for his failure to seize his chance. Then he made his lucky discovery and I couldn't cope with his totally undeserved success. So I alleged that he was fucking the local boys who worked for us on site and he was sacked.*

*The dig finished and I applied for the job at St Julian's where my published reports, as well as my experience in the field, gave me a headstart. I should have settled down, put it all behind me but I* couldn't. It was a terrible itch I had to scratch. It wasn't just sites for artefacts that I knew must be stolen or looted, that I accessed.

So when they contacted me they knew and I knew, that I was guilty and therefore vulnerable on two counts. Of course I suspected what they wanted my experience for. It's a very specialist but lucrative market, the luxury end of the trade you might say.

The pier fire wasn't one of mine. Too crude and not very well researched. I had seen about the glass egg on your doorstep, though of course I didn't know that, or you then and, I saw its possibilities. It was also a test of how well organised they were, how capable of carrying out a complicated project requiring the kind of skills and co-ordination you have to have to set up a dig.

The order was for something bizarre, beautiful and deathly. I even made maquettes of how each scene should look. I destroyed the last one tonight. They were a kind of Fabergé in their field, a development of the Victorian tableaux if you like. But I truly had no idea that they would use real boys until it was too late. When I protested once, they told me that the boys were already dead when they got them, that they were merely latter-day body snatchers, plundering the dead but no more guilty than the old anatomists.

As for who 'they' are, I don't know. We dealt only over the internet on websites that were constantly changing and anyway I was too afraid of exposure to the college authorities to risk trying to track them down. That was the real hold they had over me: the loss of my job, the public disgrace, my name on a register that would bar me from ever working in academia again or anywhere near children. I'm too old for fieldwork, and anyway a lot of countries prefer to employ their own rather than be patronised by us.

Now what I feared and tried to avoid by digging myself in deeper will inevitably happen. The police will go on until they've hunted down everyone involved. I can't face that. I haven't even the physical stamina let alone the mental resources.

I'm merely anticipating a little and it frees you and everyone else to go on.

I believe they were responsible for Linden's death and would certainly have been for mine, one way or the other.

*By the way the pieces from the Prittlewell Prince's grave were my undoing. I saw them advertised on one of the specialist websites and when I tried to buy them they pounced. Then under pressure, blackmail I suppose you call it, I told them how to use them, almost superstitiously to give the boys some kind of rite of passage like the obols placed in the mouths of the dead. They gave me the coin that I gave you as a kind of devilish contract. If I believed in such things, in anything, I'd probably say it was cursed. Lock it away from you, just to be sure.*

Then came his signature. *JS Stalbridge*

When I'd finished reading I looked up. Hildreth waited silently. Now he held out his hand and I passed him the letter. He studied it minutely while I stood in an agony of anticipation and shame.

Finally he spoke. 'Well we see some bizarre things and weird people in this job but this is up there with the best of them. This is only his version of events, as you might say the Stalbridge edition, and now he's put himself beyond questioning. So Alex, when and where did you meet him and what did he tell you?'

'Yesterday, at the London Library.'

'Why there?'

'It's a members-only library, by subscription, just off Piccadilly. You can find somewhere private to talk and we couldn't be followed in except by another member of course.'

'And were you followed?'

'It seems not, at least he doesn't suggest it in the letter.'

'And what did he tell you?'

I did my best to remember and repeated our conversation as accurately as I could. At the end Hildreth nodded.

'And who set up this meeting? Did he ask to see you?'

'I'm afraid it was my suggestion.'

'Why Alex, after I'd warned you about going off on your own?'

'I thought I might find out something, that because I was in the same sort of business and had known Jack that he might confide in me. Then of course I would inform you.'

'But you didn't.'

'He asked me to give him a day before going to the police. He was ill. I thought he needed time to recover.'

'Time to destroy or bury any evidence he might have given us.'

'I didn't think for a minute that he would kill himself.'

'No, you didn't think. Well that's all water under the bridge now. I intend to keep you in my sights in future. That means you'll have to take some time off. I'm going to Amsterdam and you're coming with me. Unless I charge you with impeding a police enquiry and lock you up. Which is it to be, Alex?'

His gentle half-mocking tone didn't deceive me.

'I'll tell them at work I'm taking some of my leave now.'

'Right. Meet me at my office at ten o'clock tomorrow. Don't forget to turn up, with your passport. I don't want to send someone in uniform knocking on your door.' Hildreth heaved himself away from the buff tiled mantelpiece he had been leaning against.

'I'll be there.'

'Yes, you will. Reckon to be away at least one night.'

'There's just one thing.' Desperately I tried to assert a more favourable image of myself, in my own eyes as well as Hildreth's.

'What's that?'

'Stalbridge thought at first his blackmailers would use dummies, replicas, something like that. Then he seems to have believed the boys were already dead when they were used in the tableaux. Were they, and was that the point of it all?'

'Forensics support that view. As to why, the answer has to be porno pics for internet circulation, either for love or money. But you must have sussed that.'

'And have they been circulated?' Again I felt a fool with my naive questions.

'Oh, yes. They've been turning up all over the web. Now we have to find out who's doing it and, most of all of course, where the boys' bodies are coming from.'

I didn't remember the drive home or how I managed to get there without accident in my agony of humiliation. It would have been hypocritical to feel grief for Stalbridge but I should have felt renewed pain for the unknown, lost boys. I had slipped back into my old cocoon of numbness and alienation from ordinary human emotion that Hilary had briefly dispelled, so much so that I couldn't bring myself to ring her but sat emptying the whisky bottle until I fell asleep in my chair, and woke chilled to stumble to bed.

When I reached Hildreth's office the next morning he was already waiting with his overcoat on. 'Have you remembered your passport, in case we get separated?'

For answer I held up the plum-coloured pasteboard.

'Right. A car will take us to Waterloo. We're going on Eurostar. I don't like flying. I'm relieved they've decided it's bad for the environment.'

It was Friday and the space in front of the ticket barriers was already packed with young people, off on their weekend jaunt to hoped-for difference in erotic, exotic Paris while the young French were setting out from their end with the same motive, and there were long queues inside the ticket hall itself.

'Here's your boarding pass.' Hildreth handed me the cardboard strip and I fed it meekly into the machine that spat it back at me as if it was alive, and swung open the metal gate. We flashed our passports at immigration and passed through to the security checks. The whole thing took only minutes. I should have felt some sense of excitement I suppose but I was still too hung over from last night.

'I don't think you'll need much in the way of euros since you're my accompanying expert but you might feel like buying me a drink some time.'

Obediently I went to the nearest bureau de change.

'Do you want a drink now?'

'Why not. What about you?'

I toyed with the idea of hair of the dog but settled for a double tomato juice with ice. As I carried the drinks over to the little round table Hildreth had chosen by a window, the absurdity of the situation, of the pair of us like two people off on a city break without a care in the world, relaxed, smiling even, raising our glasses – 'Cheers' – as if we weren't looking for possible child molesters, murderers, struck me with all its surreal force, with the very banality of our everyday actions in such a context. The tomato juice tasted salty as blood and I regretted my choice even as I downed it.

'Are you feeling alright?'

'I suddenly saw the irony of us sitting here calmly with a drink when we're supposedly in pursuit of criminals.'

'Ah, well, I'm afraid you wouldn't make a policeman, Alex. We can't afford such thoughts. If we're the sort to have them when we join the force, the job itself sees them off. You've too much imagination. You should have had a proper drink to buck you up.'

I thought it best not to tell him my glass seemed full of blood. 'I had too much last night, that's my trouble,' I said trying to put over a more macho image.

'We're business class,' Hildreth said when the Brussels train was called.

'They were the only seats left, I don't usually travel in style. We're booked into the Novotel in Amsterdam. I'm told it's clean but not fancy.'

The rest of the journey passed quickly, through the flat fields of Flanders that blurred past the window, after the twenty minutes deep under the channel. The air seemed full of the cries of the wounded, and the thunder of Big Bertha being punctuated by the stutter of machine guns. And then we were bowling across the great continental plain that stretched from the Channel to the Carpathians, taking in the land of my father and the repro-Gothic of Budapest, the plain that had offered no resistance to the Panzers sweeping east and west. I glanced across at Hildreth. He had settled himself in a corner and was deep in the day's Suduko grid. It seemed wiser not to intrude and foster my image as hopelessly imaginative and therefore impractical. I took a paperback out of my briefcase and tried to concentrate on the latest research info on the evolution of seaside structures: betting machines, beach huts, Canvey Island bungalows and caravans.

Soon it seemed we were inching through the suburbs of the Belgian capital, the train became a tram gliding between the usual city outskirts of industrial and old housing. At the station we ate a slice of pizza in the bar before boarding the Thalys express to Amsterdam, clean and bright as British transport, however new, never seems to achieve. As we crossed the border immigration officials, I suppose some kind of police, moved through the carriage checking our passports. Handing back Hildreth's the official tipped him a kind of half salute, as if recognising a European fraternity, that Hildreth acknowledged with the slight nod of a co-conspirator, a freemasonry of the just holding back the barbarians.

'They're expecting us at police headquarters,' Hildreth said. 'We'll take a taxi. At least,' he went on sinking back into the cushioned seat, 'nobody here expects you to speak Dutch.'

'Have you been here before?'

'Oh yes. They're some of our closest support. The Dutch decided years ago it was better to regulate the sex trade than try to suppress it. That way you know what's going on so they have decades of valuable experience, especially useful to us, always working in the dark with our hands tied behind our backs. He's a good bloke the man we're going to see. Beemsterboer is his name. A bit of a mouthful but you get used to it.'

I stared out of the window at the crowds on the street. Some of them were tourists I thought. The natives themselves stood out taller and heavier. I'd read somewhere that they were now the tallest in the Western world and had outstripped even the Americans. They exuded confidence from their calm demeanour and handsome faces. I thought of an average British crowd with its centuries of industrial poverty and hard labour in mills, mines and warehouses that had left us pale and stunted by comparison, with frames that ran to fat rather than height and breadth like the Dutch men and women. Hildreth himself I judged was about five-foot-eleven and heavily set, a true Wexford.

The taxi wound its way over bridges, along the sides of gleaming straight-edged canals, lined by tall town houses in handsome brick with cut-out scrolled gables and pediments, dodging the ubiquitous cycles ridden by all ages with the aplomb of knowing yours is the right of way. Maybe all the cycling had contributed to the length of Dutch legs.

'I don't care for water much myself but I suppose if you lived here you'd get used to it. You'd have to,' Hildreth said as we sailed over another stretch of canal.

The driver had been silent all this time. Now, he waved his hand towards the right. 'Anne Frankhuis,' he said, before turning left and turning right again. I caught sight of the street name: Elandsgracht, but it carried no resonance except as the possible habitat of a species of African deer. 'Hoofbureau van Politie, Police Headquarters,' the driver said and drew up with a flourish.

'Captain Pete,' the big man behind the desk in shirtsleeves, stood up and put out his hand, dwarfing Hildreth by several centimetres.

'This is Alex Kish, Harry. He's helping me with the background for all this.'

My hand was gripped and wrung. 'Pleased to meet you. Have a chair. I got your email, Pete. What can I tell you?'

'We've had this series of bodies turning up, young boys, pre or early teens. Forensics say some of them died of suffocation but not in the usual way, manually if you get my meaning, strangulation or a pillow or plastic bag over the face. There are some signs of bruising to the ribs as if the chest was being constricted. And they're all foreign. I got to thinking of all those dead migrants, illegals, under the base board in the back of a lorry. I remembered we'd once talked about that sort of thing and I wondered if you'd any more experience, any advice you could offer. It's not something that's come my way before.'

'People-smuggling, of course. Amsterdam is a good jumping-off place for the US and the UK. We try to intercept them coming through but this is a port where trucks come from all over the world and there are so many ways to hide such illegal cargo. You sent me some pictures. I ran them against our missing young persons database. I think I have a match for one of them. Come. Look out here.'

We got up and went to stand on either side of him where we could see over his shoulders at his computer screen.'

'This is the one. He was found by the docks wandering. He was probably trying to get on a ship. He spoke no Dutch of course but no English either. It was easy to see he was under the age so he was taken into care. He disappeared from the children's hostel after two weeks. Either he ran away or he was, what do you say, kidnapped?'

I found myself staring at the boy whose slightly smiling face I had last seen looking down through the glass egg on the beach at Canvey. 'Do you have a lot of cases like this?' I felt it was time to justify my presence, even with something that sounded like the detective equivalent of 'Do you come here often?'

'Mostly it is girl children from the sex trade. They are promised education or jobs as children's nurses. What do you call them?'

'Nannies,' I said automatically.

'And the boys? What happens to them?'

'They pay to come here mostly or their parents pay for a new life. The boys work and save to pay the smugglers. When they get here they are put on the dump, on the streets alone. Sometimes a gay man will find them and taken them in, this is Amsterdam, the gay capital of the world. Or we find them. In Holland we have strict age restrictions. Under sixteen is a child still. We take them into care to deport, like the girl children, and like them they run away.'

'The poor little sod didn't get far.' The anger and compassion in Hildreth's voice surprised me.

'You think perhaps he died en route to the UK?'

'It's a possibility.'

'And then what happened? How did you find him?'

'He, his body was made part of an artwork, an installation. It was enclosed in a glass egg.' I answered for Hildreth.

'An egg? Like the German artist who uses body parts, dried foetuses as earrings. I forget his name.'

'The difference,' Hildreth said, 'is that pictures of those death scenes are finding their way onto the internet. A kind of S&M soft porn.'

'This we have too but not with dead boys. We have the usual whips and chains. That is not illegal as long as the woman is the age. We also of course find the child pornography. It comes most from Russian or US sites.'

'Yes, we know about that. This is something different. This mixes in religion and art. Death and decadence.'

'But if the boys are already dead? Is it even a crime? How would we prosecute it? Might it not be seen as censorship? Here in the Netherlands it might not be possible.'

'We should be able to get them on something.'

'Even in England? Obscenity? Now if you could find the people-smugglers and stop them. But it is very difficult. They have many other outlets we believe like drugs, money laundering, as well as the world-wide sex trade both virtual and physical. I wish you luck. If we can help let me know. In any case keep in touch. We too would like to stop this traffic.'

'You may have wondered why I got a bit worked up there,' Hildreth said when we were outside on the pavement. 'Let's find a bar. I could do with a drink. There must be an O'Reilly's Irish house somewhere.'

We wandered up the road the way the taxi had come.

'What's that? Is that a bar?'

'I think it's a boat museum,' I said.

'More water. I suppose we'll have to cross that bridge.'

I got out the guidebook I had bought at Waterloo. 'You'll be pleased to hear we're close to the Torture Museum.'

'That's all I need. What's that over there? Surely that's a bar.'

'De Zothe,' I read. 'It seems to mean "the Sot" so it should be okay for a drink.'

'Come on then.'

'It'll all be some sort of lager,' Hildreth said when we had settled at a table. 'Belgian's better than German. I'm a bitter man myself though it's hard to find now in London. I used to drink Newcastle brown but after a certain age it doesn't taste the same.'

We ordered two large glasses of local brew that came with a deep head on it. 'At one time we'd have sent that back saying it wasn't a full glass,' Hildreth said, wiping away a foam moustache with the back of his hand. 'Still it's better than nothing. I was going to tell you why this business upsets me. I grew up with it you see: religion, art of a sort and sex. You probably didn't think it to look at me but I was once a pretty little altar boy, lighting the candles, swinging the censor and always overlooked by Jesus's bleeding heart or Mary in the Lady Chapel, a pale girl in a blue dress with hands clasped waiting to be fucked by an angel. And after the service Father Brown, only that wasn't his name, would take us back to the rectory, "the rectum" we called it among ourselves, for tea and cake and gropes. We were still in short trousers.' He took a long pull at his beer. 'We didn't tell anyone: you didn't in those days. We just joked about him among ourselves. I'd almost forgotten until all this stuff came up and I found I was getting angry.

It can be a distraction, that kind of personal involvement. In theory, coppers shouldn't feel it but sometimes we have to admit we're only human. Any skeletons in your cupboard, Alex?'

'Only an absent father,' I said without thinking. I wasn't sure that I wanted this level of intimacy with Hildreth. And then I thought: he'll think I'm a mummy's boy and we know what that means, and added, too hastily and brutally, so that my own words shocked me, 'And a dead wife.'

There was a silence. Then Hildreth went on, 'These boys – Beemsterboer seems pretty certain they're smuggled illegals, certainly one at least for sure. It has to be part of a chain that starts maybe thousands of miles away in some foreign country with a kid desperate to get out. Are the smugglers the same people who put up the pictures? Who set up Stalbridge? How do we break into the chain? We can check missing persons through Interpol but if the parents think they've gone to find a new life they won't even have notified the boys as missing.'

'They must be very desperate to start out on such a journey not knowing where they'd end up.'

'We're a nomadic species. That's how we populated the world with just a small group coming out of Africa.'

'You believe that? What I really meant was: how do you know that, an ordinary copper risen through the ranks?' He saw through me at once and laughed.

'I told you I was an armchair archaeologist. Besides I feel it myself. I came south looking for something. Me Dad was a redundant miner, embittered by the loss of his world. But I hadn't wanted, dared, to step out of my class, think of college and all that. There were no jobs in Blyth. After bumming around London for a bit I joined the police. In those days it was a bit like the army – you didn't need any qualifications. What about your missing father?'

I had to answer. 'He was Hungarian. Came over after the uprising. Met my mother at a language school where she was teaching. Disappeared when she got pregnant.'

'See. There's all sorts of reasons why people go on the run from wherever.'

'What do we do now?'

'We look around Amsterdam. Get the smell of the place. Unless you want to go and choose a girl in a window. You're on your own there. My wife only lets me out because she knows I behave myself.'

'Not my kind of scene,' I said.

'I have to go through some more stuff with Beemsterboer in the morning. Course you could just get on the train back.'

I thought of my empty neglected house. 'No I'll stick it out. What about something to eat?'

'Right, supper. A walk and early bed in that order. Let's have another beer.' He waved at a passing waitress.

But the walk came first. 'Our hotel's up by the Amstel,' Hildreth said. 'I fancy the big park and some fresh air after being shut in all day.'

I took out my map. 'Vondelpark's not far. But it's going in the wrong direction.'

'We've got all night. As I remember Amsterdam's quite small. More like Paris than London.'

'We'll have to cross a bridge.'

'I'll be brave and try not to look down.'

We strolled along beside a broad winding waterway. It was growing dark and the tall houses were black silhouettes against the paler sky while the water gleamed with highlights from its fringing of street lamps. And then the buildings around us began to change. The seventeenth century dropped away. The houses were huge with stained-glass windows and entwined vines rimming the art nouveau doorways. Next we were in a wide, brightly lit street of boutiques and diamond merchants.

Looking at the map I said. 'This is the museum quarter.'

'You'll be in your element then.'

I thought how we'd once supported the Dutch against their Spanish overlords, then fought them, then married them and put their prince on our throne, and finally struggled with them for empire in a trade war across the world.

'We've come too far,' I said. 'We'll have to go back a bit. The park's over there. This is only the Museumplein.'

'It looks like a park of sorts. Still you're the navigator.'

We turned right along Van Baerlestraat and suddenly there was the sound of music, and trees sketched in charcoal against the wash of sky. As we came through the edge of the park we could see a lit stage ahead with musicians and a crowd of people sitting on the grass or standing in front of them. The music was a waltz, Strauss I thought, though I couldn't identify which one.

Hildreth paused on the fringes of the crowd. 'Do you like music?' I asked him.

'I played in the colliery band as a boy though there wasn't really a pit anymore. The band kept going for a bit though.'

I let my eyes wander over the audience as the band moved through the polka rhythm. The seated front rows seemed to be given over to young men with their arms round each other, swaying to the music. As it ended with a flourish of baton they clapped loudly, smiling into each other's eyes and then turning back towards the rostrum, laughing with an easy pleasure that caused a wave of envy to run through me.

I looked back at the stage again where a new piece was beginning: Mozart's clarinet concerto and a girl soloist caressing the reed with her lips, her hair falling in a blond half veil across her face and then back as she raised the shining instrument for a higher cadence. Suddenly I ached for Hilary. It wasn't fair, right, to make the decision for her by excluding her, and cause the pain I had heard in her voice. I would ring her as soon as I got home.

'There's a café along there,' Hildreth waved his arm towards a cluster of lights round an awning, above small tables, each with a flickering candle. 'Let's see if we can eat there.' So we ate under the city's starless night sky like any ordinary tourists, and then, with me anxiously trying to follow the map in the half-light, made our way back towards the central station.

'Any more bloody canals?' Hildreth asked as the road from the Riksmuseum crossed its fifth, making him hunch his shoulders and his breath come faster and thicken into almost a snort.

'Just one more. But it's the biggest: the Amstel itself.' To divert him I went on, 'I'm surprised you didn't have a problem with the train when we went under the Channel, all that water overhead.'

'I'm used to tunnels, it's in the blood. Anyway, what the eye doesn't see … This stuff's there underneath, waiting to catch you.'

'Sailors used to worry about mermaids pulling them down.'

'That might be worth it.' His face set grimly as he marched out over the threatening waters.

The hotel when we reached it was clean and anonymous, part of an international chain with everything you could need but devoid of character or distinction, my room a coffin-sized box in pastel colours with a minimalist shower room.

'What about a nightcap?' Hildreth had said as we waited for the lift. 'See you in the bar in fifteen minutes.'

'Right,' I said, though I had hoped to be alone for the first time that day, partly to take stock but also because I wasn't used to the constant pressure of another presence, especially one as all-pervading as Hildreth. It made me realise how cocooned I was, alone in my office with only occasional interruptions from staff or the telephone and then home to my empty house, insulated from the noise of the world by my job and the way of life I had chosen.

The bar when I went down was dark with only pools of light here and there and above the long corridor, with its rack of high-lit bottles and glasses behind the white-coated barman. One or two small groups of men were dotted about, and a handful decorated the barstools, not speaking but gazing into their drinks or at newspapers in assorted languages.

Hildreth had already bagged a table and was sitting with a half-empty glass of blond beer in front of him. 'What will you have, Alex?' He lumbered to his feet.

'I'll get them. Another for you? What is it?'

He nodded, drained the glass and held it out. 'You order and they'll bring it. It's the Jupiter, Belgian draught, not bad.'

The boy serving had the impeccable English, under an accent I couldn't identify, that puts the British traveller to shame. I ordered Hildreth's beer and a whisky and dry ginger for myself and sat down at the table. The walls where the meagre lighting fell on them, were the colour of old dried tomato ketchup.

'Looks as if they're trying to set the tired businessman up for a trip to the red-light district,' Hildreth said, waving a hand at the décor. 'Still we can't say much. Our pubs aren't what they were. They're still better up home. When Julie and I go back for a family get-together the lads can still down ten pints of an evening.' He picked up his new glass. 'Cheers. I like the way they throw in the free nuts and crisps. That's not something you get at home. So what's next in your life, Alex?'

I told him about the summer exhibition only a few weeks away now. Even to me it sounded an irrelevance in a world of smuggled and desperate people and dead boys.

'How do you plan it? You see I'm trying to understand the mindset of these people, whoever they are. These jobs took a lot of planning, across thousands of miles. We're dealing with a global syndicate, maybe more than one. How does it start? How do you start?'

'I can't see that planning an exhibition in a local museum or gallery can have anything to do with this.'

'Bear with me, Alex. Tell me what comes first.'

'Well. I suppose it's knowing I've got to come up with something. Then the concept, the theme if you like.'

'So there's a need that has to be fulfilled. Then the idea. Then what? The mechanics, the how?'

'Budget, timing, feasibility. And all the time someone, usually in my case the chairman, snapping at your heels.'

'You have to be driven? So what drives these guys? First money, money from parents or the boys to get them to a new life. The idea? That you can provide the service, the transport. Then the organisation, the nuts and bolts. But all this doesn't get us to the end product, the equivalent of you opening the doors and the public coming in. The end product here is someone wanking over the picture of a dead boy, tastefully arranged. We've got two parts that don't fit, except that we know that they do. I can't help thinking it would be easier somehow if we were dealing with girls. Girls get lured away with the promise of a decent job. Then they get raped and put on the game. Girls you can track down. They're on the street or a member of the public says a particular house is being used for funny goings on. Or the girls themselves run away and ask for help. Straightforward. This is different. One for the road. My turn to get them in.' He drained his glass again and went over to re-order.

My whole body seemed to ache with weariness. Hildreth, for all he looked less fit than me and couldn't, I reckoned, be any younger, had more stamina or more sheer will that kept him going.

'Maybe,' he said when he had settled himself down again, 'I think girls are easier because we've got a daughter and we've been through some rough times with her. You never had kids I take it.'

I shook my head. 'When she was fourteen,' he went on, 'she ran away from home, took off for Liverpool, and was found by the police passed out in a phone box. That's how I realised what it was like to be on the receiving end so I put in for this job when it came up. By the way, I ordered their version of a double. Help you to sleep. You look as if you could do with a good night. Breakfast at eight. They start early here. Then we can be back by mid-afternoon. I don't like to leave the shop too long.'

And I did sleep, as soundly as if Hildreth had spiked my drink. The telephone ringing beside the bed woke me. 'I thought I'd better give you an early morning call, you looked so knackered last night. Can you be down in half an hour?' He had put the phone down without waiting for an answer. It was an order not a question. I sat up and swung my legs over the side of the bed hoping that when I tried to stand up I wouldn't simply fall over. Somehow I managed to shower and shave and make it downstairs in time. There was Hildreth of course with a piled plate in front of him, knife and fork at the ready.

A couple of cups of coffee and two slices of toast later I began to feel as if I might live. 'I've paid the bill so we can be on our way as soon as you're ready. Eight forty-five in the lobby?' His hair was ruffled as if he'd run his fingers rather than a comb through it and his normally crumpled shirt now looked as if he might have slept in it.

As if reading my thoughts he said: 'Julie keeps me tidy. I'm not much good on me own. I've ordered a taxi. We did enough walking yesterday.'

'You are lucky,' Beemsterboer said when we were shown into his room. 'I asked for the DNA and blood group results on that boy and this morning they came through. They show he is from somewhere in East, the border between Europe and Asia, old Russia, Uzbekistan or Kazakhstan. Quite distinctive.' He tapped the boy's picture now lying face up on his desk and I remembered the oriental cast to the young features, even through the distorting mirror of the curved glass shell, the high cheekbones and slightly hooded eyes, above the smiling mouth.

I remembered too a school trip, a sixth form exchange with Russian students that took us first to Moscow and then on to Tashkent and Samarkand, the Tomb of Tamerlane and the necropolis of the royal princesses, at the end of the Silk Road. I had seen women in bright local dress bringing teenage daughters to the tombs to rub the dust that accumulated on the stones on the girl's cheeks. For good luck in marriage? Fertility? I couldn't ask but I remembered their faces, with flushed cheeks and dark, dark eyes framed by strong black hair, at that confluence of tribes and religions.

'Thanks, Harry.' Hildreth stood up and held out his hand. 'We'll keep in touch. Let me know if anything else turns up.'

'I will. Good to see you, Pete. Let you keep me informed also. We don't like children in our care to disappear, especially not to turn up dead even as an art work. You are going to Central Station? From here you can take the metro or the tram.'

I slept most of the way back to Brussels while Hildreth immersed himself in his Sudoku puzzlebook. Then we were speeding through Kent, the fields and orchards still a luminous spring-green after recent rain. A kind of numb silence had settled on us. Hildreth finally broke it with a weary sigh.

'We'll have to try Interpol but their writ doesn't really run that far east. Frankly, Alex, I don't really know where to go next to push this forward. I don't like admitting it but we seem to have come up against a brick wall. Expenses aren't going to be pleased with what they'll see as a wasted trip. They'll say I could have got this much from an email. But I'm a bit old-fashioned. I like to meet people face to face. That way you get the feel of things.'

'Did you get any "feel of things"?'

'I could see the chain stretching right across so many different countries.'

And times, I thought – there's another chain to this that isn't geographical like the Silk Road, but somehow chronological. Somewhere I'd read that time was space or was it the other way round? Two lines, horizontal and vertical, converging at a point in the present, the two bits Hildreth had said didn't fit together. A flush of excitement went through me as if I'd been out with a metal detector and turned up a horde of silver. Just like the Bateses, I thought. And look where that had led. Or Jack Linden, stumbling across his tomb in the desert and setting off a wave of envy and resentment. In any case, my idea smacked of New Ageism, ley lines, stuff I'd never had time for. Hildreth would think I'd lost the plot and maybe I had through being so out of my depth in this surreal world of international crime, caught up in what could be seen as a kind of sexual terrorism. As quickly as it had come my excitement drained away and I said nothing, feeling a sick hollow in my stomach.

Could I even discuss it with Hilary? She might think I had flipped completely. Pseudo-philosophical theorising hadn't been part of our discourse. My decision to tell her everything weakened. After all, nothing had changed. She could still be at risk but I longed for the comfort of her voice. Hildreth was going back to his Julie who would send his suit to be cleaned and him out for a haircut. I both envied and despised their domesticity.

The journey seemed endless. At Waterloo I took the Tube to Embankment, changed for Liverpool Street and then on through Essex. Today I could only see the familiar fields with their painted signs advertising 'Bonza spuds for sale' as a featureless continuation of the European plain I had just crossed, and once part of it before the sea flowed in and cut us off.

I put the key in the front door lock, dreading the silence I felt reaching out to suck me down. Dumping my overnight bag in the hall, I went through to the kitchen to see if Doris Shepherd had left me one of her enigmatic notes, propped against the pepper grinder. As I stepped through the doorway my eye slid automatically to the tiling in front of the sink. Every day I put down an offering to whatever god of missing persons. At first it was bowls of cat food and saucers of milk that in the evening when I came back, were dried and fly-blown or curdled and with a skin of dust. Lately repelled by scraping and tipping them down the lavatory, I'd left only the hard pellets of Caesar's favourite brand.

The dish was empty. I stepped forward and picked it up, stifling a rush of hope. Another cat, a hungry stray could have found its way through the flap while I'd been in Amsterdam, and gratefully gobbled up the contents. Putting the dish in the sink I ran hot water into it and then went through into the sitting room, not daring to call out and moving as quietly as possible so as not to alarm any feral creature that might still be lurking there. There was no one. I went out into the hall again and began to climb the stairs. The whole house must be searched before I could be sure I was alone. Maybe the stray could be persuaded to take up residence. Maybe it would be a she cat with a clutch of kittens.

My bedroom door was slightly ajar. I pushed at it, stood still for a moment in the doorway and looked towards my bed. A small, round, dusty ammonite of black fur was curled up in the middle. I just managed to hold back from starting forward to touch him. Was he still alive? He didn't seem to be breathing. Was it really Caesar come back or a stranger, looking unnervingly like him?

He must have sensed my presence. I moved gently forward, stretching out a tentative hand. He tried to sit up but almost toppled over and sank back again. Clearly I must get a vet to check him over. I stroked the blunt head between his ears with a forefinger. His coat was matted and dirty; one eye was half closed. I wanted to howl with a mixture of grief and sheer relief. He must be alright. He mustn't die from whatever hidden damage he might have suffered.

I shut the door to keep him safe. It didn't matter if he peed on the bed or worse. I went downstairs to phone the vet. 'I'll be over after surgery. Keep him as quiet as possible and give him plenty of water. The worst fear if nothing's broken or he hasn't suffered some internal injury, is dehydration.' I took him up a bowl of water and more food. This time when he looked up, I saw that one ear was torn and there was a gash across his nose. Then I settled myself to wait for the vet, not daring to celebrate yet with a whisky but making myself a comforting cup of coffee instead.

The vet, thankfully the one he usually saw, was gentle and firm, inspecting the injuries to Caesar's head and lifting him to feel his legs and abdomen. 'How long has he been away?'

'Five weeks.'

'He's very thin of course and that tear in the ear won't knit together again. You've lost your handsome head, old chap, but nothing actually seems injured. You've been very lucky but don't try it again. Unusual for a neutered animal to go off like that.'

'I think he must have been shut in somewhere,' I said defensively.

'Keep him in for a few days and build him up. I'll give him a shot of antibiotics just in case. Bring him in at the end of the week, to make sure everything's going along nicely.'

Alone again I allowed myself my postponed celebratory glass. Caesar had come back and he was going to be alright. He had been courageous and clever. If only he could tell me where he had been. I bolted the cat flap from the inside and left my bedroom door ajar again. Then I sat down to ring Hilary.

'Caesar's back,' I said and felt tears pricking in my eyes and the proverbial lump in the throat threatening to choke me.

✳

From the Historia Ecclesiastica Britonem c. 580

*Those are called the days of the Saints, after St Germanus had utterly defeated the Pelagian heretics, who denied the dual nature of the Lord, the original sin of our forefathers and the efficacy of the priesthood, in argument, and after another fourteen years, returned again and without a sword being drawn put to flight the army of the Picts and Saxons in terror with the great shout of Alleluia from the British warriors, and at last the church enjoyed many years of peace, and many monasteries were founded among the Cymri.*

*First came St Dyfrig to Hertland and after him St Illtyd, the most learned of the Britons in Testaments and all kinds of knowledge. He caused to be built, on the banks of the same river at Llantwit, a monastery, with seven churches, each with seven companies, and seven colleges in each company, in all two thousand saints leading a life of godliness, fasting, prayer, almsgiving and charity. Here St Samson was educated and ordained who after went to Caldey Island and lived as a hermit for seven years and then in a vision was commanded by God to cross over to Cornwall and thence Armorica with other Britons where he founded the monastery of Dol.*

*And after them came other saints as Cadre who founded Llancorfon and Teilo who founded Llandeilo and was with St Dewi in his journey to Jerusalem. In these days there were many comings and goings between all these monasteries and Ireland, Armorica, Cornwall and even Iberia where there was a colony of British Christians.*

*Yet for all this, as St Gildas says in his Excidie and his Epistolae, the land suffered for the sins of the princes and people, and even the very priests fell under God's wrath for their wickedness, for all too much throughout all this land men feared not to commit the most heinous crimes as incest and murder, oppression, torture and drunkenness after many droughts of golden sweet honey mead as Aneurin says for which the saints often had occasion to curse them and call down God's punishments. St Gildas himself calls those princes 'tyrants'. 'Britain has judges – they are unrighteous; ever plundering and terrifying the innocent, aye guilty brigands, having a multitude of wives – nay harlots and adulteresses, warring but in unjust and evil warfare, rewarding the brigands who sit with them at table, despising the humble and guiltless, raising to the stars the bloody, the proud, murderers, comrades and adulterers, enemies of God.' Especially he names the five princes Constantine of Damnonia, Aurelius Conan, Vortipar, and Cuneglas, but chiefest of all in wickedness is Maelgwn Gynedd, 'the dragon of the island' who in his youth murdered his uncle the king. After repenting of this crime and taking the vow of a monk he was led astray by his nephew's wife, murdered his nephew and his own wife and married his temptress.*

*So that it was no wonder that the heathen Saxons advanced upon us daily until they had consumed almost all the island for our sins, and that the men of God retired to such places as Illtydd's Lantwit, for when he first came there the saint found it pleased him well, with a fertile plain with no ruggedness if mountain or hill, a thick wood with trees of various kinds, the dwelling place of many wild creatures, and a river flowing between pleasant banks – Pulcherrimus iste locorum.*

## Monarchus Ignotus

'Where were you, Alex?' Hilary said. 'I rang you a couple of times, both at home and at the museum. I didn't leave a message. There didn't seem any point.'

I felt a rush of relief or pleasure; I wasn't sure which. I hoped it meant she'd forgiven me. 'I was in Amsterdam.'

'Amsterdam? Why? And why didn't you tell me you were going to be away?'

'I thought you were, well, angry with me.'

'That wasn't the best way to stop me if I was.'

'No. I'm very sorry. Look, do you think our phones are safe, that no one can hook into what we're saying?'

'Are you alright, Alex?'

'Honestly, I'm not getting paranoid. I went to Amsterdam because Hildreth asked me to go with him to the Dutch police. Only of course he doesn't really ask. It's like that old Latin construction, expecting the answer "yes". Quo or quid or something with the subjunctive. I'm rambling. Okay, what I haven't told you and why I thought we shouldn't meet, is that I'm being watched.'

'Alex …'

'No, hang on. Caesar didn't just go missing. He was kidnapped. Whoever took him sent me a note with a piece of his fur.'

'What did the note say?' The suspicion in her question made it hard to answer rationally without stuttering.

'That we'd see if he could find his way back, if he was clever enough. But the point is: someone must have been watching the house to know about him, and me of course, and catch him.'

'Why didn't you tell me?' I could hear the doubt in her voice again.

'I suppose I thought you wouldn't believe me. I'm not sure you do now.'

'Did you tell your friend Hildreth?'

'No. If I didn't think you would believe me, I was pretty sure he wouldn't. And now Stalbridge is dead and that's my fault too.'

'I don't understand any of this. Stalbridge is dead?'

'He took an overdose.'

'I didn't see it in any of the papers.'

'I suppose it wasn't important enough. Elderly Oxford don takes own life. But it was my fault because I'd met him the day before and told him I was going to the police.'

'Why? I still don't understand.'

'He designed the death sites. Some of them anyway. Apparently he thought at first that they were going to use dummies. Then when he read the newspaper reports he realised they were dead boys. He was in too deep to go to the police. Afraid of losing his job, his reputation, being put on the sex offenders list. All that.'

'Where did you meet him?'

'At the London Library. I thought we could both meet there without any suspicion and, I hoped, without being followed. But I can't be sure whether we were or not. That's why I thought you and I shouldn't risk meeting, in case it put you in danger. If they could take Caesar, what might they do to you.'

'Is all this true, Alex? You're not making it up?'

'It's all true. I know it sounds far-fetched. It's not the sort of thing you associate with people like us. But four boys are dead, Jack, and now Stalbridge. They think the boys are being trafficked.'

'They?'

'Hildreth and the Dutch police.'

'Does all this mean that you're in danger? Next time it might not just be Caesar they take away.'

'That's why I thought we shouldn't be seen together. There's you, and your daughter.'

'Beth? But she's got nothing to do with any of this.'

'With Caesar it was their way of warning me off. But they didn't stop at kidnap with Jack. They killed him. I'm sure of it now.'

'We must keep in touch somehow.'

'I think, oddly enough, that phone is the best. Email they could hack into, at least I think so. Old-fashioned landline seems the safest.

Think of the royal mobiles that were as leaky as sieves and that was just journalists tapping into them. We'd better phone at home rather than the office where calls go through a common centre.'

'And technology was meant to be progress!'

I had used the one argument no parent, especially a mother, can ignore: a threat to her child, an instinct basic to our animal nature, shared by lapwings and elephants, with us somewhere in the middle. I hadn't done it deliberately. I had simply and suddenly realised the danger, the chain of hostages that had begun with Caesar and whose end we couldn't foresee.

As soon as Hilary put the phone down I realised I had some necessary shopping to do. Caesar was still asleep, knocked out by the shot the vet had given or just exhausted and collapsed after making it safe home. I topped up the water bowl and went out into the now rainy afternoon, hurrying down towards the useful parade of shops on the main road for some sort of tray and a bag of cat litter, blessing his annual holiday at the cattery that had taught him what they were for.

The evening still had its summer lightness but dampened and overshadowed by the lowering sky. I found myself nervously peering about to see if I was being followed but the road seemed quite empty, apart from occasional passing cars. My neighbours were sensibly at home having post school tea or getting ready to go out to supper, the cinema or theatre. It was the kind of road where you knew the people next door slightly, and they had both been kind to me when Lucy died, and then again when Caesar went missing and they had seen me pinning up the 'lost, stolen or strayed' pictures of him. They had rung the front door bell and offered cups of tea with shots of brandy or whisky, and invitations to weekend lunches, after Lucy, and had only given up when they sensed or understood that I preferred to be alone.

On one side was Colette whose husband had died of a brain tumour, leaving her to bring up Darren alone, and on the other Dick and Margery, retired teachers, keen gardeners who had helped me look for Caesar even though he sometimes dug up their flower bed for his lavatory.

Margery was just drawing the sitting room curtains as I passed and I waved at her and she waved back. Everything that had happened in the past weeks seemed out of place on that road. At home I found a piece of hard elderly cheddar in the fridge and melted it onto a stale slice of Ryvita. Watching an undistinguished evening of summer repeats, I found myself falling asleep, to wake with a start when Caesar pushed open the door and tentatively put his black head round it. He crossed the floor on wobbly legs and sat down on the rug in front of the unlit electric fire.

Next morning I shut him in carefully, rang Doris Shepherd with the news that he was back and to be sure not to let him out, and set off for the museum. The chairman had left a message that I was to ring him as soon as I got in.

'Ah, Kish, how's the exhibition coming on? I've booked Lord Rochford for the opening.'

'We're working on it now, chairman,' I lied.

'Good, good. We must meet so you can give me a progress report.'

He put the phone down not waiting for my reply, and I went in search of Lisa.

'I'm in a panic,' I said as I pushed her door open. 'I've just had the chairman on the phone asking about the seaside exhibition and I've done nothing about it, not a single damned thing,' I went on, hastily adjusting my language, remembering that Lisa had once said she thought 'the f word' downgraded something important. In my heart I'd agreed with her.

'It's alright, Alex. I knew you were busy so I've been working on it. I've got some sketches to show you that I did while you were away.' She got up and opened one long shallow drawer of a cabinet in which maps, drawings and posters were kept flat.

'Lisa, you're a star!'

'We can do most of it from our own collections especially the stuff we can't usually show because of lack of space. We'll have to move some other things temporarily to make room. I've also tracked down some additional material but I haven't placed any definite orders until I talked to you about the budget for it.'

'You're a supernova!'

'Aren't they the ones about to explode or collapse into black holes?'

'Not before the opening. The chairman's booked Lord Rochford.'

'Couldn't we have had a celeb? Tony Robinson or dishy Tristram Hunt, someone the visitors will have seen on the telly?'

'Not within my power, I'm afraid. The chairman likes a local and preferably a lord. Now what have you got?'

'I thought a chronology as the resort developed, starting with a bathing machine, an exhibition focusing on bathing costumes from men's drawers to bikinis, then the fairground sideshows, food, whelks and so on, candy floss of course...'

'I can see I needn't have worried to come back. Let me know if there's anything you want me to do.'

'Can we talk about the budget? I've got some draft figures here.'

For the next hour we talked money, getting and spending, until Lisa left me convinced I was quite superfluous and 'everything was under control'. I opened up my computer and began to consider the annual report to the Arts, Libraries and Tourism Committee who were our overlords. Later I held the weekly staff meeting at which Lisa explained her plans for the exhibition and I fielded questions about whose part of our permanent exhibition would have to be mothballed for a few weeks. It all seemed so familiar it was hard to think I had been in Amsterdam yesterday talking to the Dutch Vice Squad, if that's what they were, if not just Missing Persons. That is until Hildreth rang.

'How's everything, Alex?'

'I don't think anyone even missed me.' I knew there must be a reason for his call but I had decided to play it cool.

'While we were away the techies were looking into Stalbridge's computer. He was much deeper in than he let on to you. What's Ganymede, Alex?'

'You mean "who".' I knew I was sounding rather tetchy.

'Ah. I thought you'd be able to tell me.'

'One of your techies could have looked it up on Google.'

'The internet? I don't trust that stuff. You never know what you're getting. I prefer a reliable source for my information. So, who's Ganymede?'

'He was a beautiful boy carried off by Zeus in the form of an eagle. Greek mythology. Zeus was the most powerful of the gods. A father figure. The Romans called him Jupiter or Jove. So you got: "By Jove!"

meaning, politely, "by God!"' I heard my own voice taking on its best lecture to the local society tone.

'The most powerful of the gods was a paedo?'

'It was accepted as part of Greek society, the pursuit of beauty in men and women.'

'I'd have been out of a job then?'

'Something like that. Anyway what's the significance of Ganymede?'

'It was the name of some sort of society or ring that Stalbridge belonged to. They all had names you'll probably tell me came from the same source. I'll send you a list. A society for swapping pictures.'

'And the dead boys?'

'They're all on his computer. He seems to have been at the centre of it. I hoped we could get some addresses off it but they're all scrambled in some way. The IT department is working on it but they're not very hopeful. There's some sort of customised block, maybe even an auto destruct if it's tampered with, so we could lose the lot.'

He rang off threatening to keep me informed. My quiet normal day had been destroyed and all my fears for Hilary and even myself, my sense of a darkness waiting to envelop us all flooded back. Was the point of all those myths of rape and abduction, the dark cloud, the shower of gold, the eagle's claws and beak a metaphor for the ever presence of uncertainty, of terror in some shape or form. The Ganymede Society sounded like something the Victorians might have come up with only it would have been tangible, real boys picked up from the dank alleys and yards of the Jago smelling of horse piss, and lured with promises of lucre and the good life. And did it matter? Wasn't the attempt to ban it, the Labouchere Act, worse than what it tried to stop with the consequent downfall of Wilde and so many others? Did prohibition in any form ever work? I reminded myself that this was different. These boys were dead, possibly murdered and the subjects of gruesome display, a cyberspace of Grand Guignol.

Stalbridge had kept all the pictures of his handiwork on his computer. He must have sent the designs off to someone somewhere who had the resources to set up the tableaux, including access to the essential ingredient, dead teenagers or even younger. Hildreth and company must have worked this out and hoped for leads from

Stalbridge's computer but they'd been unable to break into whatever codes were masking the identities of the Ganymede club. The very name of the club suggested that the members were sophisticated, educated, possibly academics like Stalbridge himself. And there was plenty of precedent for them among my Victorians when the age of consent was thirteen. There were an estimated 80,000 prostitutes in London with virgins at a premium and gentlemen could enjoy rent boys at the Cleveland Street brothel, if you couldn't get a guardsman, and you were rich enough. Every way I turned there seemed to be questions and no answers.

Perhaps Hildreth suspected me of being involved and was also keeping me under surveillance, keeping me close in the hope I would break or let something slip, and that was why he fed me these gobbets of information and took me with him to see how I would react: I felt like a fly entangled by filaments of web in the corner of the window-pane, buzzing and whirling my wings to break free and creating the very vibrations that would bring the spider down on me with her immobilising bite. I couldn't concentrate on the pile of papers demanding my attention. I had to get out and walk, 'to clear my head', as I told Lisa on my way out. Yet even strolling towards the front and down the stairway to the promenade with the open sea beside me I couldn't relax, the sensation of being observed, spied on, was too strong. Now they, whoever they were, had only me to watch since Stalbridge had escaped them, and added to that, there was now the question of Hildreth and what suspicions he might have. I was sinking into a quicksand of paranoia and I'd deliberately excluded Hilary from throwing a lifeline.

Maybe I was just tired. I should go home and get a good night's sleep and start again in the morning. Turning back towards the museum I glanced behind to see if anyone turned after me. I would call and tell Lisa I was going home. Driving back up Victoria Road I caught myself constantly glancing in the rear-view and wing mirrors to see if I could spot anyone following me and even when I turned into my own drive I was still looking over my shoulder so that I only just braked hard in time to stop the car slamming into the garage door. When a silver saloon seemed to almost meander past the gate a wave of sick terror went through me, and for a few moments I went on sitting in the driving seat not trusting myself to get out.

It was a relief to find Caesar curled up on my bed. I scratched his head between his pricked ears and he put out a black paw with spread claws to dab playfully at my hand when I drew it away. Downstairs as I switched on the radio and poured myself a drink, he stalked into the kitchen and crossed over to the still bolted cat flap to scratch at it expectantly. 'Sorry boy, you can't get out, not for a while yet.'

We were both prisoners, banged up together, and who could say for how long, unless and until Hildreth and his boys could make some arrests and put an end to our imprisonment. Caesar looked back at me and mouthed, 'Out'. All I could do was put down a dish of his favourite pellets, rattling it seductively to try to entice him away from the lure of the great outdoors. Next morning, after cleaning out the cat tray that he had finally been forced to use in desperation (though thoughtfully with an easily removed, neat chipolata of crap) I set out for work feeling as if something of the bright summer morning might yet rub off on me. If Hildreth left me alone.

Trying not to let my mind wander over what he might be doing, whether they had anything else on Stalbridge's computer, who had killed Jack and all the other unanswered questions, I set about the annual report again, never a job calculated to engross me even with nothing else on my mind. Eventually the routine of work, of everyday, took over so that everything that had happened began to seem like a receding nightmare I might at last emerge from. At lunchtime I ate my sandwiches on the beach with a stretch of ribbed sand in front of me smelling of stranded seaweed in rubbery heaps glinting in the sun, and far out a silver bowstring of water drawn across the horizon.

The afternoon was spent with Lisa, overseeing the mailing of the exhibition posters to sites all over town, and finally posting them up on our own noticeboards outside and inside the building. So when I heard Hildreth's unmistakable voice coming out of the end of the handset and into my unwilling ear, I had to fight hard to resist a strong impulse just to put it back in its cradle and pretend I wasn't there.

'Ah, Alex, I thought I'd pay you a little visit tomorrow. There are some things I want to check on in Bradwell and I thought I'd drop in on the way. I've got something for you. I suppose you wouldn't like to come with me?'

'I'm up to my ears at the moment.'

'Well another time. I should be passing your door about eleven. Would that suit?'

'I'll be in my office.'

'See you then.'

Was it just a romantic fallacy or had the day really clouded over? On my way out I took comfort in our shiny new posters. The chairman at least should be pleased with their bright colours and laughing faces, showing off some of the pier head entertainments. Then I remembered Hildreth's threatened visit. Why was he really coming and what was this mysterious 'something' he had for me? Perhaps it was just an excuse to check on me, that I was where I said I was.

Caesar was waiting when I got home, demanding to know why he couldn't go out and reclaim his old territory. His wounds had quickly healed and his coat had got back its shine. Like any other recoveree he couldn't see why he wasn't allowed to get back to his old routine.

'You might not be so lucky next time,' I said sternly. 'Now they know how clever you are, they might not let you go.'

I considered whether I should send him away for a bit to the safety of his usual cat's hotel but the thought of my empty house without the comfort of a living, warm-blooded presence I could at least communicate with, made me reject the idea, even though I knew it might be selfish to do so, and putting him in danger again. I even wondered briefly if I should take him to the museum with me every day. Then I imagined the chairman walking into my office. I rang Hilary.

'Hildreth's threatening to pay me a visit tomorrow. He says he's got something for me.'

'Does that mean they're making some progress at last, that he's actually got something to tell you?'

'I think it's a more tangible something but I can't imagine what it could be. I'll let you know. Will you be around?'

'Yes, yes I will. Beth's back in Cambridge so I'm on my own again.'

'Hildreth didn't say that they were making progress. It seems like a complete stalemate.' I heard the laughter in her voice and made no effort to keep it out of mine.

Suppose the whole thing went cold and there were never any obvious answers, we would never feel safe again. I could imagine being lulled into a false sense of security only to be snapped awake by some unexpected happening, like a nearby gunshot, even if it turned out to be just an exhaust backfiring.

I slept badly, haunted by confused and whirling dreams of trying to find something or someone, I didn't know which or where, so that when Phoebe showed Hildreth into my office at ten minutes to eleven the next morning, I was in a decidedly uncooperative mood, wanting him away on his travels as soon as I could get rid of him but, as usual, he was affable and unruffled by my refusal to respond, making me feel like a tetchy, over-tired child in danger of a serious tantrum.

'Exhibition keeping you busy, Alex, I imagine. I saw the posters as I came in. I see you've got the Laughing Policeman up there with Aunt Sally. Must be a lot of work to organise a thing like that.'

'My chief assistant did most of it while I was in Amsterdam.'

'Delegation, that's the thing. We have to do a lot of it in my profession. Now that technology, forensics and all that, are all-important poor old PC Plod is out of his depth. I blame Sherlock Holmes. He was a bit of a technocrat for his time, wouldn't you say?'

I refused to be soothed. 'You said you had something for me – Dr Caistor and I were wondering if you were making any progress. It's hard to get on with life when you're looking over your shoulder all the time.'

'You feel you're personally in some kind of danger do you, Alex? Has anything happened that has made you feel that?'

'It's just that everything is so unresolved. I'm sure Jack was murdered by whoever was putting the squeeze on Stalbridge but we still don't know anything concrete, do we?'

'You mean the police don't. The trouble is, Alex, I can't discuss what we're doing with the lay public, even someone as closely involved as you. I can only say we're working on it, and if you come across anything, however trivial it may seem, you get in touch. Sometimes it's the little things that tell us most. That hasn't changed since Holmes, even though he was a fiction. He used all the tools available to him, and his imagination, powers of reconstruction, that sort of thing, because criminals themselves are very imaginative as I always tell recruits when I'm asked to lecture at Hendon. And nowadays of course they've got the internet, the virtual world. Don't underestimate them, I tell the students. It's a battle of wits.'

I wanted to say, 'I don't need the lecture,' but managed to keep the words back. Instead I asked, 'So what have you got for me?'

'Ah yes. I nearly forgot.' Hildreth pressed the catch on the brief-case he was carrying, opened the leather flap and took out a small, soft cloth, drawstring bag. Pulling apart the puckered mouth he emptied the contents into his large open palm where they lay in a glistening heap. 'We've done with these so I think as they're technically yours you're entitled to have them back.'

I stared at the small golden squares with their engraved lettering resting in the cup of his hand. I knew I must make some suitable response but they seemed to glint with a malevolent eye as the light caught the metal surface, so that I couldn't put out my hand to take them from him. He slid them deftly back into the pouch and held it out to me. 'Oh, and there's this.' He took out a small black notebook. 'We found it among Stalbridge's things. My boys have gone over it but they can't make anything of it except the physical forensics, prints, DNA traces, that sort of thing. I'd like you to have a look at it and see if you can come up with anything.'

'Thanks,' I said. 'I'd better put them all in the safe,' and found I was able to reach out and take the little bag and the notebook from him. 'Do you need a receipt?'

'Any time. Next time we meet will do. I'd better be off. Don't bother to see me out. We'll keep in touch. Anyway I'll see you at the opening. I take it I'm invited. Let me know if you have any eureka thoughts.'

My legs were shaking. I sat down and stared at the small sand-col-oured pouch, lying on the desk in front of me where I had dropped it as soon as Hildreth had left. If he'd wanted to watch my reaction to seeing the plates again I had given him a fine display of terror that could easily be judged guilt. It was almost as if he was in league with the enemy and had been delivering their warning. But he was the one who involved me, who dragged me along. He hadn't told me why he was going back to Bradwell, what he hoped to find there. In fact when I came to think it over, he told me nothing while seeming to take me into his confidence. And now I understood the power of fear, to dissolve all certainties, call everything and everyone into question, to shake the foundations of one's own mind, of the state, the world, the universe. That was why governments used it as Orwell had seen. Our responses are those of any animal: fight or flight, or if we can't manage either, that of the rabbit frozen in the headlights with death bearing down. And it seemed that I was just the petrified rabbit.

It was fear itself, the fear of being shamed if anyone, Lisa or Phoebe, or even the chairman dropping in, should find me in this almost catatonic state that finally made me lift my head, open the desk drawer, take out the tin cash box where the safe key was kept, and open the safe door. The companion to the gold squares, the round disk or coin that Hilary and I had found in the amulet with them, looked back at me. I put the little bag on top of it, unwilling or unable to open the drawstring and put the coin inside, the notebook on top, and closed and set the lock on the door, more as if to contain any malign influence within than to keep out intruders.

'I'm going out for a sandwich,' I said, putting my head briefly round Lisa's half-open door. The Laughing Policeman and Aunt Sally grinned at me as I passed.

***

From a lost chronicle of Abbot Albinus of Canterbury. Transcribed by Nothelm, a priest of London AD 721

*580: In this year the Blessed Gregory, not then risen to the papacy, passing through the market at Rome paused to buy from some traders newly come to the city and among the wares exposed for sale were some boys of fair complexion, fine features and bright hair. Upon his enquiring of the merchants who they were and what land they came from and whether they were Christians, he was told that they were Angles from Deira and pagan. 'Non angli sed angeli', that is in English; 'not Angles but angels,' and further: 'they shall be saved from De Ire, that is the wrath of God.'*

*597: In this year the Blessed Gregory sent Augustine to this island to begin the conversion of the English according to his promise when he was papal representative to the city of Rome and first saw the Anglian boys in the market place. Augustine, after many hesitations, for the prospect of coming to a barbarian country put him and his forty monks at first in great fear, landed in the island of Thanet in the kingdom of Aethelbert, King of Kent who had a Christian wife from Gaul, Bertha by name.*

*601: In this year at Augustine's request, Pope Gregory sent more workers to Britain and among the most to be remembered were Mellitus, Justus, Paulinus and Rufinianus. And Mellitus was made Bishop of London, Augustine himself having established his see at Canterbury. Paulinus was consecrated Bishop of York and Justus of Rochester. Altogether twelve bishops were made all from Rome sent here for our salvation: since not only did we not know the Lord but we were unlettered in Greek and Latin and even in our own language, for we would not learn from the Welsh whose armies we fought constantly for the land we had taken, as God willed it, nor did they make haste to teach us. When these learned men first came among us they brought interpreters from Gaul so that they could speak to us and we to them until they learned our tongue and we began to know both to read and write in Latin.*

*The Holy Father Gregory in Rome, did not abandon us as the Roman legions had Britain but was continually in correspondence with Augustine and the others while he lived, following the example of the Apostle Paul.*

Someone, Lisa I suppose, had put a newspaper on my desk detailing the rape of the antiquities of Mesopotamia – Iraq, the sale of ancient sites of two-thousand-year-old mud brick buildings to be melted down to make new bricks, and of all the beautiful and priceless objects that came back into the light of day as a result of potholing and demolition. I thought how distressed Jack would have been and was glad he couldn't see this latest grotesque act, destroying all traces of the oldest of civilisations to build new fast food takeaways and shopping malls.

The evening before our grand opening I gathered the staff together for a celebratory drink. The schools had already broken up for the summer holidays so I had decided to site the exhibition in what was usually the Discovery Centre, a special education resource in term time with SID, the database of local photographs, concentrating on our Victorian collection. The planetarium showed the night sky on 15 August 1890. After all, although the stars might have moved a bit, they were still fundamentally the same.

Lisa had solicited the Kursaal for help with the end of pier entertainments. There was traditional fairground hurdygurdy music accompanying the slowly revolving carousel of painted cocks, and gilt horses with flowing, carved manes and flaring nostrils riding their barley sugar poles. When the show was switched on by Lord Rochford the music would start the carousel and the Laughing Policeman, Aunt Sally and their friends would burst into jolly laughter and pop out from behind the curtains on their boxes. Off would go the toy train from a replica Victoria Station and SID's screen would light up with the photos and posters of a day at the seaside a century ago. We gave Lisa a burst of applause and the bottle of Waitrose Chardonnay went round again.

In the morning I was up early so that Caesar and I could get through what had become our morning ritual of putting down his food and water for the day and cleaning up the cat tray. He had accepted his incarceration and no longer pawed at the cat flap, looking up at me with a theatrically pitiful cry to be let out.

Phoebe had already metaphorically opened up the shop. 'Nice day, Mr Kish. The sun's come out for us.'

I glanced in at the Discovery Centre on the way to my office. All was still as if the exhibition was holding its breath for the moment to spring into life. I made myself a cup of coffee and sat down to work on the annual report, now almost complete. I wondered whether, when it was finished and the exhibition over its inevitable teething problems, I could take a few days off and persuade Hilary to come away for our first holiday together. Surely we would be safe in Paris or Prague, the first places that came to mind. I sat day-dreaming a little, until Lisa opened the door.

'The drinks and snacks for the VIPs are all ready. I thought we'd adjourn as soon as the chairman finishes thanking Lord Rochford.'

'Let's hope he doesn't go on too long. Once he gets into his stride he can't be stopped.'

'What's his lordship like? Have you met him?'

'Once. Young, Labour life peer. Local boy, hence the title. One of the few IT companies that didn't crash when the first 'dot com' bubble burst, though not in the Bill Gates league of course. Sits on the Parliamentary Science and Technology Committee. I hope he doesn't think the whole concept is too…'

'Old-fashioned?'

'I expect he'd call it analogue. I just hope he sees the development of science and technology as a continuum not something that sprang up overnight by courtesy of the first computer.'

Phoebe put her head round the door. 'There's a man from *The Echo*, Mr Kish. Says he'd like a statement from you.'

'Tell him to talk to me afterwards, Phoebe.' It was too early to dig out the usual platitudes about our heritage and the value of a sense of history to society, even though I believed them. A feeling of weariness washed over me. I wanted the event to begin and then be over. I clung to a fragment of my dream of a time away from it all with Hilary, however brief. I only hoped I hadn't left it too late to book Caesar in to his usual holiday home.

Lisa went off to check on the final arrangements, Phoebe to unlock the front door and wave through early arrivals. It was time for me to go to the staff washroom and make myself as tidy as possible. The chairman wasn't a fashionable open-necked shirt proponent. I stood up. Then the door opened and there was Hildreth. I had forgotten his threat to attend.

'All ready for the grand opening, Alex. I'd like a little chat after if you've a moment.'

'I'll try,' I said. 'But I'll have to chat up the chairman and Lord Rochford first. And then the local paper wants an interview.'

'Not to worry. I'll just hang about. Good luck.' He shut the door quietly but firmly behind him. I gave him a few moments to get clear then followed him out, now desperately needing to get to the washroom and suddenly understanding what it might be like to piss yourself under stress. And yet he had said nothing alarming. It was just his presence that made me uneasy.

I took up my place in the entrance hall, poised to greet the chairman and Lord Rochford as they arrived. The chairman was first, rubbing his palms together as if to make sure they were suitable to shake hands with his lordship. The invited public were arriving in dribs and drabs. Some I had to greet with different degrees of warmth, others I could just nod to as they passed.

The Bateses were there as representatives of the local historical society. Harry's wartime relic of a Flying Officer Kite moustache was neatly trimmed and combed to compensate for the tanned dome of his head and Jean still showed a trim ankle in high-heeled court shoes though they must both be in their eighties.

'Thank you for coming,' I said, shaking their hands in turn.

'A bit late for us', Harry said, 'the Victorians. But we wanted to show support.' His camera dangled round his neck. 'Just take a few pictures for the newsletter.'

The chairman had moved away to stand expectantly inside the door apart from the local riff-raff as he probably saw them. I walked over to stand beside him. The trickle of last-minute comers dried up, ushered into the Discovery Centre by Phoebe and Reg, its usual curator. I could hear the buzz behind us as the chairman and I stood side by side, shifting slightly and looking out expectantly. I'd seen the same sort of body language from civil servants waiting for the minister to arrive at a conference on local archives I'd attended in Westminster.

Suddenly there was a flurry and Lisa appeared, followed at a smart pace by a dark-haired, dark-suited man about my own age, and close behind him a young woman in light jacket and skirt who was either his wife or his PA. No one had warned me which. The chairman stepped forward. 'So good of you to do this, Kevin.'

'My pleasure, Ted.'

'This is the museum's director, Alex Kish.'

'I thought we could just step into my office for a moment to agree the running order,' I said as I shook hands. I led them towards my room.

'Can I get you anything?' I asked, not knowing how he liked to be addressed. 'Tea, coffee?'

'I'm fine. Some water might be useful. I seem to have woken up with the start of a summer cold. Got in rather a sweat running last evening.'

'Of course. I'll make sure there's water there.'

'Right,' the chairman said. 'I've got my speech here.'

'I'll say a few words to introduce you, chairman. Then if you could say a little bit about the service here and the particular relevance of a Victorian seaside exhibition. About ten minutes I think we agreed.'

'Yes, yes. I've cut it down.'

'Then you introduce Lord Rochford and hand over to him.'

'I'll just say how pleased I am to be here,' Rochford said. 'Something about how I used to be brought here as a kid. And then press the button and bingo. You'll show me where it is before we start.'

I tried a joke. 'All a bit Heath Robinson rather than PowerPoint but at least it's in period.'

'Shall we get on with it then. Drinks after, Kish?!'

'At the back of the room, if you don't mind,' I turned to Lord Rochford. 'I'm afraid people like the celebrity to mingle a bit.'

'That's fine. I'm well trained. I imagine a donation from my company would be useful. I looked up your website.'

'We'd be extremely grateful,' I said, leading the way back into the entrance hall and through to the Discovery Centre, the buzz dying away as we entered, except for the usual one or two too intent on their conversations to notice.

We walked along the aisle between the flanking rows of seats to the little dais at the front with its three chairs and low table, on which I was relieved to see three glasses and a bottle of fizzy water, and the lectern for the speakers.

'There's the button you press,' I said, pointing it out to Lord Rochford. 'Let's hope we don't have a power cut at the crucial moment.'

We took our seats at the back. I poured out some water for us all and then stood up and moved to the lectern.

'Good morning, ladies and gentlemen. Thank you all for coming. I hope this microphone is working'. I tapped it for the reassuring echo. 'Can you hear me at the back?' There were some murmurs of 'yes', and we were off. I heard my own voice mouthing a few banalities and then brought my part to a close with 'So here is our chairman who will introduce our distinguished guest, Lord Rochford, to open this year's summer exhibition.' I sat down as the chairman strode to the lectern as if about to quell a riot or admonish the guilty.

Looking out over the attentive faces I let my mind wander, not hearing his words. Whatever he said there was nothing now I could do to unsay or prevent it. It was better to switch off and deal with the flak later. Harry Bates wasn't listening either but snapping away at the exhibits. Suddenly at the back of the room I saw Hildreth's black curly head of hair like that of a young bullock and looked away hastily in case he caught my eye.

The applause signalled the end of the chairman's speech. Nervously, I would have prayed whatever gods that the electrics might work. He stretched out an arm to wave Lord Rochford forward to the microphone. Rochford began on his childhood memories, obviously a seasoned performer, I saw his hand hovering over the button. Would it all work? I caught sight of Lisa's anxious face where she stood just inside the door.

'And so it gives me great pleasure to declare "A Victorian Day at the Seaside" open.' His hand came down. There was a burst of music, the little train began to rush, the horses went up and down on the carousel, the curtains parted and the Laughing Policeman and Aunt Sally came rocking into view, laughing raucously. And then a gasp, a kind of yelp, went up from the audience and a loud buzz of conversation broke out. Aunt Sally was gone. The figure that had been projected forward in her place, backed by the mocking laughter, was that of a dead boy, his face smeared with what looked like blood where Aunt Sally's red cheeks should have been, under the incongruity of her black hat.

With great presence of mind Rochford hit the button again, the music died and everything came to a standstill. I was aware of Hildreth forcing his way to the front and stepping up to the lectern.

'I am a police officer. Everyone please sit down for a moment. There's no danger to you all, the public that is, but nothing must be disturbed. Alex, will your people please get everybody out now, a row at a time, starting from the back. Your names and addresses will be taken down outside in case we need to ask you questions later. Will you two gentlemen stay behind, please. I've called for some of the local police. They should be here shortly.'

The two figures of the real boy and the Laughing Policeman had been caught, half in and half out of their stalls. My staff moved forward with the discipline learnt from our fire drill practices for evacuating the public. Only I seemed to be paralysed. Until the chairman hissed at me under his breath like some villain in a Victorian melodrama: 'I'll expect your resignation for this.'

Even the unfairness of his words failed to rouse me. Sleepwalking, I moved forward to the familiar comfort of helping Lisa and others clear the building. Hildreth came over to exchange brief words with the first of the local police to arrive.

'Can we use your room, Alex?'

'Of course.'

He turned to the chairman and Lord Rochford. 'If you would, gentlemen.' He ushered them out of the room. Those in the audience were filing quietly outside where they clustered in the entrance, exchanging shocked views, as uniformed police moved from group to group taking down names and addresses.

I could see it all through the open door as I followed Hildreth and the others but it was as if I was walking through some nightmare, a numb unreality with the sensation that my ears were full of water and sound came through filtered as in a dream.

'So,' Hildreth began when we were all inside my office, 'another staged bit of necroporn.'

'But this one's quite different,' I said, not knowing that I was going to speak but as if I too were some kind of automaton whose button had been pressed.

'How do you mean?'

'There's nothing of beauty. It's grotesque, a mockery of death. Nothing redeemed, no voyage to the Blessed Isles.'

'What are you talking about, Kish?' The chairman turned on me angrily.

'Go on, Alex.' Hildreth held up his hand.

'All the others, the ones designed by Stalbridge, that is, were an attempt to deny the ugliness of death, to put art and a kind of love or at least desire for the beautiful against it in some sort of ritual. This hasn't any of that.'

'What you're saying is that the others were designed for a different market.'

'If you want to put it like that.'

'I don't follow any of this,' the chairman said. 'I hope you don't want to keep us hanging about here. Someone has to deal with this mess.'

'That's right, sir. We all have to deal with it in our different ways.'

A girl I didn't know appeared at the door. 'Sergeant Thomas,' she said. 'Can I help?'

'The sergeant will take statements from you and then you're free to go. Alex, you can come with me. Mr Kish,' he turned back to the others, 'is being a great help to us in our enquiries, providing the kind of background expertise we don't have to hand on the force.'

Obediently I followed him out. 'Your chairman,' he said, 'strikes me as being out of the same mould as our super.'

'You may have saved my job. He's demanded my resignation.'

'I think we need a drink. Where's the nearest pub.' We turned right along Victoria Avenue towards Prittlewell Church and the Blue Boar where I had sometimes gone for lunch in what seemed like another life.

'Now then,' Hildreth said when we were settled at a table with our drinks in the near empty saloon. 'What did you mean back there? You do think this is different?'

'It seemed obvious to me then. I suppose I'm not so sure now. This seems quite different in feeling, in tone almost. The people who set this up don't have the same intention. There's no underlying religious symbolism.'

'So why have they done it?'

'I don't know. I don't know what it means or why.'

'The other scenes were designed by that Professor Stalbridge, partly for the pictures they would make for the benefit of the Ganymede Society, and others with similar tastes. Hebophiles, as we call them in the unit, with a dash of necrophilia, all tastefully arranged. Then you say there's some sort of religion mixed in. But what sort? Does that give us a clue.'

'That may just have been Stalbridge's private input, nothing to do with whoever is behind it all. Stalbridge called them "some people who play rough". They must have been the ones who got him to do the designs. Then they had someone also quite skilled in a different way to set them up. This time they simply took the Aunt Sally figure away, dressed up the body in her clothes and put it in her place.'

'There couldn't be any little gold square involved either, like the others.'

I'd been hoping that Hildreth wouldn't bring the amulet into it. Now I mentally took a deep breath and said, 'That's of course because they're all in my safe,' I paused and took a deep breath, 'along with the one Stalbridge sent me.'

He put his pint down carefully. 'What else have you been keeping from me Alex?'

'I would have told you. But I thought you'd just laugh if I said they'd stolen my cat.'

'Your cat?'

'You see. That's exactly what I was afraid of.'

'How do you know he was stolen, that he didn't just run away or get run over? Cats do.'

'They sent me a note with some of his fur. Then they let him go and he found his way back.'

'Where is he now, this Houdini of a cat?'

'I keep him shut in.'

'They were warning you off – is that it? And if so, this latest stunt could be directed at you in the same way.'

'Me? Why?'

'Look at it like this. You agree this is different, that it isn't done for the same purpose as before, the same market as I said, so what's its purpose? To frighten you off. It's a threat. Now you've told me about the cat it's clear. They've seen you with me. Maybe they even followed you to Amsterdam. They wouldn't have known we were meeting Beemsterboer but if they were keeping track of you they'd have seen that we went to the Dutch police headquarters. You're in danger, Alex. What about your girlfriend, Dr Caistor?'

'We haven't been meeting recently. I thought it best.'

'Alex, we may have to use you as bait, to draw them out. Would you be willing to help? You see, this isn't just aimed at you but through you at all of us. They've got cocky and that may be their undoing. Beemsterboer thought there was nothing we could do but if they step outside their original activities, providing a little tasteful soft porn for kinky professors who'll get all the references, then we may have them. They'll make a mistake.'

'If you could prove they killed Jack …'

'That trail's gone cold. No, we need something new. Who knows, we may get something from forensics on this one. I must get back on the job. I'm afraid they'll have made rather a mess of your exhibition.'

I left him at the entrance to the Discovery Centre and went straight to my office without the courage to look in at the, no doubt, orderly chaos where 'A Victorian Day at the Seaside' should have been. Shutting the door I took the key from my desk and opened the safe. I had to be sure that the little bag holding the pieces from the amulet was still safely inside.

Opening the drawstring neck, I shook the four thin pieces of gold and the coin into my hand. I'd never been one for crossing my fingers or not walking under ladders but now I felt again the same tremor of fear the prince and his grave goods had always provoked in me. I thought of Shakespeare's curse on 'the man who digs my bones', and the so-called curse of Tutankhamun. It was a commonplace: the desire to lie quiet in the grave, in hope perhaps of a resurrection that would reverse the 'ashes to ashes and dust to dust' grim dictum of a burial service. Had Lucy known she was dying? Had she been afraid? We never talked about it.

The other animals were lucky not to have the burden of this consciousness, the real curse of Adam, the penalty for the knowledge of good and evil, or just knowledge. Yet even they mourn an absence, a loss. Now science gives us a new immortality! Our dust breaks down into its elements and is whirled about the world to be reincarnated. Transmigrate, in new life forms, satisfying all the old suggestions for life everlasting. But for our egos, the individual apprehension of ourselves, the biological unit, it isn't enough. We still want to survive as an 'I', a 'me', subject and object, to outwit the extinction of that unique consciousness.

We've invented art to try to combat our fear, to give permanence where there's otherwise only mutability as the Elizabethans called it. Jesus hangs on the cross, beauty in death, like the sculpted figure of the dying Gaul. Even without a resurrection Jesus is immortal in paintings, in music and words; art and religion intertwined, something we can believe in without belief. Was that what the scenes Stalbridge set up had meant?

He had thought, or so he said, that there would just be an effigy at the heart of his designs and by the time he realised the truth he was in too deep. He thought he was making a kind of art but it had the frisson of a real death. The phone was ringing. I picked it up. It was the chairman.

'Well, Kish, I meant what I said. Just because you think you've been indulging in some kind of sleuthing with police involvement it doesn't excuse the neglect of duty that's led to this serious breach of security. It can't go on. Who knows what people got up to while you were swanning off to Amsterdam to play detective.'

'If you mean my staff, I trust them implicitly.'

'It seems to me there's been too much taken on trust. No, as I say, it won't do.'

'I take it you're still asking for my resignation?'

'Well I'm glad you agree you have no alternative.'

'I expect the terms of my appointment to be honoured in full.'

'We can talk about that.'

'I believe I'm entitled to a month's notice. I shall date it from today.' A sliver of ice had entered my heart at the unfairness of his reaction. He wanted a scapegoat or, maybe all along he had been wanting someone he could browbeat even more than he did me, always the mark of the petty tyrant. 'A dog's obeyed in office.' Now more than ever I needed the comfort of Hilary's voice. I would have to ring her when I got home. She must hear what had happened from me, not just read about it in the papers.

I decided to leave by the rear entrance to the museum so not to have to pass the Discovery Centre, now crawling not just with police but sniffer dogs. At least I told myself that was the reason but the truth was a reaction had set in that made me afraid of my own shadow. If Hildreth was right and this latest happening was aimed at me what might I find when I got home: a trashed house and a dead Caesar? The sense of relief when I closed the front door and walked into first the kitchen and then the sitting room and found it all as tidy as Doris Shepherd had left it that morning and Caesar safely curled up on my bed, was so intense that it left me feeling sick and exhausted.

Hilary wouldn't be home yet. I poured myself a drink and rang the cattery. Caesar would be safer there. Then I began to search my old green metal filing cabinet for the copy of my contract. I was determined to go down fighting. I had just pulled it out when the phone rang. It was Hildreth.

'Alex, I thought you'd like to know what we've come up with so far.'

I wanted to say I'd had enough but I knew it was no good. 'Go on.'

'You were right that this is different but you couldn't know how different.'

'Yes…'

'This boy is British, Scotch I should say. Ran away from home, brutal stepfather, usual story, taken into care, ran away from the hostel, been living rough, died of malnutrition and drugs. On the Missing Persons Register.'

'What about the blood?'

'Animal. They think pig, you know, bleeding like a stuck pig.'

Hildreth's brand of gallows humour had begun to grate badly, reviving the overwrought sensations that the whisky and familiar surroundings had begun to soften.

'You're talking about a dead boy.'

'This job is like being a surgeon. You have to develop a shell or you can't wield the knife. What I don't get is, why they think they can frighten us off with these tactics. Or is it just the self indulgence of revenge.'

'Well they've succeeded. I've agreed to resign. In other words I've been sacked.'

'Is that my fault?' Hildreth's tone was one of simple enquiry not denial.

'In a way I suppose, though I don't blame you. You were doing your job. I went along with it. Maybe I was flattered and so it is my fault. I'm accused of neglecting my duty, playing detective, ironically being negligent about security.'

'I'm sorry, Alex. I didn't foresee this. I hadn't sussed out your chairman sufficiently. What will you do?'

'Oh, they'll have to pay me redundancy. I've got a five-year contract. Maybe I'll join the police. You like graduates these days, I believe. Immediately though, I'm insisting on a month's notice to put things in some sort of order for the poor sod who takes over. I wish him luck. Are you issuing a statement yet? I'd like a copy before the press come calling.'

'I'll see you get it.'

'Tonight?'

'I'll make sure it's emailed to you. There's not much in it. There's not much we can say at this stage. Get some sleep. With luck there'll be more to tell you tomorrow.'

'I'm not sure I want to hear it,' I said and put back the receiver, only to feel very alone as soon as I'd cut the link, like a dog that's slipped its lead and finds itself in a strange street and hungry for home.

The boy had slipped his lead; thousands do every year, the papers tell us, and thousands are never found, spirited away, gone underground with the rejected asylum seekers, illegals, druggies, an underworld we treat as the festering residue at the bottom of our society, a murky sediment we try not to disturb in case it muddies our clear waters, underclass in the underpass, with 'subprime' the new word for the next layer up who still have aspirations to be part of the common weal or wealth.

Trying Hilary's number I got her answering service. There was no help to be had there; nowhere I could give my self-pity a workout. Perhaps I should take up Buddhism or Stoic philosophy. What about a book: *Meditation for Non-Believers*? Instead I poured a good measure of Famous Grouse and, suddenly seeing its relevance to my present state of mind, felt my mood lighten and raised my glass. 'Here's to you, kid,' I toasted myself.

Next morning I called the staff together to tell them I would be leaving at the end of the month. It was Phoebe who showed the strongest reaction, putting up her hand to her mouth and almost sobbing, 'Oh, Mr Kish!'

'Will you put in for the job?' I asked Lisa after the others had left. 'I'd give you a glowing reference of course, but I don't know that that would do you much good'.

'I don't think I could cope with the chairman,' Lisa laughed. 'I may apply somewhere else.'

Selfishly I hadn't thought about the impact my going might have on the staff. Locked in my own bleak bubble I'd been oblivious to their loyalty, even affection over the years. It was something, a real plus to set against my low self-esteem.

'What will you do, Alex?' Lisa asked. She rarely called me by my first name, nearly always using the non-committed 'you' without attribution.

'I honestly don't know. It's all been so sudden I haven't had time to think.'

Phoebe brought in a stack of newspapers. The tabloids had gone to town, 'Lost Boy Found Dead.' 'Billy's Last Grisly Gameshow.' The *Daily Muckraker* had tracked down his parents. 'We don't know why he ran away. I never lifted a hand to him.' 'Sinister Gang Targets Homeless.'

The phone rang. It was the man from *The Echo* I'd managed to dodge yesterday. 'We think you owe us a statement, Mr Kish.'

'You can tell your readers I've taken full responsibility for the security failure that made this grotesque happening possible, and have given in my resignation.'

'Yes, but who was the kid? What's it all about?'

'You should ask your national colleagues. They seem to know more than I do, I'm only a local government agent not the police. Try them.'

'I have. They're not giving us anything.'

It was true. The press release Hildreth had emailed through to me was of the classic 'No comment. We are continuing with our investigations' order.

'So why exactly are you resigning?'

'I've told you. If you like, I'm old-fashioned. I believe in taking responsibility for what happens on my patch.'

'Alex, are you alright?' It was Hilary breaking our rule not to use our work phones.

'You shouldn't be ringing me; it's not safe.'

'I've seen the papers. I had to ring.'

'I tried to get you last night to tell you but there was no answer. You must have been out. I didn't leave a message.' I hoped I didn't sound petulant.

'I was at the Lyttleton. *Coriolanus* is one of Beth's set texts or one she's chosen. Anyway she wanted to see it, so she came up and stayed the night. Can't we meet?'

'Hildreth thinks it isn't a good idea.'

'He seems to want to govern everything you do. And without getting any closer to solving anything. It's just going on and on.'

'I should tell you I've resigned. At least we're calling it that. Actually I was effectively sacked, told to fall on my sword.'

'What will you do?'

'Find another job if I can. Maybe there'll be a vacancy in your outfit or the V&A.'

'Alex, I'm so sorry. I feel so inadequate…'

'It's a help to hear you. I'll ring this evening. Will you be in?'

'I'll be at home. Let's talk then.'

The museum still swarmed with police and was closed to the public. Hildreth turned up at the end of the morning. 'Let's go back to that pub where we can talk.'

'When can we have the building back, and re-open?'

'Shouldn't be long now. I'll tell them to get a move on. Will you go on with your exhibition?'

'It'll certainly pull in the crowds.' I remembered the queues outside on the day after the break-in and the theft of the amulet. 'They'll probably come in busloads. We found the original Aunt Sally in a cupboard. As soon as your boys get out we can put it all back as if nothing had ever happened. Did you get to the boy's parents first or was it the press?'

'We tracked them down as soon as we found him on the Missing Persons Register.'

'And nobody knows where he's been all this time.'

'The post-mortem showed he'd been fed before he died and then took or was given too big a shot of speed. We've got enquiries going on to find where he used to hang out. The homeless often have their own beat where they're known and feel safer.'

'But he wasn't safe, was he. Someone got to him as they did to the others.'

'The Ganymede site has closed down. They'll start up again under another name of course. But they're not the real villains. Some of us even question whether just looking should be a crime, or rather such a serious one, being banged up and put on the register, with all the consequences. Those who go in for grooming and trying to fix up meetings are the really dangerous crims. But there you are: it's the law and we're the grunts who have to enforce it.'

He was off on some crusade of his own where I couldn't follow. 'So what happens next?'

'They're getting desperate. They'll make a mistake, that's what I'm waiting, hoping for. They've lost a market. Presumably it was worth something to them. They must have had some pay-to-view system going. We might find there was a credit fraud involved as well but of course their customers couldn't come forward to complain without involving themselves, probably risk their jobs at least.

'Anyway they'll need to find another line. This wouldn't have been their only business. The fact that the Scotch boy died of an overdose suggests an involvement with the drug trade. Who knows what else. The trouble is if they're just able to switch tracks, to start again without being caught, then we'll be searching blind.'

We were able to open again the following week. As I'd predicted there were queues all day to see the reconstituted exhibition. Phoebe and Reg were kept busy moving the crowds through the displays in groups, and excreting them the other end. I shut myself in my office and concentrated on finishing the annual report, the inventory, and the financial statement that would show I had done a good job, and that the museum was in as good shape as the budget would allow.

The police did a safety check as part of their own enquiries and for good measure I got in a security firm to go over all our precautions. The verdict was the same. Nothing we could have put in place, or done, apart perhaps from employing a night watchman would have kept them out if they were determined, and even then they could easily have killed any guard since they obviously had no qualms about a body or two.

Hildreth himself seemed to have gone into limbo and I was glad of his absence. Hilary and I spoke often on the phone in the evenings, which helped, but I was aware that I was waiting, sure that this wasn't the end, that they would strike again and that no one was safe until there were answers, a resolution. I had never asked for anything so much since the last weeks of Lucy's life. And outside every day the sun shone and the sea glinted back its light as if in a mockery of human terror and disaster.

It was the second week after the aborted exhibition opening. I had only a fortnight to go before I had to clear my desk, say goodbye to everything that I had known for the best part of my working life and be out on my own. Something had prompted me to take the finds from the amulet out of the safe and lay them on my desk as if they were the pieces of a jigsaw puzzle that, if I could only fit them together, would reveal the answer. I pushed them about with a forefinger trying to remember what Jack Linden had said. Jack had been able to read the script. He had said it contained instructions about what the soul should do after death, engraved on the gold by an Orphic priest and worn by a Christian convert hedging his bets with a good luck charm.

I picked up the little notebook too and began to look through it. I saw at once that it was some sort of sketchbook. Stalbridge had clearly been in the habit of making drawings of things just as I'd seen him doing at the Forgotten Empire exhibition. And there indeed, as I turned the page, was the winged disk. There were other sketches too that I recognised. The boy in the soft cap from the Museum of London, a flagon from the prince's grave. I came to the last pages. A few were empty, intended for future use. Something made me turn to the very end. There was no picture, only what seemed a list. I stared at it.

*Egg*
*Orpheus*
*Crucifixion*
*Bull slaying*

I was looking at a list of the death scenes. There was nothing that suggested the fire on the pier. Perhaps that was what had given him the idea for the whole thing. Someone had wanted to get rid of the body and make it look like an accident. Stalbridge had refined on the original plan and gone on from there. But what was meant by 'bull slaying?'

I picked up the phone and dialled Hilary's number. 'Does "bull slaying" mean anything to you?'

'Mithras,' she said at once.

'What do you mean?'

'That's what he does, did, in the myth. He slew the primeval bull from which came life. Its death set life going if you like. We've got a sculpture of it that was found in the Walbrook. Why?'

'It's something in a notebook that belonged to Stalbridge, part of a list. I wondered what it meant.'

Someone came into the room and she rang off hastily. What did it mean? Was it going to be Stalbridge's next project if I hadn't got in the way? Did I have anything I could usefully tell Hildreth? Stalbridge was dead and that was presumably the end of it. But they had wanted to threaten me or get their own back for meddling, as they would see it. There might still be a supply of dead boys they wanted to use to make more pornopics from or there might even be girls as well if they decided to expand into another market, as Hildreth had called it. Perhaps Stalbridge had given them a last set-up. Maybe they still wanted the religious element to give that added frisson. Judging by the previous installations it didn't matter to the commissioners what the religion was. Or was that Stalbridge's own input, reflecting his interests and the pieces from the amulet? Zoroastrian, Orphic, Bacchic, Christian. There were all the Christian virgin martyrs, some of whom must have been young girls, to choose from. There was the sacrifice of Abraham and Issac, Proserpina whose rape led down to Death, Kronos devouring his children. Oh, they'd got plenty to work their way through, endless depictions of lust and murder under the guise of art, art which was meant to achieve catharsis, resolution, but was being subverted to titillate. I was beginning to sound even to myself like 'Disgusted of Tunbridge Wells'. Yet the alternative was the 'woolly liberalism' ridiculed by traditionalists.

Somehow you have to cling on to 'No man is an island', with all its consequences, even if you go down pinioned to the great white whale, and drown in your own failure. I had to risk being thought a fool by Hildreth.

I rang Hilary again. 'Any news?' she asked at once. 'I'm sorry I had to ring off like that before.'

'If you were thinking of staging something to do with Mithras, another scene, where would you do it?'

'Not us again! I don't think I could bear it.'

'I don't think so. At least they've never repeated themselves before. Where else might it be? Somewhere within what you might call their catchment area.'

'Do be careful, Alex. Don't get too involved. Let the police get on with it. It's their job, not yours.'

'I can't refuse to help if Hildreth asks me.'

'You're all like little boys playing cops and robbers, and dressing it up in duty or idealising'.

I thought of the last of the great Victorians, Kipling:

*What is a woman that you forsake her*
*And the hearth fire and the home acre*
*To go with the old grey widow maker?'*

I knew that Hilary was right. I felt myself carried along on the wave of Hildreth's enthusiasm, the energy that emanated from him, in a game of follow my leader, even while I was sick with a complex fear I couldn't share with anyone.

The next day passed uneventfully. Unable to believe that in a week I would have cleared my desk and left, I went about the building like a sleepwalker, knowing the chairman and board were already interviewing the shortlist for my job but unable to apply for any new post myself.

The house was lonely without Caesar. Every few days I went to see him in his comfortable prison, climbing the steps to the row of cages, stepping into the obligatory tray of evil-smelling disinfectant and opening his individual meshed door, under the supervision of Jane or Alice who ran the cattery. Sometimes he would come out to see me with a little cry of recognition; at others he would stay sullenly inside the wire hut with its cushioned ledge, bowls of food and water and litter tray. Those days I knew I was being punished. I couldn't even explain to him or his minders why his incarceration was necessary since I was clearly around and not on a world cruise or away at an archival conference.

Then Hilary rang. 'There's a place called the Roman Bath. I think people once thought it was something to do with Mithraic rites. Now it's generally accepted that it's neither Roman nor a bath but some sort of Tudor water tank with a spring under it.'

'Where is it?'

'Surrey Street, I think. In a little alleyway, leading down to the Embankment and the Thames.'

'Where does the bull slaying come in?'

'It seems to have been part of the initiation rite for young boys. Symbolically they went down to the underworld, rather the same idea as going under in Christian baptism. The real Temple of Mithras is by the Walbrook, the stream under Victoria Street but there's nothing left except the outlines of walls. You've seen all the artefacts they found in our display here. You remember…'

'The singing head. But wasn't that Orpheus? He's in the list I found at the back of the notebook.'

'The two were very closely linked.'

'Like on the coin from the amulet.'

'That's it.'

'You know I'm leaving next week.'

'What will you do?'

'Write my memoirs. No, honestly I don't know. I don't seem to have the will to start sending off my CV and filling in forms. Something will turn up, I suppose.'

Hildreth rang the next morning while I was on my second piece of toast. 'Any luck, Alex?'

I took a deep breath. 'I was going to ring you. We might be on to something. I found a list at the back of that book. It seems to refer to the scenes. They're all listed except the first, the fire. I suspect that was what gave them, or Stalbridge himself, the idea for the rest. But there's a fourth. It looks as if they were intending to stage at least one more. Suppose they are? Hilary thinks she knows where and what it might be.'

'Go on.' His voice, which had been rather flat, lifted.

'The last entry says "bull slaying". It's a long shot but she thinks it might refer to some kind of initiation ceremony. And she thinks she might know where it could be.'

'Go on.'

'Apparently there's something called the Roman Bath in Surrey Street that was once thought to be connected to Mithras, the god who went in for bull slaying. I know it all sounds very hypothetical…'

'It's all we've got. We'll check it out. I only hope you're both right. The lack of progress is beginning to get to our chief.'

'What will you do?'

'Suss it out and then stake it out, twenty-four seven. It'll have to be done carefully. We don't want to frighten them off. This could be our best chance yet.'

'But you don't know when. It could be anytime or never.'

'That's why the stakeout. They'll need to set something up if they're going to film. But my guess is it'll be soon.'

'You know I'm leaving at the end of the week.'

'I've got your home number. You're not thinking of going away, are you? I'd like you to stick around until this phase at least is over. You're my good-luck talisman, Alex. We'll sort this in the end.'

Once again I could feel myself being swept up by his energy and confidence. 'No. I've no plans to go anywhere. I'll have to look for another job.' The faint memory of a plan to take Hilary away some-where, just the two of us, passed over my mind like the merest waft of the after scent of a lover's skin.

The real world was being replaced by the virtual. We no longer needed to meet. We could talk or write instantly. We could blog and email, conference call on video links, find lovers and friends in space without their interfering physical reality. I wanted to prick myself to see if I still bled but, like most of the rest of this technologised, sanitised world, I'm unused to pain. Even Lucy had faded into a half-remembered ache. I felt myself sinking into a dulled stupor. After next week I would be alone in the house without the comforting presence of a job to go to, people to see, decisions to make, and without even the company of my cat and his needs. It was a forced early retirement and I could quite see why people 'taking' it simply gave up the ghost.

'God, Alex, you do sound low. Should you see a doctor?' Hilary was making what had become her ritual evening call. 'I wish I could see you, put my arms around you. Could you take a holiday?'

'Hildreth wants me around. He thinks this is the big break and he wants me in on it.'

'I went to look at the Roman Bath in my lunch break today. I've never seen it before. Never thought it was worth it. It's very weird: a deep brick well, square or rather oblong. I can see why people thought it was a bath. In the nineteenth century it was tricked out with marble walls, a changing room and Roman busts. David Copperfield swims in it in the novel. It's closed to the public except on Wednesdays between one and four so I couldn't get in. But you can peer down into it through a big glass window and there's a switch on the outside wall that lights up the inside. It's very deep and dark. Rather spooky. I imagine you can hire it for events. I can see some people might fancy an alternative wedding there.'

'Was there any sign of Hildreth's boys?'

'If there was, they were well disguised as passers-by or the curious like me. But then that's what you'd expect.'

'Did anyone see you?'

'Other people walking through the alley must have done but I did my best to look ordinary. I took a guide book with me and was ready with my attempt at a mid-Atlantic accent if accosted.'

I decided not to tell Hildreth about her expedition.

The staff had organised a farewell party for me on Friday afternoon. Lisa had brought in a couple of bottles of wine and Phoebe had baked a cake to go with the obligatory crisps and nuts. We all did our best to be cheerful but it was hard work.

'Have they appointed anyone yet?' Reg asked.

'Not as far as I know.' I washed down a handmade, cracked pepper and sea salt crisp with a mouthful of Chardonnay too sweet for my taste.

'The chairman rang me today,' Lisa said. 'He asked why I hadn't applied and if I would be acting director until they found someone. Apparently "someone of the right calibre", his words not mine, isn't rushing to live by the seaside in our exciting town.'

'What did you say?'

'I said I was considering my options but I'd take over temporarily until they found someone.'

'Maybe they'll increase our budget and let the extension plan go ahead,' I said bitterly, 'that'd be an incentive.' I didn't think I could bear it if they got the Prittlewell prince back from London and I wasn't any longer in charge.

'You'll come back and see us, Mr Kish?' Phoebe asked.

'Of course I will, if the new director doesn't object, or the chairman.'

'Oh, him,' Phoebe said. 'We'll invite you to the Christmas lunch.'

Fearing my own inability to cope with goodbyes, as soon as the bottle was emptied, I packed my remaining papers and books, and left Lisa to lock up. The house, as I feared, was painfully silent. I poured myself another drink, moving on to real wine, and sank down in an armchair in front of the television in time to switch into the doom-laden evening news.

An hour later I had fallen asleep when the telephone woke me. It was Hildreth.

'We think we're on for tomorrow.'

'How do you know?'

'Our stakeout reported activity at the bath. Stuff being brought in. Comings and goings.'

'It might be for some completely different happening.' I was trying not to be swept along again.

'It might but we can't risk it. I'll keep you posted.'

'Surely you don't need me there. What could I do?'

'You might be able to explain what they're up to. Anyway I want you there. I imagine whatever they're doing they'll want it dark and as few people around as possible. That's what I'm banking on. Can you get up here about seven? The evenings are light until half-past eight at least so I don't think anything will happen before ten o'clock but just to be on the safe side... We can wait in my office.'

After he had rung off I set myself to finish the bottle in hope of a night's sleep but it was broken by whirling and violent dreams so that I woke at two and again at four sweating under only a sheet, aware of my pulse beating so furiously in my carotid artery that I could hear it reverberate inside my skull. Grimly I thought that if I died of a stroke or a heart attack now Hildreth would have to get by on his own.

In the morning I woke again feeling sick and exhausted, to trail downstairs for rejuvenating cups first of tea, then coffee with toast and orange juice. It was Saturday. I could ring Hilary at home. Should I tell her? If I didn't she would never trust me again. I rang.

'I'll be at home. You've to let me know as soon as you and Hildreth get the word. I want to be there.'

'I don't know if I can ring you from his office.'

'Go to the loo and use your mobile.'

I decided to pass the time with a visit to Caesar. He was in his for-giving mood, pleased to see me and allowing himself to be stroked into a purr. It was Jane's day on duty. 'If anything happened to me while he was with you,' I said, 'you would get him re-homed. You wouldn't let anyone put him down?' I heard my voice about to break.

'Of course not. No question. We look after our guests and he's a favourite. I'm surprised you should ask, aren't you, Caesar boy?'

I drove home chastened, to trawl the internet for jobs. It was time I started looking forward, beyond this evening. I wouldn't tell Hil-dreth about my promised call to Hilary until I'd made it, in case he objected. I set out for the station, and parked my car wondering when, or even if, I'd be unlocking it again to drive home. It was five o'clock. The countdown had begun.

I decided to get out at Westminster and walk across Parliament Square and up Victoria Street rather than go on to St James's, the nearest station to New Scotland Yard, anything to postpone the moment of being shut up in Hildreth's office with him, waiting. Coming out of the Tube station I was struck by the blinding evening sunlight from the expanse of open sky above Westminster Bridge and the river below. Crowds of summer tourists flowed towards the absurd yet somehow impressive fake Gothic Houses of Parliament while Westminster Abbey itself seemed moulded in pale marzipan above the green dais of the Garden of Remembrance. Around me were all the skin tones and features of the human universe bathed in sunshine. Surely it couldn't be true that I was going to spend the next few hours sitting in an artificially lit office waiting to be called out to witness some grotesque ritual.

The centre of Parliament Square had been railed off. I presumed it was against terrorist surprise like the crash barriers along the pave-ments. I picked up an evening paper to give me something to do if easy conversation with Hildreth dried up. Suppose the summons never came and we sat there all night. How would we pass the time?

'I've arranged for any call to be put through on my mobile,' Hil-dreth said when I reached his office. 'Let's go and find a coffee.' So I found myself sitting again in the lounge of St Ermin's where we had first talked. I saw at once that he was hyped up like a nervy racehorse making its way to the starting gate. This was what you signed up for, the adrenalin surge of the heist, a piece of the action. His strong clean fingers with the short pared nails were drumming on the table.

'Suppose it isn't the night?' I said.

'Oh, it's the night. I'm quite sure. I can almost feel it.'

After our cups of coffee we went back to New Scotland Yard to wait in his meticulously tidy room where only the computer, printer and telephone sullied the tops of his desk and filing cabinets. All detritus had been banished from sight.

'I've got a report to do,' Hildreth said. 'Can you amuse yourself?'

'I'll read my paper,' I said, taking it out of my briefcase.

'Good.' He began to tap away at the computer with his forefingers. I looked at my watch. Eight o'clock. Outside the sun would still be streaming down on the crowds. In here we were hermetically sealed from the world. Time seemed to alternately scurry and drag, as I was able to concentrate on what I was reading or overtaken by panic, the sensation of rushing down to disaster on a run that ended in a precipice, unable to stop or turn aside.

The call came at nine fifteen. Hildreth picked up the desk phone. 'Right. We're on our way. Looks like we're on,' he said to me, putting the handset back.

'I need a pee,' I said.

'Down a floor. You'll see the sign but don't be long. We don't want to miss the fun.'

Quickly I left the room, pulling out my mobile as soon as the door closed behind me, switching on and bringing up Hilary's number.

'We're off in a few minutes.'

'I'll be there. Alex, be careful.'

Now I was inside it seemed wise to empty my bladder. Hildreth was standing outside his door ready to go.

'I've got your briefcase.'

'How do we get there?'

'A car will take us to the Aldwych. Then we walk. No sense in turning up like the US cavalry. I've got officers staked out within call if we're lucky enough to need them.'

The dusk was deepening as we drove up the Strand and were

dropped off at Bush House. Hildreth led the way down the steps and across the surprisingly empty road. It was vacation and the usual term time overspill of King's College students wasn't thronging the pavements but one or two hopeful travellers hovered at the bus stop.

A man stepped out from the dark arched entrance to Somerset House. 'This way, sir.'

We followed him past the vaulted gateway, the heavy doors of the Courtauld and the courtyard where the fountains and lights had been switched off, down a narrow street between tall stone buildings and through another arch. I glanced up as we were swallowed by a dark tunnel smelling of piss. A plaque above the entrance read ROMAN BATH. PROPERTY OF THE NATIONAL TRUST. 'Surrey Steps,' our guide whispered as we began to climb down. Two figures had stood silently at the top, one on either side. Hildreth raised his hand in salute. Now we were going up a narrow alleyway.

The police guide stopped us with his hand and pointed. At first I could see nothing. Then I noticed a rim of light spilling out along the edge of an arched window that must be about five metres in length ending in a closed door. A square piece of card was stuck to it. Hildreth moved forward, surprisingly soft-footed. Then he came back and beckoned us to move further down the alley.

'It says "Filming in Progress." Who's this?' A figure was coming up the alley towards us. 'What are you doing here, Dr Caistor?'

'I came to make sure you didn't get Alex into trouble.'

At that moment notes of music, though not from any instrument I recognised, began to come from the building. 'Tell the boys to close in,' Hildreth said. 'We're going in. Have you got the key?'

'Yes, sir. The Trust was very helpful when I told them we thought something illegal might be going on. The booking was for an independent film company, said they were making a programme for Sky Arts. Everyone's ready, sir.'

I was aware of figures approaching up the alley. 'Alex, you and Dr Caistor stay here. Just in case there's any rough stuff. I'll call you when we're in. You might be able to explain what's going on. Now, very quiet everyone. We want to surprise them. Is there any other way out?'

'No, sir.'

'Let's go. Silent as you can.'

Hilary and I stood still as the silhouettes of half a dozen backs moved up the alley with hardly a sound of boots on the paving. Below, what must be the Embankment traffic roared past the entrance, helping to mask their progress. In the light from a drunkenly leaning street lamp we saw them pause at the door. Then suddenly there was a shout of: 'Police. Stay right where you are!' The figures disappeared with a clatter and more shouted orders, except for two left on either side of the door like dummies outside a shop.

We moved up closer to be ready if called. After a few minutes one of the guards came towards us. 'Inspector says to go in, sir.'

We went through the door, down a few steps into a small ante-chamber that must have been the nineteenth-century changing room and paused at the entrance to a long narrow well blockaded by Hildreth's back. Peering over his shoulder I could see the bath had a wide ledge running round it. A camera had been strung up at one end. In the reddish glow from a couple of spots I could see several costumed figures topped with animal heads or bird beaks. In the middle was the figure of a boy, naked except for a bull mask, held upright with cords against some kind of throne but motionless as if dead.

'Is this the sort of set-up you expected?' Hildreth turned to me.

'It's a re-enactment of a Mithraic bull slaying initiation ceremony,' Hilary said, stepping forward.

'Nobody move. Hawkins, take some pictures. Then bring the lot along except the boy. Untie him and lay him down. The doctor should be here shortly. Get some proper lights in here. Lock them up separately. I'll have them out one by one for interview.' He turned to Hilary. 'If you could write me an explanatory note about what you think was going on it would help.'

There was no question of my going home that night. We went back to Hilary's flat where she poured us both whiskies and then we drank a bottle of wine, going over and over the same ground until we fell into bed too exhausted to do anything but sleep.

In the morning Hildreth rang. 'I thought you'd be there. Can you come over, Alex, and I'll fill you in with what we've got. We've caught a big fish at last.'

Obediently I set off for New Scotland Yard while Hilary steeled herself to go to work. 'You'll let me know, Alex, won't you. God, I hope this is the end of it all.'

'We've got one serious,' Hildreth said. 'The others were just actors hired for the job. We've let them go on police bail.'

'What was meant to happen?'

'The boy was to be stabbed ritually. The actor who was supposed to do it believed he was using one of those daggers with a retracting blade that they kill people with on stage. He didn't know it had been substituted with a real one. The boy was already dead so he couldn't be killed but there would have been a lot of animal blood of some sort. Our catch is going to sing, we think. Anyway we've seized his computer and mobile and a lot of other stuff. We'll get Interpol to follow it up. Looks like it leads back to Bulgaria and then, Christ knows, on from there. Your girlfriend emailed us her background note. She's been very helpful. We might have taken a long time to get there.'

'I can't see it makes much difference what it was all for.'

'That's because you're not in the force. Every bit of knowledge is valuable because it helps you understand the psychology and piece the bits together. The crims are always looking for new ways to do things. Seven of these new porno sites go up every day. Cruder stuff. Not this tasty necroporn as I call it.'

'How do you manage not to feel disgust for the human race?' I said wearily. 'Everything we invent seems to cause some terrible new pollution. The factories and mills filled the air with smoke and the rivers with filth. Now we've found a new form of pollution, of the mind. Global tides of it washing all our shores.'

'You're tired, Alex. Go home and have a rest.'

'Is this the end of it?'

He shrugged. 'Who can say? I hope we've broken the ring, and maybe we'll get the whole gang. At least we'll have stopped this end of the operation. For a while anyway.'

＊

## Saeed's Story AD 2007

After my parents had paid the money we waited for instructions. It seemed a long time although it was only ten days. Then I was told to pick up an e-ticket for the bus that would take me on the first part of the journey and the documents that would see me across the borders first into Turkestan and then across through Europe. I could take only one small bag which my mother packed for me. At the bottom she put a copy of the Quran and I added the poems of Hafiz. Then she stuffed it with as many changes of clothing as she could until it was as tight as a drum and filled the front pocket with washing stuff and medicines, painkillers, plasters and quinine. Anything else I needed I could buy as soon as I started the job that they had waiting for me.

The bus is to leave at dawn. It's still cold in the chill wind coming down from the mountains with only a smear of light showing in the sky. My father comes with me to the village square where the bus is already waiting with some boys on board.

'Hi, Saeed. What are you waiting for? Let's go.'

It's Hamid from my class at school. I hadn't known he'd be on the bus although we had often discussed going to the West, to Europe but he had always said his parents couldn't afford it. He's a beautiful boy, everyone's favourite, slim and athletic where I am stocky and short.

My father hugs me and orders me to let them know that I'm safe as soon as I get to Engelestan. We've been told the journey will take three days. My mother I know will be weeping at home and praying to God for my safety. They have given me all the money they can spare. A man stands by the open door of the bus inspecting tickets and hurrying us on board. When my father first contacted him through our cousin Ali he said he was from Bulgaria and we had wondered if that was the way the bus would go. It is old, with the paint peeling and with faint writing on the side in letters. I can't read but think it might be Greek.

The Bulgarian shuts the door. He isn't coming with us. The driver starts the engine and the old bus shudders and groans with the effort. I hope the brakes are the best part of it when we come to the mountains. The driver guns the engine and we begin to move.

I look down at my father and wave. He raises his hand and there are tears on his cheeks glistening in the light from the rising sun. I crane my head to see him falling away from us, growing smaller until he seems to vanish.

'Why didn't your parents come to see you off?' I ask Hamid.

'They don't know I'm going. I saved up for the fare myself doing things for people, cutting their hair when they were too poor for a proper barber. That's what I want to do in England, become a real barber. People always need their hair cut.'

'Hey, you can cut mine when we get there. Save me money.'

'I'll shave it smooth as an egg,' he laughs and gives me a little punch.

I don't have a watch so I don't know how long we've been going but it must be several hours. The sun is right overhead and the bus is stifling until we begin to wind up and down the mountains on narrow roads that fall away on one side down to the valley, and on the other are walled in sheer rock. My mother has given me a bottle of water and some little cakes that I share with Hamid who has nothing. I try not to think about his parents' despair when they find he has gone. He tells me he has left them a note so that they at least know that he is safe.

The bus judders to a halt in the high mountains above a lake, big as an inland sea, gleaming under the fierce sun. The driver tells us to get out and relieve ourselves. He gives us bread and cold tea. 'We are going to cross the border,' he says. From his accent I think he is an Afghan.

'But I have no passport,' I say.

'I have your passport and documents. That is partly what you pay for. Your parents gave me the photographs and I got the passports.'

'But my parents didn't know,' Hamid says.

'I have a spare one for such as you. The soldiers will only count them when I hand them over and then count you, not check your faces with the pictures. Remember if anyone asks you, this is a school project. You are tracing the boundaries of the Persian empire.'

I like this idea very much, and part of it is true in a way, at least as far as the Danube as we have been taught. We get back in the bus and go on. The road is very narrow and runs between the mountains, climbing all the time. At the top we are stopped by a barrier manned only by two soldiers who come out of a hut. The driver gets down from the bus. One points a rifle at him. He opens a bag and brings out a bunch of papers that must be our passports.

One soldier goes into the hut with them while the other keeps his gun pointing at the driver. The other soldier comes back and climbs into the bus. He begins to count us. I sit up and try to look smart and confident. He gets out of the bus and speaks to the driver. Then he goes back into the hut. After a bit he comes out again and gives the documents back to the driver. The other soldier lowers his rifle. The driver offers them cigarettes and they stand there smoking and talking. Then the soldier who took the passports, nods. The driver gets back in the bus. The other soldier raises the barrier. The driver starts the engine which coughs and belches smoke and we drive slowly through the gap. We are in Turkestan.

After another hour or so I fall asleep in spite of the swaying and bumping of the bus. Hamid wakes me. The driver has stopped at a small village in the mountains. We climb down to sit at wooden tables and a big man with a moustache brings a pot of soup and ladles some into wooden bowls with flat flaps of bread. The driver goes into the taverna to eat and talk to the people inside. He seems to know them well and they were obviously expecting us because the food was already waiting.

The driver hurries us back into the bus and we're off again. The journey has become monotonous and I no longer bother to look out of the window at the mountain passes, the high peaks and the valley bottoms where goats wander. By nightfall we are in the outskirts of a town, the first we have come to, very dusty and poor-looking. There are as many women as men in the streets and a lot of them don't wear the hijab.

We pull up in the rear of a grim block of flats with dim lights behind shuttered windows. The driver gets out from behind the wheel. 'You will sleep here.' We climb down. My whole body aches with the vibration of the bus. He leads us through a back entrance and down narrow dark stairs to a basement room that must have been used for some kind of store. There's a pile of tattered-looking rugs or covers in one corner and a pail in the other.

'No pissing on the floor. Use the bucket. The door will be locked so don't try to go out. I don't want you wandering round the town.' Then he leaves us. There's one dim bulb high up in the ceiling. I can hardly make out the faces of the other boys. There are twelve of us altogether. We use our bags as pillows and cover ourselves with the mouldy rugs smelling of damp and mildew.

Although I'm tired I sleep badly, starting awake from time to time to wonder where I am. One of the boys is weeping quietly with a snivelling sound. The Afghan wakes us early in the morning. There's a big jug of hot tea and some stale cakes. Then he takes us to a kind of washroom where laundry lies in piles on the concrete floor.

'You can wash here. Then you must take it in turns to use the lavatory. Today is a long drive.'

We are off again, this time on unmade roads so that the old bus shudders and clatters as if it might fall to pieces and we rattle about in it like lentils in a pot. All day we batter along with only a stop, more bread and tea, and to stretch our legs in the stony scrub at the side of the road. Sometimes we pass boys herding goats who wave at the bus and we wave back glad of a moment of human warmth.

Darkness comes down and finally we stop on the outskirts of a village at another taverna, where we are allowed to sit at the tables and a woman brings us lamb stew and rice. I think of running away. All my taste for adventure has gone and I just want to be home with my father's arms hugging me to him.

'You can sleep in the bus tonight. Use the lavatory first. One at a time.' He stands at the door to make sure we don't run away. Then we climb back into the bus and are locked in.

'Have you said your prayers, Saeed? I think we should pray God to keep us safe. I don't trust that man.'

'I've got a copy of the Quran in my bag. My mother packed it. Which way is Mecca?'

'We're travelling West so it must be behind us.'

We knelt down in the aisle. 'What are you doing?' another boy asked.

'We're going to pray. You should too.'

One by one all the boys kneel facing the back of the bus, some in the aisle, some on the seats.

In the morning I ache all over. A big lorry drives into the yard. We go through what has become our morning ritual.

'We are going to drive to the ferry. Just before we get there you will all get into the lorry and be absolutely silent until I open the doors again.'

After a couple of hours bumping along, the bus and the lorry pull off the road into a small wood. The driver gets out and we climb down. The back of the lorry is open. It smells of rotten fruit. Far away through the trees I catch a glimpse of something shining. It must be the sea. We climb into the back of the lorry behind a row of boxes. The lorry driver comes in after us and makes us huddle together close to the front and lie down. He throws a pile of dirty sacks over us and rearranges the boxes.

The door is shut. The engine starts up. I can hardly breathe in the smothering dark and the fumes from the old diesel engine are making me feel sick. The lorry clatters over some wooden boards and stops. The floor is rising and falling. I mustn't throw up. It seems that we're waiting here forever. Now the engine starts and the rolling sensation grows worse. Then there are shouts and a shudder as the ferry hits something. It must be a dock on the other side. The lorry starts up and rolls forward. We must be going ashore. Where will we be? How long before they let us out?

The lorry stops at last. There are voices. Police? Soldiers? Eventually we start up again and move forward. We go on for what I think is about half an hour more. The lorry stops again. The doors are opened. Light comes in above the boxes. The boxes are moved aside. We throw off the sacks and crawl out.

The bus driver is standing at the back. 'Welcome to Thracia. To Yoonan.' We are in Europe. I realise how we have been deceived. There are no real passports. This is a journey of illegals. Yet we can't go back or protest. Now we have to go on.

I get up my courage and ask, 'Why are we hiding? Why don't our passports let us in? This isn't what we paid for.'

'If you're not happy you can stay here. I've taken you to Europe. That's all I need to do. Get out now and see how you get on.'

I am defeated. I know I can't manage alone. At least in England I can speak a little from my classes at High School. Here I can't even read the signs. I keep silent.

The days blend into each other. We are always hungry and dirty, and always tired, our bones and flesh aching from the constant battering and the cramped seats of the bus where we sleep. There are no more stops at friendly tavernas for stew and bread. Again we are packed into the lorry to cross water. Then on. Sometimes in the night we hear voices and I can judge our progress by the different sounds and rhythms though I can't make out the words.

At last we draw up again on a deserted strip of beach. I can see the waves grey under the clouds from the bus windows. We climb out of the bus.

'Over there is Engelestan,' the driver says, waving out to sea. 'Here I leave you, my lovely little ones. My job is done. You will cross in the lorry and you must be very silent. The police here are very cunning.'

We take up our places in the lorry. There's a long wait before the engine starts. It coughs several times until it settles into its usual noisy clatter. We drive a long way before there are the noises of not a boat, I think, but a train. The engine is switched off but the lorry is full of its fumes. I lift up the sack to get more air. Hamid is very quiet beside me. Perhaps he is holding his breath. I can't tell how long we've been in there. The engine starts its bronchial coughing.

I drop the piece of sacking back in place. The lorry begins to roll. It goes a short way then stops with the engine running. There are voices. Suddenly the back is thrown open.

'What's in the boxes?'

We hear one being lifted out. 'Empty. What's behind.'

'Nothing.'

There's a sound of someone climbing into the lorry. 'What's here then?' The sacks are lifted. 'I thought so. Arrest the driver. There's a load of kids here.'

Another voice. 'He's done a bunk.'

The man in uniform stands over us. 'Come on out. Anyone speak English.'

'Yes.'

'Come out quietly. Tell the others.' He moves to stand over Hamid who is lying very still. 'You! Get up.' He tries to move him with his black boot. 'Barry, call for a doctor. I think this one's dead.'

**Acknowledgement**
This is a work of fiction nevertheless I should like to acknowledge the help of the Metropolitan Police, the London Library and Madge Puttock, for local research, during the writing of it.